Return the Favor

Adah Armstrong

This book is a work of fiction. The characters and events in this book are fictitious. Any similarity to real persons, living or dead, is purely coincidental and not intended by the author.

Dedication

To the real John Morrissey,
a kind and gentle man,
gone now more than sixty years
but still alive in my memory

Return the Favor
Prologue

On a sunny Friday afternoon in December, Loren Holloway left his sprawling Texas-sized ranch house in the most upscale neighborhood of Amarillo and drove to his spread 40 miles southwest of town. It was a working cattle ranch only for the tax write-off, with this year's stock sold and the ranch hands dispersed to wherever winter took them and their nomadic lifestyle. Holloway would be alone except for the female company he'd arranged for the weekend's recreation. No worries about his wife. She was visiting one of her Texas high society girlfriends in San Antonio.

Holloway was a combination good ole boy and spoiled rich kid living on his family's oil money, dabbling in real estate and the cattle ranch. His sense of entitlement had persuaded him that he wasn't subject to the normal rules. His personal history reinforced the notion. Two date rapes of beautiful Tex-Mex girls during his early 20's, hushed up and made to go away through threats and intimidation before any charges were brought. Later, in his 30's, land grabs through the foreclosure and orchestrated auction of tracts worked by struggling farm families, aided by penalties and interest imposed by good ole boy banks that deliberately overleveraged the farmers and set them up to fail.

Is this a great country or what, he thought as he sat at the large stone fire pit near the ranch hands' bunk house. Good friends with old Texas money doing business favors for one another, and nobody cares that the peons take it in the neck. Tonight would feature the bottle of Jack Daniels in his hand and the glorious and talented female body arriving in two hours. Life was good.

At least it was until a voice behind him said, "Good evening, Mr. Holloway. Don't move. We need to talk."

Fifteen minutes later Loren Holloway was dead, a bullet through his brain, an untraceable .38 caliber Police Special revolver in his hand, five unfired rounds in the sand at his feet, and one blank cartridge at 4 o'clock on the revolver's cylinder. The visitor who had spoken to him had long since vanished by the time Holloway's intended entertainment discovered his body early that evening.

Chapter 1

As retirement parties go, it went, accompanied by all the usual screwed-up dynamics. For the attendees, it was an awkward obligation: attendance expected, with a festive air that was artificial and forced. For the object of the occasion, John Morrissey, it was more complicated. In his view, the party was unnecessary and unwelcome. Sam Chapman knew that because Morrissey had told him so two days before, in the department's favorite cop hangout, at two o'clock in the afternoon.

"Sam, come with me," he'd said. "You're senior enough to disappear early, and I've finished cleaning out my desk."

"Something on your mind? You want to vent?"

The disarming Irish smile that had trapped so many perps creased Morrissey's face. "Nah. But I figured as my former partner you're the designated eulogist, the one who says all the flowery things about me as they ease my scrawny ass out the door. I thought I'd give you a little perspective beforehand."

They walked out of Portland police headquarters, then three blocks down and one street over to the edge of the Old Port, the city's once-seedy waterfront district, now in the process of gentrification. Their destination, the Full Clip, was a cops' bar through and through, a shot and a beer place. It had dark mahogany paneling and backdrop, tarnished brass fixtures, and stained Formica tops in the booths. The proprietor, Mick Garnish, didn't bother to put premium booze in front of the mirror behind the bar. It was all well brands you'd find beneath the counter anywhere else.

Chapman and Morrissey chose the booth opposite the end of the bar. The most elegant; the Formica wasn't chipped.

"So alter my perspective," Chapman said.

Morrissey's '60s-'70s upbringing was still evident. "This whole affair is a downer," he said. "Not my retirement, which is fine, and inevitable after thirty-five years. But the party – the party tradition – is stupid. I know my friends wish me well, because they've already said so. Those who think I'm a prick and a pain in the ass – especially the higher-ups – haven't said so, but they all want me gone, and my feeling about them is mutual. Whole thing is a waste of time.

"And nobody really wants this shindig anyway – I feel damn uncomfortable being a command performance that steals an evening from everyone, and I'm annoyed that my evening is being stolen too. The suits want the spotlight, and the feeling that they're doing me and everyone else a favor with their platitudes. That's the only reason this is happening."

He took more than a sip of his drink. "And then there's some regret. There's always unfinished business in the handful of cases you couldn't crack, or if you could, couldn't get the DA to indict and bring to trial."

"Oh, come on, John," Chapman said. "You aren't going to be one of those cliché detectives haunted by your unsolved cases or miscarriages of justice, are you? For Chrissake, you solved hundreds of cases, and always the toughest ones. They even made you an admiral two years ago; you could name your own task force of detectives on the most high-profile cases. I lost my partner – bad news for my career education – but really, how much more respect can you get? Don't hang on to a handful of cases we couldn't close and let them spoil your days."

Morrissey surprised him. There was no sad smile in his response to that, only the same Irish grin as back in the office.

"Oh, don't get me wrong," he laughed. "I'm not *haunted*, for Godsake. Just some regret that I didn't bat 1.000. Or more like a 1000-piece jigsaw puzzle missing the last few pieces. Offends my sense of order.

"Just wanted you to know that you shouldn't go all 'Kumbayah' in your speech, that's all. And for Chrissake, be brief. Otherwise it's embarrassing."

He turned to the bar. "Hey Mick, what the hell does a broken-down old flatfoot have to do to get another Jameson's in the middle of the afternoon? Two more over here, if you please."

They downed their glasses after a silent toast. Morrissey's face turned serious.

"Sam, you are a very good detective, and you're going to be a great detective. You have rare instincts and intuition. Don't let yourself be hemmed in by what can't

9

be done. I hate this expression, but don't be afraid to think outside the box.

"And take care of that new partner of yours. I like her – haven't had a chance to work with her more than a couple of times, but she's really bright from what I can tell. Her name is Harwood? "

"Kate. Kate Harwood."

"Yeah. I see a lot of you in her. She's way better looking, though."

He clapped Chapman on the shoulder. "See you Friday night. Be safe."

Chapman thought the party two nights later was anticlimactic after their conversation. The Mayor and the Chief blowharded their honorifics, then Sam said all the right gauzy things about mentor and protégé, about how much they'd all learned from the legendary street snoop who'd refused time and again to become Chief of Detectives because he said it would be a demotion.

When his turn came, John was John – tweed sport coat, gray slacks with a worn crease, a tie that was deliberately twenty years out of date. He was soft-spoken and generous, all smiles and thanks and humility, no immodest war stories about the hundreds of intractable cases his genius had solved. But his eyes glinted a little at his throwaway jibes at the higher-ups, and they darkened just for an instant when he mentioned the cold cases. "Keep after them," he said. "Your measure is how you do on the toughest cases. After all, our business is justice, despite the reality that a whorehouse is the only place you can get it for sure."

That last line brought down the house. He stood there at the podium, a wisp of amusement on his face at his own handiwork. Then, a round of handshakes and backslaps later, he was gone. Off to his Casco Bay island, to the old Army fort guardhouse he'd renovated over the last ten years, to the place where he and his longtime girlfriend Dottie Taylor were going to relax, kick back, and drink tequila on the restaurant deck like Ernest Hemingway. Except cancer had taken Dottie in three short months two years ago, and as Morrissey left, they all looked at each other and thought, "What the hell is he going to do with himself now?"

Chapter 2

Morrissey rose on Saturday morning and contemplated the rest of his life. First order of business, he supposed, was to finish his house and blend into his new full-time community. He had owned the old guardhouse for almost ten years, and had transformed it from dilapidated jail to luxury home. But while he had been one of the first owners at Atlantic Estates, he'd stood only on the periphery of the evolving development.

Atlantic Estates had a long and complex history. In the late 19th century, the U.S. government had used eminent domain to seize the seaward half of Granite Cliffs Island for construction of a coastal artillery fort. Elihu Root, Teddy Roosevelt's Secretary of War, had overseen the construction of barracks, officers' quarters, and support buildings during the first decade of the new century. Virtually all the construction was Queen Anne Colonial Revival architecture – magnificent buildings.

During World War II, the Navy had made the waters off Granite Cliffs the primary anchorage for the destroyers that escorted supply convoys to England and Russia. The old Army fort expanded to accommodate Navy personnel, and the island population doubled from its original number.

With the war's end, the military lost interest. The installation was sold to a private company that stripped the buildings of all useful and easily accessible building materials. Most harmful was the removal of all the copper flashing and gutters in the buildings' roofs – guaranteeing rainwater leakage, rot, and deterioration. The old fort, falling into disrepair, became a vandal's playground for residents of the island's "private" side, and for boaters bent on an afternoon's mischief.

A real estate boom brought a visionary developer who saw possibilities in the decrepit buildings. He removed all the debris and discarded junk on and around the fort's central parade ground and put several million dollars into two buildings – a 109-man barracks, turned into eight townhouse condominiums; and a dockside quartermaster's building, rehabilitated and repurposed as an upscale restaurant. Then he set about advertising the place as a luxury gated community, and named it Atlantic Estates after the Navy's anchorage during the Battle of the Atlantic.

Most of the people on the "private" side of the island – year-round and seasonal residents alike – were outraged by the new development. Like many Maine residents, and almost all islanders, they were opposed to virtually all change. This was coupled with bitter resentment that their playground had not only been taken away but put off limits. They hated the developer and by extension were prepared to hate any new residents of Atlantic Estates.

It was into this atmosphere that Morrissey and his girlfriend had stepped ten years before. They had taken Morrissey's one luxury in life – a 28-foot cruiser with

13

cuddy cabin – out to the dockside restaurant, about which they'd heard good reviews. The developer was in the restaurant that Friday evening, overjoyed to see some interest attributable only to word of mouth. He invited them to stroll up the fort's main access road after their dinner to look at the parade ground and surrounding buildings.

As they completed a circuit of the parade ground, Dottie noticed an offshoot lane seemingly headed for the edge of a cliff. They came closer, and a long series of wide stone steps came into view, leading back down to the restaurant and the pier.

They neared the steps, and Dottie glanced to her left along the top of the cliff. She promptly fell in love.

A large brick building sat on the ridgeline, above the pier and the ocean cove that protected it. A wide porch spanned the entire front of the building; overlooking the porch was a high hip roof and a wide central gable featuring a Palladian window.

"That's the most beautiful building I've ever seen," she breathed. She looked at Morrissey. "I want it, John. I want to live in it."

"Honey, it looks like it's falling apart," Morrissey said. "That building might be in the worst shape of anything here.

"Half the slate roof is gone – there must be tremendous water damage inside – and look, the main front door is hanging by one hinge, and other door in front is completely off its hinges and leaning against the brick. That thing is a money pit."

14

Dottie wouldn't be deterred. "We can at least ask about it, can't we? Let's see if David is still in the restaurant."

Minutes later, they sat with the developer at a table in the bar's lounge. "How many of these buildings do you intend to rehab?" Morrissey asked. In the back of his mind, he was concerned that the developer might pull a disappearing act. Wouldn't be the first time in the development world.

David Borman laughed. "You're afraid I might cut and run, right? Not a chance. I have too much of my own money invested here, and a bankruptcy would destroy my credibility for anything I might want to do in the future. Besides – I consider this my life's work. Everything I am as a person is wrapped up in this place."

He looked off into the future. "My master plan? Stabilize all these buildings so they don't fall into more disrepair. Rehab a couple more barracks buildings into townhouses to try to get a critical mass of owners. The commandant's and XO's houses, the surgeon's house and the officers' duplexes, the sergeant's quarters – sell them all as is, and help the owners find reputable contractors to rehab and renovate."

"Are you going to do anything with the surrounding support buildings?" Morrissey asked. "We saw the fire barn and the heating plant."

"We'll certainly sell them if someone has the imagination to want to try. Who knows, someone might even want the old jail."

"Oh?" Morrissey asked. "Which one is that?"

And that's how it had happened. The following month, Borman conveyed the guardhouse – the jail – at the top of the cliff to Morrissey and Dottie for a very modest price. "It's worth it to me for people to see some activity," he said, "and that building is very visible."

That started an effort that had taken most of a decade to turn the run-down building into a home for their retirement. They'd spent weekends their first winter of ownership traveling out on John's boat, walking around the empty space now free of debris from their summer demolition work – too cold in wintertime to do any construction – and taking measurements. Then they'd go home and share some wine while drawing up alternative floor plans for the open space they'd created.

The summers had gone by, along with the occasional winter weekend to cross-country ski on the nearly deserted island. The house had become more and more habitable. Hardwood floors and installed carpeting made the house seem more like a home. Slate countertops made from the brig's communal shower stalls made the kitchen unique. What remained now was some final painting and finish trim on doors and baseboards.

Morrissey sighed. What a story. Dottie would have loved telling it to new acquaintances, along with showing them the in-process pictures they'd taken over the years. A labor of love.

Now his love was gone, taken by ovarian cancer two years before, a Stage IV diagnosis too late to do anything. On her final visit to the island a week before her death, Dottie had said to him, "Promise you'll finish this for me, John."

He was sure they all wondered what he'd now do with his time. Well, this was it. Promises to keep, miles to go before he'd sleep. He would keep his promise. How long he could live here without her was another matter.

As to his entry into the community: he and Dottie had been very private as they worked on the jail during summer weekends over the years. They hadn't come to know many people as the old fort grew from a handful of owners to a sizable year-round population and even more significant summer colony. He needed to get to know his neighbors, along with the lay of the land. He'd heard rumblings of continued friction still between the "private side" and the "fort side" despite the built-in market for construction help and lobster sales created by the Estates residents.

Word had it that his new community harbored a few unpleasant personalities of its own. One guy in particular, a former real estate developer, had interrupted Morrissey's drink at the restaurant bar one evening the summer before, after Dottie was gone.

"When the hell are you going to be done with that jail of yours?" Don Kagan had asked. It wasn't a friendly or joshing tone. "I'm getting tired of wondering."

Morrissey was annoyed. Kagan's reputation for offensive behavior had preceded him. "The exterior is all rehabbed, enclosed, and finished. That's all you need to know," Morrissey had said. "And that's all you're going

17

to see if you keep acting like that. You have a good chance right now of never setting foot in the place."

Ah well. Morrissey wondered if there were any more like him. Maybe. He imagined any upscale development had its share of self-important obnoxious jerks. And, of course, there was the rumored murder that had taken place three years before. Looked like an accident, man overboard drowning in the ocean, but a body had never been recovered. Hard to prove foul play without a body or an autopsy.

Whatever. He was out of the proof business as of this morning. It was a beautiful Saturday, the first day of his retirement. He was here to kick back, take in life's pleasures, enjoy the people he liked, and tolerate as best he could the people he didn't. He went back inside to get a second cup of coffee. Some habits of police work died hard.

Chapter 3

Sam Chapman walked into Portland police headquarters the Monday after Morrissey's retirement party reflecting on how different it now was. To be sure, it looked the same. PPD was the same squat five story building it had been on Friday. It sat across the street from county lockup and the criminal courts building, with its ground floor devoted to public access, interview rooms, and a handful of holding cells. Second floor was patrol lockers and squad rooms; the various investigative departments were on the third and fourth floors, with administration on the fifth. Robbery/Homicide Division, along with Vice, was on the fourth floor, more than halfway to heaven. Or close at hand so the Chief of Police could keep an eye on his problem children – Morrissey's legions.

Unlike television's stunning big-city police palaces, RHD spaces looked like a 1940's noir movie set: battered steelcase desks pushed together, swivel chairs with far too much play in them, ancient file cabinets, whiteboards on the dingy yellow walls. Budget constraints meant that there wasn't a computer on every desk, so most of the detectives tried to make do for everyday needs with smartphones or first-generation iPads. Three communal machines with secure lines for confidential files sat on desks pushed into a corner.

A waist-high wall with glass partitions and blinds above separated the bullpen from the offices, the rooms with the pallid view of Criminal Courts a hundred feet away. The corner office for the captain, two more for detective lieutenants, one for Special Circumstances – what the troops called "The Admiral" -- John Morrissey's late position. It was not lost on anyone that admirals outranked captains.

Chapman had passed the lieutenant's exam a good while before, but a quota system exists in most police departments, and Portland, Maine was no exception. The quota was two RHD detective lieutenant positions, both of them filled. So Sam was still Detective Sergeant Chapman, in the squad bullpen, his desk back to back with his partner Kate Harwood's.

He was greeted by Sally Rinaldo, the division's executive assistant. Her desk was just inside the swinging gate in the baluster railing that separated RHD spaces from Vice.

"Hey Sam," she sang out. "The Chief wants to see you as soon as you show up."

"What's up? Some huge award I'm not yet aware of?"

"Oh Sam," she said, "the Chief, alas, does not work for me, and he didn't see fit to tell me."

"More's the pity. Probably wants to impress upon me that I no longer have Morrissey to protect me."

"Sam, it that were true, he'd want to see the whole division."

Chapman laughed. "Ah, you got me there, Sal. As always. Tell Kate I'll be back down here as soon as I can."

Access to the fifth floor stairwell was locked to the floors below, so Chapman had to use the elevator. He came out in plain sight of Laurel, Administration's cupcake receptionist. Laurel wasn't brilliant by any means, but she wasn't stupid either. And she was very pretty and very well put together. Since many of the visitors to Administration were heavyweights — the Mayor and his minions, City Councilors, visiting pols or dignitaries, all usually there either for a favor or a complaint — well, it couldn't hurt to have a bit of eye candy as a first impression to put middle-aged men at ease. Chapman didn't like Chief Armand Anthony, but knew that he, like Laurel, wasn't stupid either.

The eye candy gave Chapman her most brilliant smile, the one reserved, he suspected, for everybody.

"Sam Chapman! Long time no see!"

"As fond of you as I am, Laurel, long time no see is a good thing on this floor," he said.

"To what do we owe the honor?"

"Chief wants to see me."

Her face grew serious. "Okay then. I'll let Alice know." She picked up the phone and dialed.

Just because a pretty girl was out front didn't mean that there were no Praetorian guards in multiple lines of defense. Two uniformed cops stood inside the door from reception to the office areas, and Chief Anthony's last line of defense was Alice Spinder. She looked like everyone's old witch high school English teacher, utterly lacking in sense of humor – skin and bones, poorly styled gray hair, wizened face, ice-blue eyes lasering above ancient half-glasses.

"Detective Chapman," she said.

"Mrs. Spinder," he said. He wasn't foolish enough to call her "Alice."

"The Chief will see you now."

Chapman hesitated, waiting for her to rise and conduct the ceremony of escorting him to Anthony's door and announcing him. Instead, she smiled, first Chapman had ever seen, something he'd thought her incapable of.

"Sam, you're a big boy and a very smart detective. You can find your way to the door and knock on it yourself."

Uh-oh, he thought. *Major charm offensive going on here. I wonder what it's about. Must be important if she's in on it.*

"Thank you," he said, and took three steps to knock on the Chief's office door.

"Come in." *Not the usual pompous "Enter." Something clearly was going on. Keep your wits about you, Chapman.*

He walked into the inner sanctum, all brass and glass table tops and leather chairs. The spotless expansive desk befit an executive who was a marathon runner, not the squat balding man who sat behind it, piggish black eyes glinting.

Although he surely gladhanded all the visiting VIPs, Chief Anthony generally stayed seated with department types, glowering beneath caterpillar eyebrows with a disdainful stare to set the tone. But not this time. He rose and extended his hand toward one of the two black leather chairs in front of his desk.

"Detective Chapman," he smiled. "Have a seat."

"Thank you, Chief." Nothing more. Not "What can I do for you this morning, sir?" or anything else. Sam was playing his cards close.

"Nice party for John Morrissey Friday night."

"Yes it was. I know he really appreciated it." *Bullshit, Chief. He thought it was contrived, just an ego trip for you and yours. He told me so. What are you up to?*

"I know you two were close; you were partners for close to ten years before we had him head up Special Circumstances. What is it you fellows called him? The Admiral?"

"It's a seagoing town, Chief. No disrespect intended to any departmental titles. It's just that admirals command task forces. It was a high honor to be named to one of his."

"Yes," said Anthony. "And you were more often than not his chief of staff. Likely because you two were so used to working together, but I also suspect many times deservedly so on the merits.

"Anyway, Sam, I called you here to do you the courtesy of telling you that you will not be named head of Special Circumstances. Nobody will."

That's not what this is about. Something else is going on here. Be careful.

23

"Chief, honestly, it never occurred to me that I'd even be considered, let alone appointed. I'm not senior enough, and there's no way it would be feasible – or fair – to leapfrog me over Lieutenants Dayton and Canedy. Besides, maybe that position should retire with John. The Navy no longer has the rank of Fleet Admiral either."

"Good point, Detective. I may use that as we promulgate this decision. We'll still have Special Circumstances task forces, but Captain Langdon and I will form them."

Ah, Captain Robert Langdon, Robbery/Homicide's nominal man in charge. A suck-up with his nose so far up Anthony's ass that it would never again see the light of day. He was almost fatally threatened by anyone with true competence. But in a division populated with the brightest, most tenacious cops in the department, Anthony needed a mole to keep him apprised of the natives' rumblings. Langdon was his man. He fit easily under the Chief's thumb with room to spare. The Chief deluded himself that the detectives were under Langdon's thumb. They were not. They had all learned contempt for incompetent superiors at the foot of the master – John Morrissey.

The real reason Special Circumstances had been created was that Morrissey had said he would no longer abide, report to, or have anything to do with Robert Langdon. Otherwise he'd retire early and quite possibly name names. The Chief had tried to buy him off with the position of Chief of Detectives – an equal rank with Langdon, but not reporting to him. Langdon would be administration, Morrissey would be investigations. No dice, John had said. He wouldn't be "demoted" to a supervisory job; he was a working detective. They compromised by creating Special Circumstances, with pay equal to a Deputy Chief – more than Langdon. John's little twist of the knife.

Chapman smiled at the memory. The Chief thought the smile was for him. "Chief, thank you for telling me this," Chapman said. "I'm flattered that you thought I deserved a personal notification. I appreciate it."

"Sam, you have a real future here in the department. I hope our next conversation will be when we promote you to lieutenant."

Oh boy. More charm. Here it comes. The object of this whole charade.

"Tell me," the Chief continued. "What's John going to do with all his free time now?"

And there we are. He's probably afraid that Morrissey is going to write a book, in which Armand Anthony will have a prominent role as a craven political ass-kisser. For all I know, that might happen, but let's not put the Chief on guard.

"Chief," Chapman said, making it up on the fly, "John was always concerned about how rudderless a lot of cops were when they retired. Some might catch on in some ceremonial security position, but he thought most of them sort of shriveled on the vine, no power or influence or rush from upholding the law. He said a lot of them drank themselves to death. He was sure some of them actually died of boredom, or ate their gun just before they did.

"Wasn't going to happen to him, he told me. There are a thousand things on his bucket list. Learn to play the piano. Get better at chess. Read all the great books. Ski sixty days a year instead of six. Master finish carpentry so he can make that jailhouse of his out on Granite Cliffs Island a real showplace. He isn't going to lack for things to do. He'll probably be so busy we'll have to go see him rather than the other way around."

"Well, that's good to hear," Anthony said. "And reassuring. Thanks for stopping by." He smiled again. "I'll let you get back to work. Have a good day."

"Yes, sir. Thanks again for the courtesy."

And he was out of there, both he and John unscathed as far as he could judge. A nod to Alice Spinder, a wink to Laurel, and a trip down to the fourth floor and a host of questioning glances.

Chapter 4

Lt. Fred Dayton, the day watch commander for the month, stopped Chapman on his way to his desk. "What did the Chief want, Sam?"

"Nothing important, Loot. Just fishing for information on what John's going to do now."

Dayton was in his late 40's, a stocky man with a ruddy complexion. He wasn't endowed with soaring insights or intelligence, but he had a master's degree in street smarts. "Probably worried that John's going to write a tell-all book."

Chapman smiled. "Exactly. I tried to deflect that – I actually have no idea if he will or not – just told the Chief that John has a zillion things on his bucket list, and he'll have no trouble keeping himself busy."

"Good. That ought to hold him, at least for a while," Dayton said. "Go on over and bring Kate up to speed. I'll join you two in a minute."

Kate Harwood was not only the sole female detective in Robbery Homicide Division, she was the first. She had been born and brought up in Boston and came from a family of cops – multiple generations in the Boston PD. She was a college graduate, major in criminal justice, and smart as a whip. She'd joined the Portland PD to escape the family shadow in Boston, and had risen quickly through the patrol ranks. Promoted to Detective within the last year, she was Sam's partner, and he'd already foreseen her all-star future. *I'm supposed to mentor her,* he'd thought, *but I don't think it will be long before she's mentoring me.*

She was fifteen years younger than he, Black Irish through and through. Jet black hair, fair complexion, a cute scattering of freckles across her nose. Blue eyes that could be grandmotherly warm when she played good cop, ice cold when she took the bad cop role. She was dressed in her usual detective's uniform: dark tailored jacket, light colored blouse, slacks that advertised her long legs.

She looked up as Chapman approached, an inquiring look on her face.

"Nothing to it. Chief was just fishing for information on what John is going to do now."

"And what is that?"

"Hell if I know," Chapman said. "I told the Chief John has a long bucket list, and he intends to stay busy." He laughed. "Dayton and I both think he might live rent-free in the Chief's head while Anthony worries about whether he'll write a book."

Harwood smiled as Fred Dayton arrived and parked his behind on Chapman's desk top. She and Chapman spun their chairs around to face each other.

"Tell Sam what you told me," Dayton said. "I'd like his take on this."

Harwood grimaced. "As soon as you went on your way to the fifth floor, Sam, Captain Langdon called me into his office. He's assigned us all of John Morrissey's old cases that, in Langdon's words, John 'couldn't solve.' I guess there's a half dozen of them. All homicides. I just pulled the summary files to start familiarizing myself with them. I'm sure you know them already."

Chapman gave her a sardonic grin. "Indeed I do. John mentioned them just last week, in fact. Said he wasn't going to be haunted by them, but had some regrets about not closing them – the way he put it, they were like the last six missing pieces of a thousand-piece jigsaw puzzle."

Dayton interrupted. "Kate just told me this – Langdon hasn't seen fit to tell me yet – and I'm wondering why now, why you two. Portland PD doesn't have a designated cold case squad, we're not a big enough department. Even if we did have one, it would probably be a dead-letter office, staffed by guys on their way out – what the Navy calls their last cruise – and not much would get done. So why is Langdon all fired up about this now?"

Chapman shook his head. "I don't think he's fired up at all. He's sending us all a message, especially me and Kate. 'You're no longer Morrissey's favored children, because Morrissey isn't here.' He knows these cases won't go anywhere – John and the rest of us beat the hell out of those cases already – so this is to take us down a peg."

Kate looked worried. "Is this to undermine us, make lack of progress an excuse to get rid of us, transfer us out of RHD?"

Chapman looked at Dayton and they both grinned. "Nah," Sam said. "He's not going to do that. He needs us way more than we need him. He just thinks he sees an opportunity to get us under his thumb. It's all about him."

"My conclusion too," Dayton agreed. "I'll need to ask him if I should curtail your availability on the watch list, make sure that you won't catch as many new cases because they'd take time away from these. But he's going to say 'No.' He'll say if you two are as good as you supposedly are – as good as Morrissey said you were – then you ought to be able to handle both sets of responsibilities."

"Thanks for seeing through the bullshit so quickly, Loot," Chapman said. "We'll take a look at these, review everything in the murder books, see if any new possibilities jump out. But I doubt it."

Dayton agreed. "So do I, Sam. I also think he'll lose interest and let these go after some decent interval. I don't think he's persistent enough to use it as a club long-term. This is just his immediate pounce after John's retirement to try to establish an advantage for himself. Administrative bullshit is the only leverage he has."

Fred Dayton smiled. "I guess that's enough disloyalty from me for one day. But loyalty is a two-way street. This is what he gets for bypassing me and keeping me out of the loop. Life has consequences. He does this to you – and to me – and you're going to know exactly what I think as a result."

"We know you've got our backs, Loot. And we have yours." Chapman gave him a thumbs-up; Dayton did the same in return and walked back to his office.

Harwood shook her head. "Sam, explain to me how the hell a guy like Langdon came to be a police captain."

"First of all, he looks like a police captain. Tall, rugged good looks, blah blah blah. A lot of success in life depends on whether you look the part, whether you look like you belong." He paused, and a grin creased his plain face. "Which explains my meteoric rise."

Harwood smiled at him. "Give yourself some credit, Sam. You're more than okay."

"Aren't you sweet. Well, Langdon isn't. He's what we call a paperwork whore, Kate. On his way up the ranks, he had no talent for – and no real interest in – pounding the pavement, chasing down leads, interviewing witnesses and suspects. He took as much of the paperwork drudgery and report generation as he could get his hands on. And you know how we all love filling out reports – so everybody let him do it.

"Once he had control of that, he could slant the reports to make himself look good. He'd damn all of us with faint praise, or no praise at all. He'd find a way to present progress reports to the higher-ups, and act like he was in a supervisory role as he talked: 'Detectives A, B, and C are going to follow up on thus-and-so and report.' That sort of thing.

"It worked for him. Probably because a lot of the higher-ups had advanced in the same way, and

31

recognized one of their own. I keep hoping he'll prove he's risen to his level of incompetence. But that doesn't stop him from looking for more stripes. Chief Anthony just told me that Special Circumstances is no more – it's gone along with John. If we have Special Circumstances task forces, Anthony and Langdon will form them. Langdon will presumably head them up."

Kate groaned softly. "Won't that be fun."

"Yeah, a great time. It'll be a really frustrating pain in the ass. If a Special Circumstances task force breaks a high-profile case, he'll maneuver to take all the credit. If it doesn't work, he'll say Special Circumstances was a stupid idea to begin with, and just an ego trip for John. Heads I win, tails you lose. The mark of a paperwork whore."

Kate smiled at him. "This is why Mondays suck, Sam. The higher-ups have all weekend to think of ways to upset the apple cart."

"Don't let them get you down, Kate. Let's get the murder books. I'll start reviewing them while you go over the summary files. You'll catch up in no time."

Chapter 5

The murder book is a staple of big-city police departments everywhere. It is a detailed – excruciatingly detailed – chronological record of a murder investigation. Everything is included – from the report of the first officer on the scene, the initial detectives' walk-through and inspection, the EMT's report, forensics findings, coroner's report – to all the leads and avenues of investigation. Interviews with witnesses, persons of interest, suspects. Every rumor or conjecture considered, chased down, dealt with. Supposedly – although sometimes held back for a time by an experienced detective – every theory of the case, and how it stacked up against confirmed facts.

The books are a hodgepodge of typed reports, penciled notes, post-it stickers, telephone numbers written in margins. In her short time as a detective, Kate Harwood had formed an opinion – kept to herself – that a murder book tended to be a disorganized mess. Aside from the chronology, these ought to be digitized, cross-referenced, organized by subject, she found herself thinking. The computer can plow through this material and match files better and faster than we ever can. Much better chance of two random facts from different detectives matching up and popping out at us.

But, as Tevye said in Fiddler on the Roof – *"Tradition!"* This was the way it had always been done, and it probably wasn't going to change any time soon. In spite of that, experienced detectives learned to review murder books thoroughly and put them to good – if not optimal – use.

As she reviewed the books from John Morrissey's 'unsolved' cases, she was surprised to see that Morrssey seemed to agree with her. His books were far more organized than others in the PPD files. He kept the detailed chronological record just as everyone else, but he organized material by subject and inter-relatedness as well. It was a treat to see the work product of a very organized mind.

The six cases assigned to Chapman and Harwood had several things in common. Foremost among them: all the victims were people living on the margins of society, and all the persons of interest or suspects were disreputable people. It would have been easy to let some of these cases slide as inconsequential, but Morrissey hadn't. Harwood recalled the credo of Michael Connelly's fictional detective Harry Bosch: "Everybody counts, or nobody counts." Morrissey had clearly felt the same way. His intensity and persistence showed through the dry pages of the murder books.

All six homicides had occurred in Portland's seedier neighborhoods. All had been violent, up close and personal: close-range shootings, stabbings, bludgeonings. One looked to be a gangland execution: a double-tap to the head with a .22 caliber pistol. Victims and suspects were multi-ethnic and multi-cultural: Black, Caucasian, Hispanic, Asian, Islamic. None of the murders appeared random; none was a case of a pure innocent in the wrong place at the wrong time. Possible motives abounded: revenge, drugs, girlfriend competition, a perceived slight, somebody being 'dissed.'

Prime suspects were identified, and the evidence was summarized. But then the books stopped – because the other factor the murders had in common was no eyewitnesses, no one with direct knowledge. Alibis, but shaky ones, for all the suspects – one person, close to the suspect, providing an alibi – "He was with me, I saw him wherever …" -- but otherwise unconfirmed.

Morrissey and his assistants had compiled stacks of circumstantial evidence, with recommendations for arrests. But there the action stopped. Harwood wondered why. The cases looked reasonably solid to her.

Maybe she was missing something about some weakness in the cases. She suggested to Chapman that they touch base with the senior county prosecutor, an ADA named Garfield Levenson, to get his take.

"You do it. And good luck," Sam said. "I'm going to pull the forensics reports and the coroner's findings in each one. Reading about the dead will be a lot more fun than dealing with that douchebag Levenson."

Garfield Levenson was abrupt and condescending on the phone when she called to make an appointment. "If the department is making another effort, I suppose I'll have to make time for you. It won't do any good, though. You don't have enough."

Harwood trudged over to the criminal courts building and took the stairs to the DA's spaces. Levenson had a corner office that befit his senior prosecutor status. He was rumpled and unkempt, 50 pounds overweight. His office was as sloppy as he was, and his physical appearance was matched by an ugly disposition.

"Have a seat, Detective. Let's make this quick. I'm a busy man."

We're all busy, Harwood thought. *You must hold the world land speed record for establishing yourself as insufferable.*

"Mr. Levenson, I don't want to take up your time with the case details …"

"Good. Don't," Levenson interrupted.

Jesus, Harwood thought. *What a horse's ass.* "What strikes me," she said, "is that all these seem to be pretty strong circumstantial cases, yet the DA's office hasn't authorized arrests or pursued indictments. I came over here to try to ascertain what further evidence would cement these cases for you."

"You're being presumptuous, Detective. I don't work for you or report to you."

Harwood had limits, and Levenson had just breached them. "I know that, sir, and I'm not asking you to." Her voice grew bad-cop cold and the blue eyes turned to ice. "But you do *depend* on us. I think we have solid cases. You apparently don't. Why not? Tell us what else would help, and we'll try to focus our attention on those areas."

"Just do your job, Detective. Produce incriminating evidence and we'll proceed."

Oh shit, let me write that down, Harwood thought. *Produce enough evidence and the village idiot can proceed.* "Thank you so much for that advice, Mr. Levenson. That's really helpful. But if you can't offer any specifics, I'll take my leave. I'm busy too."

She stood, and made only a half-hearted try to veil her contempt. "I'll show myself out."

Harwood wasn't back in the office 20 minutes before Robert Langdon beckoned her into his office. His voice was curt.

"Have a seat, Detective." He adopted his grim disciplinary face. "I just had to field a phone call about you from ADA Levenson. A complaint. He said you insulted him – insinuated that he was subordinate to you."

"Not that way at all, Captain. He got annoyed when I asked what further evidence he needed to proceed on these cases, and said he didn't work for me or report to me. I agreed, but pointed out that the DA's office does depend on us. We investigate the crime, compile the evidence, and arrest the offenders. Just like they say on 'Law and Order' every week. The DA would be nowhere without us, although I was tactful enough not to say that."

"He doesn't much like you, Harwood."

"Neither here nor there, Captain. Truth is an absolute defense. They do depend on us over there."

Langdon was a bully, she thought. *And like all bullies, a coward. Time to push back.*

37

"Look, Captain, if you and he want to make an issue about this, I think my union rep should be involved. Give me a minute to call him."

"Never mind that," Langdon said. "We'll just chalk this up to a stressful day for ADA Levenson. I'll let this go."

Of course you will, Harwood thought immediately. *You're not that stupid. You're not going to stick your dick in that wringer.*

"Thank you, sir. Are we done?"

"Yes, Harwood, you're dismissed."

She walked back into the bullpen to find Chapman with a sardonic smile on his face. "Another trip to the principal's office? Did you get your wrist slapped?"

"He tried, Sam, but I short-circuited him. Relaxed my rule about not engaging in a battle of wits with an unarmed man."

Chapman bit his lip so Langdon wouldn't see him burst out laughing. Kate shook her head and said, "But he made it pretty clear that both he and ADA Levenson think I'm a bitch."

"Of course they do," Chapman said. "You're a female detective in an old-line male-dominated police department. But you're also a great detective, Kate. Class will always tell. Besides, deep down underneath all that bullshit Langdon knows he's incompetent. He needs your talent working for him far more than you need to be in his good graces. Fuck him."

38

Harwood smiled.   "As they say in the wine commercials, thank you for your support, Sam.   I love it when you go all alpha male in my defense."

"Yep, that's me, hard-bitten old detective.   Sam Spade. Humphrey Bogart."

They both laughed, then looked up to see Langdon scowling at them through his office window.

"Yeah, we're laughing at you, asshole," Chapman muttered. They laughed even harder, then went back to work.

Chapter 6

At 7:00 a.m. on the Tuesday after the long 4th of July weekend, John Morrissey walked down the stone steps from the guardhouse to the restaurant at the water's edge. On weekends during the previous two months he'd fallen into the habit of sharing morning coffee with Jack Harlan, the restaurant owner. Part of it was proximity, part their both being early risers. Mostly it was because, in the runup to the restaurant's seasonal opening, Morrissey had helped Jack move supplies to the restaurant when the early Saturday freight boat had left them outside in the rain on the pier. Harlan was grateful, and they'd struck up a friendship.

A pickup truck was parked in front of the awning leading to the restaurant's front door. Morrissey walked into the bar and lounge area to find Harlan in conversation with Tom Warren, a long-time year-round resident of the "private" side and the jack-of-all-trades fixer and repairman for anything that went awry on the island. He'd sought Tom out this past spring, asking if people generally held a garage or yard sale of leftover building materials when they were done with their housing rehab or renovation.

Warren had laughed. "John, remember something," he'd said. "You live on an island. You never *ever* throw anything away!" It was a bitch, he said, to have to make a special ferry trip to Portland for only one or two items. It could also be a long wait for a repairman to travel out to the island – which was why Warren had evolved into a jack-of-all-trades, and an expert one at that.

No repairs this morning. Warren and Harlan were conducting a post mortem on the 4th of July weekend. Warren grinned at Morrissey and said, "What's your take on your first island 4th of July, John?"

"Dottie and I were here for a few 4ths," he said, "but only for the day. Really couldn't get any freight shipped out, or any real work done, with all the ferry crowds and activity here, so this was my first full 4th of July holiday." He paused. "Interesting."

Harlan and Warren both gave him knowing smiles. "Really?" Jack said. "How so?"

"I've heard of some friction and protracted bad feeling on the private side about the fort," Morrissey said, "but this is the first I've really seen it. When I walked over with some Estates neighbors to the Granite Cliffs Association beach to watch the fireworks last night, I saw some private side people actually – deliberately, making a big show of it – turn their backs on Estates people. What the hell did we ever do to them?"

"Good question," Tom said. "The worst impulses of really parochial small towns, which is exactly what this is. Most of that petty behavior comes from summer people. We year-rounders have got used to you guys, and decided most of you don't have horns or cloven hooves. But the summer people still resent the fort and the

41

people in it. Worse yet, some of them are insanely jealous that Estates people have nicer houses and tend to have more money than they do. So they behave badly, like last night."

"Jesus," Morrissey said. "That's junior high school stuff."

Jack Harlan said, "John, you were a cop and a student of human behavior for a long time. You know by now that *life* is junior high school."

Morrissey chuckled. "Yeah, Jack, I guess you're right."

Warren said, "I think it may be a little worse here – the feelings have persisted for a long time – because we have a couple of really divisive sonsofbitches in leadership roles in the Granite Cliffs Association. They stoke hard feelings, make trouble for lots of people – couple of total assholes.

"I won't try to poison your mind by naming names. You'll figure out who they are soon enough. Besides, you have a handful of really nasty pieces of work in the Estates community."

"Yeah," Morrissey said, "I've already had one run-in with Don Kagan. Last summer, here in the bar."

"He's a hundred percent shit," Harlan said. "He's trying to undermine David Borman, insist on all kinds of upgrades and improvements to the Estates infrastructure, despite Borman already putting millions into it. I think he wants to bankrupt Borman, run him out of here, and take it over himself. Trouble is, he has some followers here, and they've all tried to make trouble for me as well. Restrict my hours of operation, ban functions like wedding receptions and corporate picnics, ban musical entertainment. Kagan would like to run me out of here along with Borman. Then I bet he'd try take over the restaurant too."

Harland smiled. "Not gonna happen. He's a penny ante troublemaker, at least for me. I can handle him, but he's a constant irritation."

"Sounds like he has a business agenda," Morrissey said. "Do his followers have the same motive?"

"Don't think so," Tom Warren said. "Some of them just want to be important, big fish in a small pond, tell people how to live, make rules for everybody. Others want to change everything, make island life as convenient as a big-city suburb. They don't realize that an island is *supposed* to be inconvenient – that's the tradeoff for all the privacy and beauty.

"But the worst ones," he continued, "are the people who are just angry. They hate everybody and everything, and try to make life as difficult as possible for all the people around them."

Harlan and Warren looked at each other, grinned, and shook their heads. "Thalia," they said in unison.

"I thought you were going to have Kagan lead that category," Morrissey said.

"Well, he fits," Harlan replied. "But the worst of that ilk is a woman named Thalia Sandberg. She's a tax accountant, but can't practice because she's half-crippled with multiple sclerosis. She's ugly and overweight to boot, and just mad at the world. She has her nose in the

43

development's covenants and restrictions all the time, and tells Borman and everyone else, 'You can't do this, you have to do that.' Constant pain in the ass – she's relentless in trying to restrict my activities. But the worst part is she has nothing to do but threaten lawsuits against Borman, me, and whoever of her neighbors she's angry with at any given moment. Threatens to file a lawsuit, costs people time and money and aggravation if they don't knuckle under to her. She's a real princess." He and Warren both laughed.

Morrissey was incredulous. "You think it's funny?"

"Not at all," Harlan said. "But you have to keep some perspective. Her legal threats are so petty that she probably wouldn't be able to find anyone any good to take her case. She'd have to represent herself *pro se* if she followed through. She isn't going to go to all that trouble, and she can't stand on her feet in court anyway. She just abuses the legal process to try to get her way. For me and Borman it's just a cost of doing business. If it wasn't Thalia, it would probably be someone else. But for some of the neighbors she's gone after, it's cost some serious time and money. And heartache."

"Yikes," Morrissey said. "Nice place you got here, guys." He paused. "I miss Dottie, but I'm kinda glad she doesn't have to see this. Are there any others like those two?"

"Oh, sure," Harlan said. "Maybe not as bad as Kagan and Sandberg, but I doubt that you'll end up buddies with the others either. We have a guy who's a municipal court judge, traffic court mostly, but he thinks he's God's gift and smarter than everyone else. He thinks everybody should defer to him. Another who's a physician at the VA hospital and who's so sanctimonious it makes you want to puke. And a few others who are so full of themselves and condescending, living in their "exclusive" community, that they annoy people on both sides of the island."

Morrissey looked at Tom Warren. "Island life seems a lot different from what I thought it would be. You've been here a long time. Does this kind of thing ever resolve itself?"

"Growing pains," Warren said. "New people, new personalities coming up against old grudges. Think about a snotty troublemaking kid growing up, straightening himself out and flying right within a few years. I'm hoping the same thing happens here. This island is a great place to raise a family – hard for kids to get into the kind of trouble they could find in the city – and the pace of life is quiet and peaceful. As long as you eventually get the assholes under control.

"Tell you what," he continued. "Don't take my word for it. You're here permanently; walk around the island – both sides – for a couple hours each morning, chat with everyone you see. You're a cop, John. You'll be able to distinguish people fairly fast.

"My birthday is coming up the beginning of August," he said. "I always have a big lobster bake at my house to celebrate. Come on over and I'll introduce you to all the good guys if you haven't met them by then."

"I'll do that," Morrissey said. "Thanks. And thanks for the walking-around advice. I'll do that too."

He finished his coffee and put the cup on the bar. "I appreciate the intelligence briefing, guys. Maybe I'll just work on my house today and not socialize." He grinned. "Time enough to start meeting people tomorrow, after I've psyched myself up for it. Maybe some gin will help."

Warren and Harlan were still laughing as he waved and walked out the door.

Chapter 7

Morrissey trudged back up the stone steps to the guardhouse, changed into his painting clothes – paint-spattered work pants and a similarly decorated long-sleeved t-shirt – and made his regular breakfast of bacon, eggs, juice, and coffee. Always more coffee; the cop in him.

Jack Harlan was missing a good bet, he thought. The restaurant was a pricey fine dining establishment in the evening, the sort of romantic place that guys brought their girls to propose marriage, or brought them twenty-five years later to celebrate their anniversary. Too expensive for a regular evening meal several times a week, but that was fine; Jack Harlan had only five months, from mid-May to mid-October, to make twelve months' worth of profits. Morrissey didn't begrudge him a bit of that.

The place wasn't exactly a neighborhood pub at happy hour either. Some folks came out on a late afternoon ferry to get a little lubricated before their dining experience, and Harlan wasn't about to discount his highest-margin commodity: booze. So Morrissey usually enjoyed his happy hour cocktail sitting in an Adirondack chair on his back porch. But he was a little conflicted.

He liked Harlan, and wanted to support him and his business. He wished Jack would serve breakfast, at least during the height of the summer when the island was populated to capacity. I'd be down there every day, Morrissey thought, and I bet a lot of the old farts on this island would join me. That gab session this morning was fun. Should be more of those as a counterweight to the dickheads – and as a sign to Jack that he might have a good many more allies than he thought.

The task Morrissey had given himself for the day was putting a finish coat of paint on his living room and dining room baseboard trim. No wonder finish work was so time-consuming and expensive, he thought. Meticulous attention to detail. Well, a homicide detective was no stranger to that. Let's get this party started.

He put a Credence Clearwater Revival CD in his ancient stereo rack system and set to work. He was halfway around the room's baseboard, reflecting on how much slower he must be than a professional painter, when there came a knock at the front door. Perfect, he thought. Just what I need right now.

He paused the stereo and, as he opened the door, his visitor tried to follow its swing into the living room. Couldn't do it because Morrissey didn't give way to her. He knew who she was – she'd been pointed out to him once, and he'd just been talking about her with Jack Harlan and Tom Warren.

Thalia Sandberg was a hatchet-faced woman wearing the most disagreeable expression he'd ever seen.

48

She was forty pounds overweight, dressed in a frumpy housedress, with a faded scarf tying back stringy unkempt hair. She again tried to push her way into his living room and Morrissey again stood his ground.

"We need to talk," she said. "You have a garbage disposal that needs to be removed."

Morrissey gave her a pleasant smile. No harm in trying, he thought. The good cop, with the sonofabitch in reserve. "Can we back up a little?" he asked. "I don't think we've met. My name is John Morrissey, and I believe you're Thalia Sandberg. How do you do?"

He held out his hand. She ignored it. "Your garbage disposal needs to come out. It's in violation of the covenants."

"Look, Ms. Sandberg, this isn't a good time for me. I'm right in the middle of something – painting my baseboard trim – and that's not a job that's easily interrupted. I need to finish. Why don't you call me this evening and we can agree on a good time to discuss your topic?"

"You're not listening to me. Your garbage disposal needs to come out. I need to see it to see the configuration." She tried to push past him, and he again blocked her way.

The good cop faded into the sea mist surrounding the island, and the bad cop made his appearance. "On the contrary, my good woman, I *have* been listening. I heard you. But I'm not going to debate this with you right now. And probably not ever. You are rude and arrogant, and this conversation is over. Now if you'll excuse me." He started to push the door closed.

Her voice rose to a near shout. "I said your garbage disposal has to be removed!"

"You just don't get the message, do you? We're done here. Now remove yourself from my porch and my property, or I'll call Estates security. And if that doesn't get through to you, I'll call the Portland police. I'm sure you know who I am, and I'm equally sure the police will agree to come out here and arrest you for trespassing, take you back to the mainland in the police boat, and let you cool your heels in a holding cell while they see if they can tie you to any open cases of criminal trespass. Are you sure you want to continue on that path?"

Thalia Sandberg actually tried to shoulder her way into his living room. "Stop trying to dismiss me! We are going to discuss this now!"

Morrissey took her arm and walked through his open door, backing the woman back out onto his porch. "Your reputation precedes you, Ms. Sandberg. You are a bully, and one thing you should know about me is that I despise bullies. In words of one syllable, back off, lady. Leave my property or I'll have you locked up."

She stared daggers at him, then turned and limped down his porch steps. He started, but caught and didn't allow himself, to feel sorry for her about her MS. She turned back to him and snarled, "This isn't over. You haven't heard the last of me. Your garbage disposal is coming out." She looked at the flowers growing in front of his porch, beautiful perennials Dottie had planted that continued to bloom years after her death. "And so are these flowers. They're not indigenous to Granite Cliffs Island, and they're in violation of the covenants!"

Morrissey was incensed, but his voice was quiet. "Madam, you have just crossed a line you shouldn't have crossed. I suggest you get back on the other side of it before I ruin your day. Now get your fat ass out of here."

She stormed off, and Morrissey thought about his last comment. Unbecoming a senior police detective, but he was retired. Nor more "sir" or "ma'am" required when addressing irretrievable assholes.

He went back inside, picked up his paintbrush, and let his anger dissipate as he finished the baseboards. Still need to calm down, he thought. How did Jack Harlan and David Borman keep their cool if the woman behaved that way toward them and their businesses? He had no doubt that she'd caused some serious trouble for some of her neighbors. Taking issue with a beautiful garden? Good God.

Morrissey continued his work, putting finish coats on the door trim around living room, dining room, and kitchen entryways. Getting angry could pay dividends, he thought. You could accomplish a lot more as you worked through it. He finished his painting and took a long shower – the cop's version of meditation – and cleaned himself up. Then he called David Borman at the Estates administration office.

"Hi, David," he said. "John Morrissey. Can I schedule some time with you when it's convenient? I just had a rather unpleasant visit with Thalia Sandberg, and I want to make sure I'm on firm ground before I take a broadaxe to her."

Borman chuckled. "John, when you say 'unpleasant' and 'Thalia Sandberg' in the same breath, you repeat yourself, do you not? I have some time right now. Why don't you come over here and I'll see if I can put your mind at ease."

Morrissey walked down to the administration building, which had served as the post exchange for the old army installation. It was located just off the parade ground, a large brick building with an imposing columned entry. Inside, two large rooms flanked a wide central hallway. The room to the left was administration: a large registration desk for rentals, with an alcove for the Estates bookkeeper and a small conference room with adjoining corner office for Borman.

The developer came out of his office and grasped Morrissey's hand. "Good to see you. Sorry we didn't catch up with you over the long weekend. But, wow, John – you haven't been retired a month, just enjoyed your first 4th of July weekend, and you've got Thalia Sandberg in your face already. You must have real talent." He gestured toward the central hallway. "Let's go across the hall and take advantage of those easy chairs, and you can unburden yourself."

They crossed the hall to a large open room furnished with leather chairs and couches around the perimeter, with small sets of chairs and tables arranged in the open space. Borman intended the room to be an all-purpose room for the community: a space for homeowners' meetings, and for bridge tournaments, book clubs, and lectures by local historians to talk about the old fort.

Borman pointed to a couple of leather chairs. "Make yourself comfortable," he said. "What did she do this time?"

Morrissey told him the whole story – Sandberg's frontal assault, her short-lived diatribe about his garbage disposal, and their heated parting. "My memory is pretty clear on this," he said. "Way back when, I think in our year three when we had the trades in and installed the plumbing, Dottie asked if we could have a garbage disposal, and you said yes. So we had one installed. Am I wrong? Have things changed?"

"Relax," Borman said. "You're fine. No need for your broadaxe. Bit of history. During the active life of the fort, all what are now the historic buildings were on a sewer system that the Army just discharged into the open ocean. Very environmentally conscious, huh? We had to build a sewage treatment facility – spent about three million bucks on it – to meet current environmental standards. Our discharge effluent is now as clear as drinking water, and it's tested regularly.

"The original covenants that I wrote stressed the importance of the facility and said rather vaguely that foreign objects shouldn't be washed down the sink or flushed down the toilet, that people should use good judgment. I meant tampons, and stuff like contractors' glue and bits of joint compound while houses were being renovated. The covenants were silent on garbage disposals. But when Dottie and a couple of others asked, it became clear that this was not going to be strictly the summer seasonal resort I'd originally envisioned, but a year-round community. So I gave the initial year-rounders – including you, a planned year-rounder – a break, and said, 'Sure, you can have a garbage disposal.'

"Later on, as the year-round community grew, I realized that everyone's having a disposal could put a strain on the treatment facility, so I amended the covenants to permit existing installations but foreclosed the possibility of any more. Thalia Sandberg knows all this, I've been over it with her. But she chooses to ignore it. She's working from, and showing around, the original vaguely worded covenants, and choosing to interpret them her way. She says the amended covenants aren't valid because the homeowners didn't vote on them."

"Is she right? I mean, I don't remember voting on anything like that."

"Because you didn't vote, John. Nobody did. In those days *I* was the homeowners association. The homeowners didn't take control until a critical mass – 75% of the properties – had been sold. All this happened years before we reached that threshold. You're on solid ground. Keep your garbage disposal. You're fine."

A light went on for Morrissey. "She's raising hell because she can't have one?"

Borman laughed. "No, John, she's raising hell because she's a miserable bitch who can't have any satisfaction or happiness unless she's making someone else even more miserable. In fact, she was here early enough that she could have had a disposal, but didn't choose to install one. Now she can't, because that ship has sailed – I've foreclosed the possibility going forward.

"She's just a bully. Ignore her – or better yet, call her on it every time she tries, just as you did this morning. I wish more people had stood up to her and told her where to get off long before this. She's caused a bunch of her neighbors time and money and worry with her antics and her legal posturing."

"Yeah," Morrissey said, "that's what Jack Harlan and Tom Warren mentioned this morning." Then another thought came to him. "Say," he said, "she also took issue with Dottie's flowers in front of the house. Said they weren't indigenous to Granite Cliffs, and weren't allowed. What's up with that?"

"Oh, for Chrissake," Borman said. "I remember when Dottie planted those. I was so happy that someone had made an effort to create a look of permanence around here.

"Relax about the damn flowers too. Do you really think she's going to sue someone about that? She'd be laughed out of court and sent back to her homeowners association. And if she tried to make an issue of it among the homeowners, she'd look so nuts she'd lose whatever following she has even with the lunatic fringe around here."

"Okay, thanks David," Morrissey said. "Although I don't know how you put up with nonsense like that. Not sure I could do it."

Borman laughed. "All part of being a developer. I think your job was a good deal more hazardous. You had to dodge bullets. I only have to dodge this shit. Why don't I buy you a drink at Jack's at the end of the day as compensation for her interrupting your day?"

Morrissey laughed too. "You're on. Then I'll buy one for you as compensation for setting my world right again."

Borman walked him to the door and Morrissey returned to the guardhouse and his new hobby: his computer. As a working detective, he hadn't resisted the advent of technology, but he hadn't exactly embraced it either. Now he had some catching up to do, and he was enjoying the effort. Amazing what you could discover about all sorts of people in places both far and near. And not just on Facebook, which he'd already come to regard as a cesspool and a home for cruelty and cowardice. The analogy with Granite Cliffs Island seemed obvious to him – a few bad apples could poison the whole barrel. He hoped his island could avoid Facebook's path.

Chapter 8

The 4th of July holiday was over, and tourist season was in full swing in the city of Portland. Boat excursions in Casco Bay, sightseeing in the Old Port, lobsters at legendary restaurants like Boone's and DeMillo's. Congested but happy crowds on the waterfront, and happy merchants overcharging the bumpkins for souvenirs and bric-a-brac. No one really minded – like Jack Harlan, the merchants had only a few short months to make the year's profits.

With high season upon them, PPD's patrol force was in high gear, kept hopping with all-too-frequent cases of people behaving like buffoons in the night-time: drunk and disorderly, assault and battery, falling-down public drunkenness. Summer heat and alcohol were a volatile mixture, but the force was used to the routine.

RHD investigations, however, didn't necessarily ratchet up with tourist season, and Kate and Sam handled a normal flow of robberies and a handful of aggravated assault and manslaughter cases – the latter generally coming from drunken fights that got out of hand, a fractured skull from a blow with a bar stool, witnessed by a multitude, easy to close and pass on to the DA.

So Harwood and Chapman actually had some time to review John Morrissey's old cases and look busy doing it. Naturally, that wasn't enough for Robert Langdon, who persisted in his agenda of trying to discredit them so they'd have to come under his thumb.

Langdon had been asking repeatedly why more progress wasn't being made, so one sultry afternoon Sam Chapman said, "Time to raise the curtain on a more elaborate show for that fool. Why don't you very visibly go out to John Morrissey's guardhouse and 'press him'" – Chapman made air quotes with his hands – "about those cases. I'll tell Langdon I'm making the rounds of victims' friends and families to see if we can dredge up more information or insights about paybacks, feuds, grudges, that sort of thing. Maybe that will keep him happy for a while."

"Are you really going to do that?" Kate asked.

"No, of course not," Chapman said. "Already did it, beat it to death a long time ago. I *will* go see them to assure them that the cases are still open and that they should call us if anything occurs to them. But it's mostly just window dressing to satisfy Langdon."

"I'll go see John, " Kate said. "I never got a chance to work with him that much or that closely – he may not have anything more, but at least I'll have a chance to pick his brain and see how that mind works. That'll be a treat for me."

"Have fun. Boat ride out to the island will make you ten or fifteen degrees cooler. Nice sea breeze. Say hi to John for me. Check out how he's doing on finishing his house."

Kate called Morrissey to verify that he was home and wouldn't mind the visit. Fantastic, he said, he'd welcome the break and a chance to catch up on department gossip.

"I have plenty of that," Kate laughed. "I'll see you in a half hour."

She caught a ride with one of the Portland fireboats, just setting out on a journey down the bay to check equipment – hose carts and reels, submersible pumps, antiquated surplus trucks – that the fire department kept stored on each island. The boat could give her 90 minutes with Morrissey, the crew said, as they traveled to the outer islands and back. They'd pick her up at the Atlantic Estates pier late afternoon.

Kate enjoyed the ride; the respite from the Old Port's stifling heart was almost immediate as the boat left the pier and made its way out to sea. She mentioned to the boat crew Chapman's promise that the temperature would be much cooler on the island.

"Yeah," the captain said. "But these people pay for that. The city looks at the islands like a cash cow. Milks them for all they can in real estate taxes, ocean front and ocean view properties and all, even though most of the houses are old and very modest. In return, the islands don't get much in city services. I always feel guilty about that. Maybe our new fire captain can change things."

Kate knew the new fire captain who commanded the district that encompassed the islands. His name was Dave MacKenzie, and she knew him intimately – he was her boyfriend, and they were getting pretty serious. They were also a secret – wouldn't be smart, Dave said, for two up-and-comers to put themselves under everyone's

59

microscope and become grist for the gossip mill. Besides, they were private people.

Morrissey was waiting for her as the fireboat pulled into one of the finger piers flanking the main Atlantic Estates docking facility. She hopped off the boat, thanked the crew, and turned to Morrissey.

"This place is absolutely beautiful. I can see why you and Dottie worked so hard for so long to make your house a home." Her voice grew serious. "I'm very sorry she's missing the sharing of it with you, John."

Morrissey gave her a sad smile. "Ah, I don't think she is, Kate. I feel her every day. The last promise I made to her was that I'd finish the house, and if I started slacking off, I'm sure she'd haunt me." His grin grew wider. "Come on, let's go up these steps – house is at the top of the cliff. Great exercise doing this staircase several times a day."

They settled in two roomy Adirondack chairs on Morrissey's back deck, looking out at the ocean.

"I'll catch you up on some of the gossip," Kate said. "It kind of explains why I'm here." She told him about Langdon's assignment of Morrissey's old cases to her and Chapman, and about their suspicion that it was a ploy to bring them under his dominance.

"But it's given me a chance to review your murder books, John, and I've really learned something. They're masterpieces of organization – the way I think a murder book should be put together … which opinion, of course, I keep to myself. Uppity know-it-all female detectives aren't that welcome in Robert Langdon's world."

Morrissey laughed. "Anyone with any degree of real competence isn't that welcome in Robert Langdon's world."

"Anyway ..." Kate said. "I'm sure I don't need to review or summarize these cases with you. I bet Tom Brady remembers the Super Bowls his team lost far more clearly than the ones he won, and you're probably exactly the same way.

"So -- what advice do you have? I know you said at your party that we should keep after them."

"That was mostly for form, Kate. It's pointless to keep looking. Believe me, we turned over every rock. The evidence we have now is largely circumstantial, but we're sure of the guilty party in each case. There's no more evidence to be gathered unless somebody – an eyewitness or someone with direct knowledge – flips because we nail them on something else. But we can't get indictments as things stand now."

"Why not?"

"Best way I can put it is a failure of integrity. In my experience, most every DA in this town has seen his job as a steppingstone to Congress, the Senate, or the governor's mansion. None of them is going to indict on a high-profile case unless it's a slam-dunk conviction – taking no chances, and the hell with justice."

"But John, these don't look to me like they were high profile cases. The victims were all people on the fringes."

"Yeah. Until the paper did an investigative series on crime in the Old Port. Highlighted these murders as

61

evidence of a trend, that the Old Port and the waterfront were becoming a haven for violent crime, made the place unsafe for fishermen, marine businesses, and tourists. Crime would stop the gentrification that everyone wants down there. So the 'crime wave' had to be stopped, and these cases became high profile – even though we'd already investigated all of them thoroughly, and pushed for arrests and indictments in each one.

"Then the DA got lucky. The low-lifes returned to their normal stupidity, committed assaults and a couple of murders that had multiple eyewitnesses, easy to make arrests and close, and the DA looked tough on crime all of a sudden. So he lost interest in these tougher cases and wouldn't go any further – that included the assistant DA's, who with rare exceptions are no better. They see their positions as steppingstones to the district attorney's chair or some lucrative private practice partnership. So they were loath to take any chances either."

"I'm sure you're right. I talked to one of the senior ADA's and pressed him on what they need to indict and prosecute. It didn't go well."

"Oh? How so?"

"He got huffy and said he didn't like my tone – said he didn't work for me or report to me."

"Sounds like that punk Levenson."

Harwood sighed. "Bingo. It was Levenson."

"It most likely didn't have anything to do with your tone. Just as with Langdon, it was your gender."

"Yeah, particularly after I told him it was worse than his working for me or reporting to me – he depended on me. On us. If we didn't catch the perps and make the arrests, they wouldn't have a job."

Morrissey exploded in laughter. "Oh Christ, I bet that set his fat ass on fire! He couldn't call you a bitch or anything similarly politically incorrect because that might become a black mark on his record. I bet he ground his teeth into powder!"

"Yeah, but I probably made myself an enemy."

"Hey, relax. Those clowns have all kinds of political infighting going on among themselves all the time. If the guy is small and petty enough to carry a grudge against you and try to act on it, he's small and petty enough to self-destruct. Don't worry about that asshole, kid, he's not worth your time. Just do your job and you'll outshine them all."

Harwood smiled and shrugged. "I hope you're right." She paused. "We got a little off track, John. Sorry. What if anything should we do with these cases?"

"You and Sam are both talented detectives. You can make it look like you're reviewing all the evidence, investigating every possibility, when all you're doing is going through the motions and not wasting time. Like I said – there's enough there in every case, and there won't be anything more unless it comes as a bolt from the blue."

"Okay, thanks John – for the professional advice, and for the pep talk. I wish we'd had a chance to work together more. We're really going to miss you."

"No you're not, Kate. Together you and Sam will more than make up for my old bones."

They had some time, so Morrissey walked Kate around the parade ground, pointing out all the historic buildings. They arrived at the pier as the fireboat hove into view. She turned to face him. "This place is paradise, John. I'm falling in love with it myself – the difference between here and the city is night and day."

"Yeah," Morrissey said, "on a summer day like this the island is really at its best. But Dottie and I liked the other seasons too. The fall foliage is spectacular, and the winters are a little warmer than the mainland. We'd come out here on a weekend, sleep on a big air mattress, and listen to the navigation buoys sound in the night and fog. Very romantic. You and Dave should come out and stay with me sometime."

Kate's eyes widened. "You know about us? Oh my God, John, how many people know? We want it to be a secret – we don't think it would do us any good if our relationship were common knowledge."

Morrissey laughed. "Relax, kid, no one else knows. Not to my knowledge anyway. I haven't shared it with anyone. You're safe."

"How do *you* know?"

Morrissey's smile creased his whole face. "I was a detective, Kate. It was my job to know things, especially about my own detectives. Old habits die hard, you know?"

He took her hand to steady her as she stepped on the fireboat's gunwale and then on to the fantail. "Take care of yourself, Kate. Come out anytime – on a case or just to shoot the breeze. Good seeing you. Say hi to Sam."

Chapter 9

The next morning Morrissey started the research that Jack Harlan and Tom Warren had suggested to him. The first part of his journey took him past the parade ground to the Atlantic Estates main gate, anchored between two tall brick pillars crowned with granite caps. The gate separated the Estates and private sides of the island. Odd, he thought. In his memory of years past, the gate had always been open. Now it was closed and locked. What had brought that on?

The road was the main route across the island, running from the Estates pier near the restaurant to the public pier at the other end of the island. From the gate, the road took him 300 yards over low and swampy land – what one of his neighbors called "mosquito alley" – to the first houses in the interior of the island. Small and modest homes and cottages, unlike the imposing officers' quarters ringing the Estates parade ground, also unlike the large ocean front cottages on the private side owned by wealthy mainland people.

Another two hundred yards brought him to a well-worn tennis court bounded by a high screened fence. An elderly couple was happily whacking the ball back and forth. He stopped to watch.

The man, spare of frame, average height, with a winning smile, stopped playing and asked, "Oh, are you here to play – waiting for your partner? Don't mind us, we're not signed up for the court. We live just over there" – he gestured with his racket toward a cottage 150 feet away – "and we jump out here to hit a few when the court's vacant. Give us a minute and we'll get out of your way."

"Oh no," Morrissey said, "Don't mind *me*. I'm not here to play. Just thought I'd watch you for a while. Tennis isn't my game anyway – I was all smash-mouth football back in the day."

"Oh hell, we're done anyway," the woman said. She looked at her husband. "We're getting pretty ragged, Earl. Time to quit."

She turned to Morrissey. "Would you like to join us on our porch for a cup of coffee? Or if it's too late in the morning for that, maybe some iced tea? By the way, we're the Randalls – Earl and Rosemary."

"Thank you," Morrissey said. "I'd love some iced tea and a chance to visit. I've been advised that I should make the rounds and meet my neighbors. My name is John Morrissey."

"Oh, we know who you are," Rosemary Randall said. "Actually, we feel a good bit safer out here with a high-ranking police officer on the island. Come along with us."

They followed a path through some tall grass and underbrush as Morrissey explained that he was no longer a high-ranking officer, only "an old war horse put out to pasture." Nonsense, Rosemary answered. They were glad to have him on the island.

The porch was large, roofed and screened, attached to the back of a medium-sized cottage. Four dark green Adirondack chairs were arranged around a low circular table.

"It's instant iced tea," Rosemary said as she returned to the porch from the kitchen. "But what the hell, sugar and lemon fix anything, don't they?"

"Thank you," Morrissey said, settling back in his chair. "These are beautiful old vintage chairs, I can tell. Adirondack chairs must be the law of the land out here on Granite Cliffs Island."

"Yes, at least until that Sandberg bitch decides they're in violation of something-or-other and tries to force everyone to get rid of them," Rosemary said.

"Rose isn't terribly shy with her opinions," Earl smiled.

"I was pretty jaundiced about Atlantic Estates when they first started it," his wife said. "I was afraid we'd have a thousand people over-running the island with high-rise condos and such, destroying all our peace and quiet. But give David Borman credit, he's kept it to a modest scale. And there are some nice people – like you, John – on the Estates side.

"Besides, if I continued on some jihad against the Estates, I'd have to be in league with Russ Bannerman, and I can't stand him. He's done a lot of damage here on this island. He started the golf cart war, got the City to restrict Estates people from driving them on this side of the island. So that awful Don Kagan and his ilk retaliated by closing the gate and locking it. Now people can't drive back and forth to visit the people who've become their friends. Which is exactly what those assholes want."

"Rose, you're doing it again ..." her husband said.

"Yeah, yeah, yeah," she replied. She looked at Morrissey and smiled. "Earl's a bit more mellow than I am. Comes from keeping the lid on teenagers' emotions for 40 years as a high school teacher."

"What did you teach?" Morrissey asked.

"English, at South Portland High," Earl said. "Also the coach for the drama club. Directing all those young kids with their dreams of Hollywood and Broadway glory. Lots of fun."

"Earl wants to put on a play at the Granite Cliffs Association meeting hall here on this side," Rosemary said. "Get people from both sides of the island in the cast, get both sides of the island to attend, help bring the island together. But Bannerman's the president of the Association and won't let him use the building. Total asshole."

"Rose ..." Earl said.

"I see her point," Morrissey said. "Seems like we have a few rotten apples here who are determined to turn this community into a toxic waste dump for the sake of their own egos. Tom Warren told me it's growing pains, and he hopes we can overcome them."

"Tom's always optimistic," Rosemary said. "It remains to be seen if we can attract enough nice people who become friends before people like Bannerman and Kagan and Sandberg spoil the place. One big problem is these troublemakers get a lot of publicity – the

69

newspapers played up Bannerman and his golf cart war, Kagan and his opposition to Borman and the restaurant, Sandberg trying to get Historic Preservation to restrict everything. Get enough bad publicity and the housing market dries up on both sides, nobody visits the island, the restaurant fails, and people are at each other's throats. It's not what we envisioned when we retired to paradise."

"Well," Morrissey said, "in my experience lots of these problems seem to solve themselves if you're patient. I should move along, try to get a little more familiar with the cast of characters. Thanks for the iced tea." He turned to Earl. "You know, if you succeed in putting together that play, I'd like to try out for it."

"Yeah," Earl said, "You can play the cop."

"No, no," Morrissey said. "I want to play the crook!" With a laugh and a wave he was off. "Great meeting you," he said as he left. "Love to have you come over and see the jail – where the crook lives!"

Morrissey continued on his way and gleaned a lot of information for one morning, particularly about Russell Bannerman. He used a veteran police detective's oldest trick: asking only one question, then listening, waiting for the other person to fill the silence. They almost invariably did. All he had to do this morning was mention meeting the Randalls, how nice they were, and how Earl wanted to stage a play, wasn't that nice, but Russ Bannerman seemed to be standing in the way …

70

Bannerman, most of John's new acquaintances volunteered, was a vicious predator who'd used his financial expertise to evict and dispossess struggling families from their homes and enrich himself in the process. He ran a bottom-feeding closed investment group that specialized in distressed mortgages and foreclosures. He was well-known for ruining peoples' lives and boasting that he then went home and slept like a baby.

Away from work, he was still not content to enjoy his summer home on Granite Cliffs as a retreat and a place to relax. He used threats and abuse of the judicial process to bully and cow his island neighbors into acquiescing to what he wanted. He'd tied up one family in court for years over a right of way from their beach and dock to their house and yard – a right of way absolutely necessary for them – simply because he thought he might one day be interested in purchasing the lot containing the right of way. He'd also informed on one young mother who was trying to make ends meet by hiring herself out to mow lawns and clean houses for her neighbors. She had to be licensed and registered, he said, and pay Social Security self-employment tax and make estimated payments for state and federal income tax. No one else cared if Terry Roberts dipped her toe in the underground economy – it was discouraging enough for her to have to work for her neighbors – but Bannerman made an issue of it simply because he could.

Like Jason Alexander's character in "Pretty Woman," Russ Bannerman was in it for the kill as much as

71

the money.   He'd become a rich man doing what he loved to do – crushing people. He was widely hated and feared on the island, and he loved it.

Well, that's a pretty good morning's work, Morrissey thought as he returned to his guardhouse. For certain there were at least three rotten apples on this island, maybe more. But he'd met some decent people today. He hoped the nice ones would start to overtake and outnumber the toxic ones.

Chapter 10

Morrissey occupied himself the rest of July walking around the island talking to his neighbors, mentally categorizing people. He also finished the last task remaining on his house: painting the latticework skirting the underside of his front porch and back deck. The job went a lot faster after he discovered the beauty of a paint sprayer. He'd spent a day of frustration trying to cover every surface with a roller and brush, then decided he needed an upgrade.

He was standing on the pier on the private side of the island, bemoaning the need to go to town to purchase just one item, when Tom Warren said, "Remember what I told you about not throwing anything away? Use my sprayer. I haven't used the damn thing in years, but I've kept it." He laughed. "Like everything else. After thirty years here, if I don't have it, it ain't worth having. Come on, we'll go get it and I'll run you back over to the fort."

"You're allowed to drive on Estates residential property?"

"Yeah, service vehicles are allowed. I'm a service vehicle, and this is a service call. Screw Russ Bannerman and Don Kagan and their childish games."

"You're a trusting sort to lend out your equipment, Tom."

"People are pretty good at returning things – almost as good as I am about deciding who I'll lend to. I've seen you walking around talking to folks, and I'm sure you've discovered the majority of people here are pretty decent. If we can just stop the few jerks we have from spoiling it.

"Come on, let's get you set up for painting."

Morrissey also spent a good deal of time that month coming up to speed on the computer, going through every tutorial he could find. He thanked his lucky stars that as a senior detective he'd had people to do computer-assisted grunt work for him, and that the growth industry of cyber crime hadn't hit RHD's world during his career. But better late than never for him to learn the computer's potential, if not for solving crimes than for exploring.

He especially liked the 'Incognito' browsing status. You couldn't go completely off the grid, but you could occasionally swat Big Brother and keep him from looking over your shoulder. This was fun, he thought; he could understand how people could become addicted to sitting at their computers.

Morrissey went to Tom Warren's birthday party in early August, and saw a lot of his new friends and none of the people he'd categorized as unpleasant or toxic. It turned out Tom's party was not an open house, even though with so many people it looked like one. Tom in fact had a select invitation list – it was quite long, seemed very inclusive, but it had some obvious omissions.

Morrissey decided that if you weren't on Tom's invitation list, it was prima facie evidence that you were an asshole.

"What can I bring?" he'd asked Tom before the party.

"Nothing but a good appetite," Tom said. "We'll have lobsters, corn on the cob, French fries, a couple of kegs of beer, and soft drinks for the kids. Strawberry shortcake for dessert."

Morrissey laughed. "How about I bring a cubic foot of butter to melt, for the lobsters?"

"John, you're in for a surprise," Tom said. "People who drown their lobster in melted butter are the same people who like escargot for the taste of the garlic – tourists and la-di-da people from the mainland. Watch how many islanders skip the melted butter. They appreciate the fresh taste of the lobster. Pretty good rule of thumb: butter – tourist; no butter – a true islander."

Morrissey sat at the same table as Earl and Rosemary Randall. They had a question for him. "What are you going to do this winter, John, now that your house is done?" They had been Morrissey's guests for dinner a couple of times, and were impressed with his transformation of what they remembered as a tumbledown ruin.

"I guess I could sit by the fire practicing to be old, but I'd rather go skiing," Morrissey said. "I have a quarter-share condo at a ski area – Sunday River's big resort hotel. Dottie and I only used it on a few weekends, rented it out the rest of the time. Now I'll be able to use it a lot more – one week a month, and a space available basis midweek if the hotel isn't fully booked. Really looking forward to a lot more skiing, maybe make a whole bunch of new friends!"

August turned to September, the best-kept secret in Maine. The tourists and summer people went home after Labor Day and the start of school, while the island natives enjoyed the cool dry weather and brilliant sunshine. Morrissey gradually shifted his perspective to Sunday River and the upcoming ski season. Jack Harlan stopped serving lunch a week after Labor Day, and two weeks after that limited dinner service to Thursday to Saturday only, plus a Sunday brunch. Morrissey went to Fall Festival at Sunday River on Columbus Day weekend, and returned with a big smile on his face. Jack was closing down for the winter, save for his annual midwinter party on the Friday evening of Presidents Day weekend. This Tuesday morning in October would be the last coffee session that he, Jack, and Tom had at the restaurant.

"Guess what," he told them. "I'm thinking about becoming a 62-year-old rookie ski instructor! I ran into the ski area general manager and the ski school director at Fall Festival, said I was going to be skiing a lot more this season, and was looking forward to making new friends."

"Best way to do that is spend some time teaching," they'd said. "You'll make a lot of friends in ski school and among the mountain regulars, earn your beer money, cut lift lines on weekends, get discounts on equipment and on lift tickets at other areas. You've been a teacher and mentor to all your detectives anyway, you'd be great."

"I wondered out loud if I skied well enough," Morrissey told Jack and Tom. "But they said don't worry – the GM wants people who don't need the job but just love to ski, the ski school director wants mature instructors in sync with older ski school students. They said don't worry about your skiing, we'll make it better. I think I'm gonna do it. Not full time, maybe the odd weekend, two or three days midweek, it'll be fun!"

"Better than sitting around here, cooped up in the house, drinking and gossiping about the neighbors," Tom said. "I'm glad I have fuel oil delivery and plowing to keep me busy – the toxic people start working overtime on their projects to screw this place up when they're snowbound and don't have anything else to do."

November arrived, and with it the annual race among major Eastern ski areas to be the first to open. Sunday River won, on November 4, and the combination of an early-season snowstorm and cold weather for snowmaking enabled the area to expand its open terrain quickly. Morrissey spent several midweek stretches at the area, staying in his condo and getting into the ski school routine.

He advised Jack and Tom that he'd scheduled himself with ski school for a couple of weekends too, and was thinking of working the entire Friday to Friday stretch of his quarter-share week in mid-December. He'd go to Sunday River at the beginning of the week, stay at the hotel on their space-available plan, and then work his

77

quarter-share week. He'd be gone for twelve days, he said, and asked Jack to stroll by the guardhouse occasionally just to check on things. Glad to do it, Jack said.

Morrissey went to Tom Warren's New Year's Eve party and told Jack that he was having such a great time at ski school that he wouldn't be able to attend the Presidents Weekend midwinter party. That weekend was incredibly busy at Sunday River, he explained, and he felt he owed the time to his boss. The guy had been very flexible in giving John latitude with his work schedule.

"We'll miss you," Jack said. "Always a good time."

"Next year," Morrissey replied.

Chapter 11

The striking dark-haired woman was waiting at the Little Cliffs pier, one island closer to Portland than Granite Cliffs, when the late Friday night boat stopped there on its return to Portland. She was the only one boarding, and almost the only passenger. The late boat wasn't meant to bring people back to Portland at midnight; it took island residents home after a Friday evening dinner or party in town. The dozen or so off-island visitors at Jack Harlan's party had returned on the special 10:30 p.m. boat he'd chartered. The charter was worth it, he thought. He didn't want his place full of drunks hanging around till after midnight.

The mid-winter party was an annual tradition at Jack's restaurant. "We've broken the back of winter," Jack always said. "Now to get some 80-proof antifreeze in you to help you survive the last few weeks of cold weather."

Most year-round residents of the island came to the celebration, although not Jack's constant antagonists Don Kagan and Thalia Sandberg. But even the arrogant judge and the sanctimonious doctor were regulars at the party. So for that matter was Russ Bannerman. His wife always said the island was too cold and desolate in winter, so he was alone for the evening, although the atmosphere was so convivial that a number of people made the effort to talk to him.

The big event at the party turned out to be Bannerman getting uncharacteristically falling-down drunk, nearly incoherent. He'd been sitting at the bar, passing the time in conversation with a few people, including the woman who everyone assumed must be Seth Toomey's date. She was in her mid-thirties, dark and dusky in the mold of actress Penelope Cruz, and Seth was the island lothario, an exclusive fish buyer and broker for Portland's most upscale restaurants. In that capacity, he made the acquaintance of many an attractive woman. He was known for his stable of beautiful girls, and this one looked to be no exception. Russ Bannerman did not seem at all immune to her charms. They chatted for a while, then she drifted away.

It was shortly after she'd left the restaurant and headed toward the pier to catch the 10:30 charter boat that Bannerman went non compos mentis. Nearly falling off his chair, babbling unintelligibly, barely able to stand even with assistance.

Tom Warren shook his head. "I'll take him home."

"Nah, I got this," the Estates security guard on duty said. "I'll take him home in the van, get him in bed. Strike a blow for island harmony. You enjoy the rest of the evening."

Two hours later, just past 12:30 a.m., Jack and Tom and a few diehards were wrapping up the evening at the bar when the restaurant phone rang. It was the Portland Fire Department. "The fireboat is on the way," they said.

"House fire on the private side. Chad Silverman called it in, said it looks like Russ Bannerman's house."

Tom and the others piled into his pickup and drove over. The fireboat had already arrived, and the firefighters had driven the water truck parked alongside the main island road to the site of fire. They were just starting to hose the house down when the crew from the restaurant arrived. "More smoke than fire," the firefighters said. "The house has some fairly serious damage, but it's not a total loss."

One of the firefighters exited the front door of the house, took off his oxygen mask, and said to Captain Dave Mackenzie, "Clear except for a man lying on the living room couch. Unresponsive. I'm pretty sure he's dead – smoke inhalation, most likely. There's still so much smoke in there, toxic I'd guess from the brocade fabric in the couch and the carpeting, it's not safe for anyone right now."

Tom Warren said, "I qualified last year as an EMT. Give me the mask and I'll check for signs of life. We'll get him out of there somehow if he's still breathing."

Warren returned three minutes later. "It's Russ Bannerman, and he's dead," he said to MacKenzie. "You can call the rescue boat, I think the smoke is clearing enough so the EMTs can go and remove him."

"Let me check," MacKenzie said, taking the mask. When he came back out of the house, he said to his lieutenant, "I don't like this. It looks like an accident, there's an ashtray with spent cigarettes in it, like maybe he fell asleep smoking. And all the matches in the book

81

are burned, like he struck a match and the whole matchbook caught fire and he dropped it on the carpet. But the burn pattern on the couch and carpet is weird, and you don't have a whole matchbook catch fire these days with the striking surface on the back of the book.

"It looks a little too perfect for me. Let's hold off on the EMTs for the moment. I want to call the fire marshal and have him check the couch and carpeting for accelerants. And I want a homicide detective to decide if the coroner should check and see if smoke was the only thing that killed this guy."

"Good call on the matches and cigarettes," Tom Warren said to him. "I've never known Russ Bannerman to smoke."

Along with the fire marshal, MacKenzie called Kate Harwood and the coroner. After making sure he wouldn't be overheard talking to his girlfriend, he said to Kate, "I'm glad you have the duty tonight, honey. I'm at the scene of a house fire on Granite Cliffs Island. One fatality, a high-profile guy named Russell Bannerman. I think you should have a look at this before I have the EMTs remove the body. We may be looking at a crime scene."

Minutes before MacKenzie's phone calls, the pretty dark-haired woman reached an outdoor parking lot called "Top of the Old Port" some five blocks uphill from the ferry terminal. She took the Franklin Street arterial to Interstate 295, but did not merge on to Interstate 95, the Maine Turnpike, a toll road that photographed each vehicle's license plate. Instead, she turned south on old Route 1, now a secondary road. She used it to disappear into the night. She had a great many roads and a three-day drive ahead of her. Still, she wasn't in the least bit tired. Her spirits were subdued, but she felt enormously relieved.

Kate Harwood had ridden with the EMTs and the coroner on the rescue boat's trip out to Granite Cliffs Island in the wee hours of Saturday morning. She agreed with the medical examiner that a toxicology analysis was in order as part of his autopsy. On Tuesday morning he called her at her desk. "MacKenzie was right. So were you. The fire marshal tells me the carpet had been soaked in alcohol, and the tox screen shows a heavy dose – maybe two or three pills – of roofies. Rohypnol. The date rape drug. Induces symptoms of acute intoxication – staggering, incoherence, semi-consciousness. No wonder they thought he was falling-down drunk."

She told Chapman and Fred Dayton they had a murder case, and Dayton sighed. "We'll have to tell Langdon right away. Bannerman was a well-known guy, so the captain will want his fingerprints all over this one."

They started working the island that day, asking Jack Harlan who'd attended his party. Virtually everyone, he said, only a handful of year-round residents hadn't. Kagan and Sandberg were among the absent. But they were closer to political allies of Bannerman, not enemies. One couple he knew had been off-island in town; another couple, elderly, had been babysitting their kids. That's it, he said. Oh, and Morrissey had been off-island skiing at Sunday River.

They reported their findings to Dayton and Langdon on Wednesday morning, saying the island residents looked clear.

"Where was Morrissey Friday night?" Langdon asked. "I've heard that he was very disappointed in some of the people out there. Didn't care for them at all."

"We've already checked on his whereabouts, sir," Chapman said. His mouth curled in disgust. "We knew you'd ask. Morrissey was skiing at Sunday River on Friday. He arrived back on the island on the 10 o'clock boat Saturday morning."

"Open your eyes, Detectives," Langdon snapped. "He could have driven to Portland Friday after skiing, committed this crime, returned to town on the late boat Friday night, then come back out to the island on the 10 a.m. boat." Then a new idea struck Langdon. He smiled. "Even a Saturday morning toll receipt from the Turnpike wouldn't prove his innocence. He could have driven to Portland and returned to Sunday River on secondary roads, then driven back to Portland on Saturday morning via the Turnpike."

"We've already checked on that score too, sir. Morrissey conducted a private ski lesson on Friday afternoon from 3 p.m. to 4 p.m. and had a beer with some fellow instructors after clocking out. That makes it impossible for him to have driven to Portland to catch the 5:45 p.m. commuter boat out to the island. Housekeeping at his condo hotel said his bed had been slept in when they cleaned on Saturday morning. Impossible for him to drive to Portland and go out to the island, then return to Sunday River to sleep in that bed. He wasn't on the charter boat going out to take party-goers off the island, and the late Friday boat went out too late for him to have committed the crime.

"Captain, I think you may be getting us close to the land of confirmation bias – you're conceiving circumstances that would support your belief and either ignoring or discounting any facts that would disprove it."

"Detective, don't presume to evaluate the way I do my job. You don't have the standing."

"Captain, every subordinate in every organization evaluates his superior's performance, whether it's in a formal review session or not. That's a fact of life." Chapman stared hard at Langdon.

"John Morrissey had nothing to do with this crime, sir. Accept it. Wishing otherwise won't make it so."

Chapman looked at Harwood, who said, "Will that be all, Captain?"

Langdon's face was almost purple. "No, it will not. You need to check out that other couple who were off-island. There may be something there. And I'm still not satisfied with your spirited defense of Morrissey." He glared at both detectives. "*Now* you're dismissed. Get to work."

Chapter 12

Dan Hilliard was the premier criminal defense attorney in Portland. He had achieved legendary status: in first-degree murder trials, he was, in his own words, "undefeated, untied, and unscored upon." He was brilliant and intense, flamboyant and theatrical, tireless and utterly committed to his clients. Before a jury he could be courtly and charming, or self-righteously enraged at the injustice he perceived. Most frequently he took apart the testimony of a hostile witness with surgical precision; in other circumstances, he could seem a bumbling Columbo type as he set up an adversary for the killing question.

Out of court he was larger than life, and as crude and profane as any fisherman or lobsterman on the Portland waterfront – life of the party, teller of raunchy jokes, loyal to his friends, distant and unapproachable to his opponents. He was also outrageously expensive. You didn't retain Dan Hilliard unless you were in deep, deep trouble.

He was drafting a jury summation on a Thursday morning when his secretary Carol buzzed him. "Sorry to disturb you, boss, but I have Ron Roberts on the line, and he sounds beside himself – really shaken. He says he's in trouble, and it's urgent."

Hilliard knew and liked Ron Roberts, thought him one of a kind. A college graduate, but a back-to-the-land type electing to raise his family on an island and eke out a living as a lobsterman. Roberts was Hilliard's go-to guy for the lawyer's backyard lobster clambakes, and a sometime drinking buddy at Jack Harlan's restaurant on Granite Cliffs. All in all, a good citizen – how could he be in the kind of trouble where he needed Hilliard?

"Put him through, Carol." He picked up the phone and said, "Ron, what's up? Carol said it's urgent."

"It is. Dan, I think I'm in real trouble, and I don't know where to turn. No way I can afford you, but I'm hoping you can suggest a good defense attorney who can help me."

"Whoa, whoa, whoa, Ron. Slow down. First question from a friend is free. What's going on?"

"You know that Russ Bannerman died in a house fire last week on Granite Cliffs. The police think it's not an accident, but murder by arson, and they suspect me because of some trouble Bannerman caused Terry. They want to know my whereabouts at the time, and want me to prove any alibi."

"Goddamn it, Ron, you don't have to prove your innocence, you know that. And so do they. Who did you talk to?"

"Two detectives named Chapman and Harwood came to the house. They just left. They wanted to know where I was last Friday night. They said they'd cleared about everyone else on the island for that evening, because they were all at Jack Harlan's restaurant for his midwinter party. They can all alibi each other. Someone told them that Terry and I were off-island last weekend, so they're looking at me. I'm feeling awfully vulnerable, and I need help."

"What did you tell them?"

"Not a damn thing. I got this vibe that they were looking for a fall guy, and I remembered what you told me once – lots of times the cops are more interested in closing a case than getting it right – so I said I wouldn't answer any questions without my lawyer present. I told them, 'Either arrest me or get off my property. If you want to talk to me, make an appointment with my lawyer.' They asked me who my lawyer was, and I said you."

Roberts seemed to calm himself. "That set them back a little. And you know, it was a weird thing – they looked a little uncomfortable while they were talking to me, almost like they didn't really want to be there. And they didn't go good-cop bad-cop, telling me 'things will go easier for you if you cooperate with us now.' That's standard procedure on the TV shows, but they skipped it. But I'm still scared, and Terry's hysterical. What do I do, who should I call?"

"You don't call anybody, Ron. You stick with me. Get your butt in here right now."

"Dan, I can't afford your hourly rate for today, much less any retainer. I'm mortgaged to the hilt, you know that. I have a solid alibi, and it's the truth, but I think they're itching to try to poke holes in it. I just need someone with me when I talk to them."

"And you're going to have me," Hilliard said. "And you're not to worry about what it costs. I'm pretty sure I know what this is about. I hear things. We're going to nip this bullshit in the bud."

"Well, okay, Dan ... anyway, Terry and I were –"

"Not over the phone. Get your ass in to my office now. I'm going to call PPD and set up an appointment for this afternoon."

An hour later Ron Roberts was in Hilliard's office, telling him his story. An hour after that the two of them walked into PPD. Hilliard announced their appointment with Chapman and Harwood, and they were escorted to a first floor interview room. It was the standard set-up: a table, four chairs, a tape recorder on the table, and a one-way mirror enabling observation of the room from an outside corridor.

Hilliard and Roberts were already seated, facing the mirror, when Chapman and Harwood came in. The attorney rose to greet them and shake hands. Friendly and open. "Detective Chapman. Detective Harwood. Thanks for making time for us so quickly."

Chapman said, "Counselor, you're really not necessary for this –"

Hilliard interrupted him, and the friendly tone had vanished from his voice. "Yes, Detective, I am necessary. But let's not waste time debating that question. I'm here to resolve this as quickly as possible. Mr. Roberts wants to be cooperative, so sit back and listen.

"Mr. Roberts has an unassailable alibi for the time in question. He and his wife were celebrating their wedding anniversary last Friday night – a weekend off-island, their boys staying with their neighbors Nan and Chad Silverman. I'm sure you know this since you've already been told they'd gone to town.

"Mr. and Mrs. Roberts had dinner at a very nice fine dining restaurant – he has the receipt – then returned to the hotel and enjoyed one another's company for the rest of the weekend."

Harwood felt her phone vibrate in the pocket of her slacks. "Excuse me for a moment," she said, and left the interview room.

She was back 90 seconds later. "It is still possible that Mr. Roberts could have left the hotel and gone out to the island in time to murder Mr. Bannerman, and then returned to the hotel."

Hilliard's glare was ice cold. "Detective, I'm disappointed. Not in you, but in that goddamn fool behind the mirror. Your idiot boss, Robert Langdon." He half-waved at the mirror. "And good afternoon to you too, Captain."

Hilliard looked at Chapman and Harwood. "For the record, Mr. and Mrs. Roberts ordered champagne from room service when they returned to the hotel, then another bottle" – he looked at Roberts and grinned – "an hour later. Mr. Roberts signed for room service both times, which establishes the impossibility of his returning to the island."

The attorney's voice was now almost a snarl. "It annoys the hell out of me, Detectives, that I have to do Robbery-Homicide's job for it. Any competent detective could have discovered Mr. and Mrs. Roberts' whereabouts and verified them long before we had to come in here. But you don't work for a competent detective, do you? Don't think for a moment that I'm unaware of what's going on here. Robert Langdon is making you hassle Mr. Roberts because someone, just for show, has to be braced before he can hassle John Morrissey. Morrissey had nothing to do with this either, but Langdon's hatred of him is so palpable he'll do anything to discredit him and harm his reputation – like making it known that he's a 'suspect' or 'person of interest' in a murder investigation.

"This little three-act play is total bullshit. So, Detectives, stay the hell away from Granite Cliffs residents on this one. They're all accounted for. Russ Bannerman ruined plenty of people in his career here on the mainland. I'm sure cheers went up when his death became known. So check out those people."

Hilliard raised his eyes to the one-way glass, and pointed to it. "And I'll tell you this, Captain Langdon. You keep fucking up like this, and I'll put Robbery-Homicide Division on trial in every case I have that involves it. I'll tell every other defense attorney in town to do the same, and I'll help them do it. We'll have your balls for breakfast."

He looked at Chapman and Harwood, and his voice was friendly again. "Thanks for your time, Detectives.

91

But we're done here, are we not? Come with me, Ron, we're out of here."

He and Roberts rose and walked to the door. It was still locked, and it remained so for the thirty seconds it took Robert Langdon to disappear on his way back to the fourth floor. Then the knob turned, and Hilliard turned as well, to face Chapman and Harwood. "Must be really embarrassing to work for him," he smiled. "I've always had enormous respect for John Morrissey, and I hope you guys at RHD can survive now that he's gone. I'm amazed that Armand Anthony still hasn't realized what a moron your boss is."

As they left the building, Roberts looked at Hilliard and said, "Dan, thank you so much. I don't know how or when I'll be able to pay you, I'm so strapped ...."

"Ah, you spent your money on the right thing," Hilliard said. "Your wife, last weekend." He clapped Roberts on the shoulder. "You can pay me by keeping me in lobsters this coming summer, how's that?"

In the interview room, Harwood looked at Chapman, a bitter smile on her face. "That went really well, don't you think? Yikes. At least no one can say we screwed up, we barely got a word in."

"Hilliard's always lined up against us," Chapman said, "but it's not hard to see why he's the best. Very quick on the uptake, isn't he? I liked the way he took up the cudgel for John. Classy."

Before Harwood could answer, Sally Rinaldo came into the interview room. "Captain Langdon says Mr. Roberts' alibi seems so solid there's no need to take up space in the archives with this tape. I've been told to toss it." She whispered, "I don't know what's on this thing, but I'll make a copy of it for you before I destroy the original."

Chapman and Harwood watched her leave, and Chapman said, "Let's get to work doing this the right way. Get the computer to sift through Bannerman's activities for the big ruinous transactions and find the people who really hated him."

Chapter 13

Harwood and Chapman began the laborious process of contacting the long list of people who'd been devastated by Russell Bannerman's predatory activities. But one by one, their alibis checked out. It was fairly easy to demonstrate that you weren't on an almost inaccessible island on a midwinter night.

The two detectives even showed drivers license photos of the people on their list to Jack Harlan, who didn't recognize anyone as having been at his party. But he did have one reaction. "I half expected you might have a picture of the mystery woman in this stack of photos," he said.

"Mystery woman? What's that about?" Chapman asked.

"We thought she was Seth Toomey's date, but Seth says no. She was here, came in about the same time as Seth, chatted with a few people – including Bannerman– had a couple glasses of wine, then left the restaurant to catch the 10:30 boat."

"Who else do you remember getting on that boat?" Harwood asked him.

"Most all the off-island visitors to the party. They're annual regulars at the thing. Let me see who I remember." He thought a moment, then gave Harwood and Chapman eight names.

The detectives went back to Portland and contacted Harlan's list. Several recalled the woman they'd thought was Seth Toomey's date, but none remembered her boarding the 10:30 ferry.

"I bet that's our girl," Chapman said. "Came in at the same time as Seth, left the building supposedly for the 10:30 boat but then disappeared. People remember her talking to Bannerman. I bet she roofied his drink, slipped over to his house and waited, snuck in behind the security guard and hid while he helped Bannerman to the couch, then set the fire."

"How did she get off the island?" Harwood asked. "We know that no one from the party got on the late Friday night boat here at the Estates pier. The only hangers-on at the restaurant were island residents."

"Maybe she got on the ferry at the private side pier, the other end of the island," Chapman said. "Closer to Bannerman's house, and she wouldn't have to pass by the restaurant."

Harwood thought a minute. "You know, I doubt that. She'd been so careful up to that point, why risk being seen by Granite Cliffs residents as she walked toward that pier or waited there? She would have been remembered. Most all the private side residents were at that party too. She wouldn't have been able to count on deserted roads at that hour, with people coming home from the party."

"Maybe she had an accomplice pick her up in a private boat at one of the beaches."

"I doubt that too," Harwood said. "You don't plan to take a small boat out in the winter with chancy

95

weather, maybe in rough seas. Water will kill you in five minutes if you go in. Besides, an accomplice complicates matters for her tremendously."

Chapman had a flash of inspiration. "Check the tide tables for that Friday night. When was low tide?"

Harwood pulled out her phone, tapped in a few words, and read the screen. "Okay, Sam, low tide at 11:50 p.m. that evening. What are you thinking?"

"At low tide the sand bar that connects Granite Cliffs with Little Cliffs Island is exposed. You can walk across it. Hell, the city public works guy on the island can drive his trash truck across to pick up Little Cliffs garbage. I bet that's how she got off Granite Cliffs without being seen. Let's check with the ferry crew to see if anyone got on the late boat at Little Cliffs."

The office at the ferry lines terminal on the Portland waterfront was a disorganized mess – the general manager was nearly as incompetent as Robert Langdon – but eventually Harwood and Chapman located the crew roster for the night in question.

The senior deckhand for the late boat remembered the detectives' mystery woman. "Now that you mention it, yeah. Attractive woman – looked to maybe be Latina – waiting at the Little Cliffs pier on the return trip. She boarded and kept to herself. There were only a couple of people on that boat anyway."

"Did it strike you as odd that she was getting on a boat returning to Portland that late?"

"Not really. It's not unheard of. Sometimes a homeowner from the mainland will take that boat into town if they have Saturday morning business. Remember, our winter schedule doesn't have an early commuter boat on weekends. Earliest boat you can take into town on Saturday arrives in Portland at noon. So we didn't think anything of her boarding when she did."

Harwood and Chapman had a police artist work with the crew member who best remembered the woman, showed the sketch to Harlan and Warren, and all agreed that was likely as good as they were going to get. They showed the picture to other partygoers on the island, who had vague recollections of the woman, but no one knew her.

No one had seen her at the ferry terminal either — not surprising given the midnight hour. And the parking garage at the terminal had no record of anyone exiting the garage after the arrival of the late boat.

"That's our girl," Chapman said. "She was very careful, and now she's in the wind."

Lieutenant Fred Dayton praised their work in determining the likely perpetrator. But Robert Langdon was unhappy that they hadn't nabbed her. This was a high-profile case with a well-known victim, and Langdon was in the spotlight, standing there with no concrete results. It was still all about him.

"Captain, we can keep looking," Chapman said. "It's possible she's a friend or relation of someone Bannerman hurt. We could show the artist's sketch to the people on our list, ask if anyone recognizes her. But who among them is going to give her up if they do know her? She killed the guy they hated."

"It's a crime to lie to the police," Langdon snapped.

"Sir, it's an artist's sketch. All they have to do is say, 'Gee, that looks pretty generic. This person doesn't look familiar to me.' I think you'd have a tough time making an obstruction of justice charge stick."

Fred Dayton interrupted. "Are there any photos from the party, might give us a better image to circulate?"

"We already checked with the partygoers," Harwood said. "No photos. Harlan asks his patrons not to pull out their cell phones and take candids at his place. 'What happens on the island stays on the island,' he says. 'You get a little hammered in my place, you shouldn't have to see your picture all over social media.'"

"I doubt he's all that altruistic," Langdon said. His tone was condescending. "That eliminates the possibility of evidence that someone was overserved if there are problems later."

Chapman was disgusted. Langdon never missed a chance to be an officious asshole. "Harlan would tell you he doesn't overserve people," Chapman said. "He'd probably tell you right before he invited you to get out of his restaurant. He's an ex-Marine, and he doesn't take any shit from anybody. In any case, he didn't overserve Bannerman. The coroner said his blood alcohol level was .04, well below the legal limit for driving. He only looked drunk because of the roofies, and they took him home as soon as he appeared to be in trouble."

"All that's neither here nor there," Dayton said. "Bottom line is no photos. We'll keep looking, Captain, but after a week or two goes by, as it has already, the chance of a quick solution decreases pretty dramatically. I think Sam's right, sir – our perp is in the wind."

Harwood and Chapman kept on looking at friends and relatives, and kept coming up empty. Discouraged, they called John Morrissey and asked to pick his brain. "Sure," he said, "Come on out. I'll be home from skiing on Friday morning."

They took the murder book with them – unauthorized, but necessary – and let Morrissey look it over. "I like the way you have this organized, Kate," he said. "And you two have done a good job getting this far. Good theory of the case and the perp. Question is, where do you go from here?"

Morrissey thought for a few moments. "You're asking the victims of Bannerman's predatory practices if they *know* this woman – present tense. Maybe they *knew* her – maybe she's something like an old girlfriend or fiancé who had to break off the relationship because Bannerman took all her guy's property and they couldn't afford to get married. Or she might have had a big business deal brewing with someone and it went south when Bannerman came on the scene. Grudges like that can die hard. But if that's the case, what triggered this woman to take this action now?"

Harwood pondered the question. "Maybe Bannerman had a recent case, lots of publicity, that was similar to the one that threw a monkey wrench into this woman's life. I know that may be a reach, John, best I can do at the moment."

"No, it's a good thought," Morrissey said. "Maybe. I know it's a needle in a haystack, but at least it's something you can show Langdon you're doing, comparing Bannerman's deals for similarities." He looked at Kate. "Remember what I told you – a good detective can make it look like he or she is doing a lot when they really aren't. You may have to do that, because I think you're right – this woman is very likely gone, and she's going to stay gone."

"Thanks, John," Harwood said. "At least we know we haven't missed anything obvious." She paused. "How's the ski teaching going?"

"Couldn't be better. I'm having the time of my life. Busy season coming up, nicer weather for skiing." He laughed. "Tips from students make for good beer money. I'll be up there all next week."

Chapter 14

The deaths of Richard and Rachel Montgomery created a media circus in Chicagoland for the better part of a week. Schadenfreude generally sets in when the very rich come to grief because of their own excesses and stupidity. The case of the Montgomerys proved to be no exception.

The preliminaries started on a Friday morning when the couple who served as their butler and cook returned from their regular day off. The butler was shaking his head in seeming disbelief as he answered the front door for the police. Ordinarily a patrol car with two officers would have responded, but this was Lake Forest, Chicago's wealthiest North Shore suburb, and the Montgomerys were well-known – not necessarily beloved, but well-known. So the patrol officer was accompanied by a Lake Forest detective.

They introduced themselves to the butler; the uniform was Officer Delahanty, the detective Lt. Joe Plesnar. The butler, Pierre Munroe, was sensitive to publicity about his employers, even in death. He said, "A detective? Is that really necessary?"

"Two unattended deaths, sir. Standard procedure," the detective said. "Can you take us to Mr. and Mrs. Montgomery?"

The butler led them to a paneled library lined with floor-to-ceiling bookshelves. The books looked undisturbed; Plesnar suspected they were only for show. The place had the look of an old British club room. But then Richard Montgomery had well-known snobbish proclivities, and he affected a good many Anglophile trappings.

The bodies were seated at a polished oak table in the center of the room. The torsos of both man and wife were sprawled on the table top. Several lines – actually, *piles* – of white powder lay there as well, along with razor blades, rolled-up currency, and the other accompaniments of a serious cocaine session.

"Have you touched anything?" Lt. Plesnar asked.

"Almost nothing. My wife discovered them and called me to the room," the butler said. "I walked in and felt for a pulse in both the Mr. and Mrs. but I knew they were gone. Already cold. I immediately called you. Didn't touch anything else."

The butler sighed. "We knew they had a drug habit, cocaine wasn't the only treat they allowed themselves. I suppose when you're as well off as they were you can become jaded. They'd been doing this for years, not in front of us, of course, always on our day and evening off. Keeping up appearances, you see. But this dates back to when they were still working, more than ten years ago."

"We told ourselves it was only a recreational drug habit, but that seems so passé these days – a holdover from the '80s and '90s. I rather think they had really become addicts, particularly after their careers ended so badly."

He shrugged helplessly. "Must have been an accidental overdose, don't you think? Their partying got away from them?"

"We'll see," Plesnar said. "I'm going to call for the coroner's team and the forensics crew. In the meantime, is there a room where we can talk to you and your wife?"

Pierre Munroe called to his wife and led the two policemen to the living room. The couple were shocked to be asked their whereabouts the previous evening.

"Surely you can't believe we had anything to do with this," Mrs. Munroe said. "There was considerable affection on both sides of this relationship. Besides, we had absolutely no motive – quite the opposite, in fact. As of this morning, we're out of a job, or will be very shortly."

The Munroes had a solid alibi, an evening with friends, and Plesnar didn't doubt them. He was more interested in the butler's comment about the Montgomerys' employment "ending badly." What was that about, he asked. If there had been any foul play, that could become very relevant very quickly.

"I suppose I'm not betraying any secrets now that they're gone," Pierre Munroe said. "Not that all this was much of a secret anyway.

"Mr. Montgomery was the chief executive partner of a large consulting firm here in Chicago," Munroe continued. "Jackson Mansfield, human resource management, employee benefits, compensation, and so

103

forth. Mrs. Montgomery was his protégé – I've heard that she was sleeping with the Mr. within three weeks of joining the firm. They both divorced their spouses and eventually were married.

"Mr. Montgomery tried to remake the Mrs. into the image he wanted – what's that George Bernard Shaw play that turned into 'My Fair Lady?'"

"Pygmalion," Plesnar answered. "From the Greek myth."

"Right," Munroe said. "He tried to mold her – it was uncomfortable for me and Mrs. Munroe to watch him do it here at the house, schooling her on wine and art and so forth – and he also pushed her advancement in the firm. She became a very young partner, then a division head. But I'm sure you'll find some people from Jackson Mansfield who will tell you they were all about making sure she got all the credit rather than making sure they served clients well.

"Anyway, things apparently got worse within her division the more pronounced her cocaine habit became. And his reaction, besides blaming others for her trouble – again, this is hearsay, but you can check with people within the firm – his focus became taking as much money out of the firm, in the form of their compensation, as rapidly as he could.

"I gather the other partners sat still for it because they were making good money too. But the firm wasn't investing at all in the future. Eventually five of the most talented people left to start their own firm – now very successful, I understand – and Jackson Mansfield eventually died on the vine. They had to sell the firm, not at a very good price, and most of the rank and file were hurt very badly.

"And the Montgomerys became, as you might expect, extremely unpopular. Reviled, even. But that was ten years ago. Mr. Montgomery tried to rehabilitate himself as a bon vivant and man-about-town – their habit was to attend a local piano bar every Thursday evening where the Mr. would hold court with the other patrons with his knowledge of wine and show tunes. Excuse the mixed metaphor, but I'm told the Mrs. would follow him around like a puppy and parrot everything he said. Then they would come back to the house for their weekly cocaine session."

Plesnar sat back in his chair, nonplussed. "If you don't mind my saying so, Mr. Munroe, you seem, for a butler, to know a great deal about their rather sordid personal circumstances. And yet you and your wife characterized your relationship with the Montgomerys as mutually affectionate."

"It *was* affectionate," Munroe said. "The basic test in our line of work, Detective, is how as household staff you are treated. And despite their business ethics and personal habits, the Montgomerys were always kind and considerate with us.

"As for knowing the secrets," Munroe smiled, "you have to understand that the butler's job is to anticipate and do everything necessary while being invisible. Virtually all butlers know virtually all the secrets. And people in our profession see much, much worse behavior than Mrs. Munroe and I saw with the Montgomerys."

Plesnar sat back in his chair. "Thank you, Mr. Munroe," he said. "You've given us an excellent start should there be any evidence of anything other than an accidental overdose. We'll wait here for the coroner and forensics teams, then you'll be free of us.

"Please let me know where you can be reached. At some point, I may want names of the people who worked at that firm, if you have them – particularly the five you mentioned who saw the dawn before the rest of the world and got out."

"I can help you with names should you need them, Detective. As for us, I think for the moment we'll be here at the house," Munroe said. "I called the Montgomerys' attorney, and he is in the process of contacting Mr. Montgomery's sons. They have been estranged from their father for years; I've never met them. But until they make some decision, I expect Mrs. Munroe and I will carry on here."

The media firestorm started even before that evening's local television newscasts. "Cocaine deaths in Lake Forest – details at 6:00!" the teasers ran. The story focused on the Montgomerys' extravagant lifestyle and their seeming indifference to the rules that applied to everyone else.

"Unfortunately, it looks like the rules of chemistry caught up to them," one smarmy co-anchor said to his on-air colleague.

"Yes, Jeff – alas, apparently not even the very wealthy are immune to life's consequences."

Well before the morning's papers hit the newsstands, on-line reporters and the blogosphere had found dozens of people who were definitely not devastated by the Montgomerys' passing. "They ruined a great firm," one former staff attorney said in a widely quoted interview. "Their excesses were so blatant that the employees referred to them as 'Ferdinand and Imelda' after the Philippine dictator and his wife."

The attorney echoed the conclusion expressed by Pierre Munroe. "The partners with the most substantial stakes in the firm weren't oblivious, but they ignored the overreach because they were making so much money themselves. Their big mistake was, they didn't mind the store.

"The downward slide had already started when Hank Reynolds and his crew split. When they left – and they were the best and the brightest – that was really the death knell for Jackson Mansfield. Rick Montgomery's hand-picked successor, one of his toadies, didn't have the talent to save the business. He turned the place from a consulting firm into an outsourcing house, and all the firm's services became commodities. New business came into Jackson Mansfield only by way of the firm's being the lowest bidder – not something that's sustainable. The firm sold at a fire sale price a couple of years later.

"A lot of employees got hurt, their career tracks were short-circuited, and they were forced to take any consulting position they could find. But it's ten years now

– I hope most everyone has been able to bounce back. In any case, now there's some rough justice – the Montgomerys are gone, and their abuses with them.

"Karma's a bitch, isn't it?"

In the hope of explosive followup footage, the media immediately tried to contact the person named in the staff attorney's interview. However, Hank Reynolds was not in the Chicago area. He was resident in Georgian Bay, Ontario, still chairman and chief strategy officer of the consulting firm he had founded, but not involved in day-to-day management.

The McCarron Group CEO, Eric Shabinsky, commenting at the firm's corporate headquarters in Libertyville, had little to say. "Hank Reynolds and I don't believe anyone welcomes a person's untimely death," he said, "in spite of any past differences. As to those, we let our actions speak for us ten years ago. Beyond that, the McCarron Group has no comment."

Not much inflammatory in Shabinsky's remarks, so the media turned for its fodder to the staff attorney's last comment. "Karma's a bitch" dominated the newspaper headlines for two days – until the news cycle that followed a telephone call Joe Plesnar fielded from the medical examiner.

"We've finished the autopsies and just got the preliminary tox screen results," the coroner said. "This is a new one for me, Joe. Both the Montgomerys had enough tetrodotoxin in them to bring down an elephant. Can't be an accident. We have a double homicide on our hands."

"Educate me, Frank," Plesnar said. "I've never heard of tetrodotoxin. Sounds like a poison. Is it?"

"One of the most deadly on the planet. Eight to ten times more toxic than cyanide. It's found in the liver and gonads of the pufferfish – the blowfish. Pufferfish is a rare delicacy, especially in Japan. But it has to be prepared with extreme caution; there are only a couple of dozen chefs in Japan with the expertise to extract all the poison before preparing the dish. Even then, there are a few cases of poisoning each year."

"How does the poison work? And how did it get into the Montgomerys?"

"Besides being incredibly powerful, tetrodotoxin is very fast acting. It suppresses breathing, essentially paralyzes the diaphragm. Unconsciouness – blackout – follows, and then death in very short order."

The coroner sighed. "As to how it got in them, I'd say the Montgomerys' cocaine was adulterated. They both had a good deal more of the substance in their systems than the usual recreational user. They were serious cokeheads. With the toxin along with the coke, I think the end came very quickly once it entered their systems. No wonder they were sprawled on the table top. No chance to process what was happening to them, no chance to call for help, nothing."

"Jesus, what a way to check out. You say the poison was mixed in with the coke? How?"

"The wonders of modern chemistry, Joe. Tetrodotoxin can be found in the form of a distilled liquid, refined to a powder, I suppose even made into a pill. I'm sure the poison was mixed in with the Montgomerys' stash of coke for their Thursday night session. They wouldn't have been able to detect it on inhalation, not with their senses dulled by the wine they'd already consumed."

"Wonderful," Plesnar said. "Just what we need. More sensationalism. The media vultures will be all over this with consumer watchdogs, poison control, TV doctors, warnings to diners … shit. Any hope of a methodical investigation is gone. This is gonna be a feeding frenzy."

And so it was. The Lake Forest police released a statement that the Montgomerys' deaths were being treated as homicides, and specified the cause. The result was predictable: media hysteria about the "superpoison" and conjecture that those with motives must number in the hundreds.

The Lake Forest police chief held a press conference, turning the bulk of time over to his detective. Plesnar noted that the investigation was proceeding along several parallel lines.

First, he said, persons of obvious interest had to be located and interviewed as to their whereabouts on the day, even the week, leading up to the murders. That process would be lengthy given the number of people hostile to the Montgomerys. But it had to be done, Plesnar said, and it would be done. Then he displayed the diplomacy necessary for a cop in a rich town.

"We do not want anyone with a difficult history with the Montgomerys to feel unjustly accused," Plesnar said. "This is a routine process of elimination. Please bear with us. Our interviews will be conducted with dignity and respect."

For their second track, the police were asking people to come forward if they had observed strangers on and around the Montgomerys' lakeshore property in the days before the murders. "We are tending toward the belief that the killer broke into the house, most likely on the day of the murders, while the Montgomerys and the household staff were absent. We believe the killer found the Montgomerys' supply of cocaine – I suspect they kept it in a relatively obvious and accessible place – and either adulterated it with a tetrodotoxin powder or substituted his own deadly mixture for the Montgomerys' supply.

"So we're asking for help from anyone who saw anything untoward that Thursday during the day, especially in the late afternoon. Please call the Lake Forest police if you saw anything, no matter how mundane it may have seemed at the time."

Finally, Plesnar said, law enforcement forensics experts were focusing on the poison itself, on what the source might have been, and how and where it might have been refined to the powder that had been mixed with the cocaine. "I want to stress that the tetrodotoxin poison is unique to the pufferfish," Plesnar said. "The general public does not have to worry about being at risk with their supermarket's supply of seafood, nor does anyone need to refrain from eating fish in a restaurant. This toxin is extremely uncommon, as is the manner of

111

these homicides, and that makes us confident that the unusual nature of this crime will help lead us to the perpetrator."

And, as Plesnar had feared, the police got nowhere, although they had plenty of press and television coverage dogging their efforts. However, those investigative reporters lasted only a few days. Chicago was a big place, with frequent violent crimes and shocking scandals, and Richard and Rachel Montgomery gradually faded into the background noise over the next two months – until Plesnar fielded an unexpected call one morning in May from a homicide detective in Portland, Maine.

Chapter 15

Spring always came to Granite Cliffs in April. The particular date on the calendar varied from year to year, but spring would always come on a warm and sunny afternoon. The Casco Bay islands and the surrounding ocean were a different climate zone from the mainland, warmer in winter, cooler in summer, earlier in spring. The first few mornings after that sunny afternoon gave rise to a rapid transformation to green – crocuses, daffodils, jack-in-the-pulpit, and maidenhead ferns. John Morrissey thought it was magical. Ski season was over, his house was finished, and he could turn his attention to landscaping. Finish his promise to Dottie; her garden of "non-indigenous" flowers was his touchstone.

But he wasn't the only Atlantic Estates resident who was busy. Don Kagan was also active, causing trouble, with good effect to his own interests. He'd made an end run around David Borman and talked directly to Borman's investors, making a pitch to purchase the old fort's carpentry and construction building on the west shore of the island.

The construction building sat on a prime shorefront expanse, level and flat, overlooking the two mile wide stretch of water between the island and the mainland shore of Falmouth Foreside. Borman had envisioned converting the structure into a yacht club for the exclusive use of the homeowners. The stretch of water offshore was almost always gentle, protected from the winds of Maine nor'easters, and perfect for paddleboards, windsurfers, and one or two-man sailboats.

The building itself was a two-story affair, with a large central room on the ground floor for milling lumber, and a wide extended catwalk above, used for storing building materials. It would be an easy conversion to a seasonal clubhouse. Borman envisioned changing rooms and showers, a small bar and lounge with a water view, a modest sandwich counter, and an outside patio for sunning.

Now Don Kagan had changed all that. He was a greedy and grasping man, sneaky and devious. He was angling to have it all for himself – to rehabilitate it, much as Morrissey had done the guardhouse, into a first-rank year-round residence at Atlantic Estates. His argument to Borman's investors had been that they didn't need a yacht club as an inducement for the purchase of their properties; they would easily sell all the historic structures and building lots anyway. His offering price would go right to their bottom line, clear additional profit with no effort, saving the conversion cost of a yacht club in the bargain. "And the homeowners won't miss the yacht club because they will never have had it. So who cares?"

Borman cared, and he was livid. "His partners have directed David to sell it to him," Jack Harlan told Morrissey at their first early morning coffee hour at the restaurant. "He's furious, not only because Kagan went around him, not even because Kagan has ruined part of his vision for Atlantic Estates. David thinks it's part of a larger play from Kagan. So do I."

"How so?" Morrissey asked.

"He's now ingratiated himself with Borman's investors," Harlan said. "He has direct access to them now, on an equal footing. David thinks his next proposal will be to 'compensate' the homeowners for the yacht club by making the restaurant a club for homeowners only, and close the Estates pier to all but homeowners' boats. Next step would be his pitch to manage the exclusive colony."

"But those changes would involve major revisions to the association covenants," Morrissey said. "I've already had the short course on that from David. And now the homeowners run the association, not David and not his investors either. Borman and his investment group own the unsold house and lot properties, and the investors are within their rights to sell the construction building to Kagan – but they can't change the covenants unilaterally. The homeowners have to vote for it."

"Yeah," Harlan said, "and David and I think the campaign for that will start any time now. Kagan will try to sell peace and quiet, exclusivity, and snob appeal, and he'll have the help of that ilk and, I'm sure, Thalia Sandberg. Going to be an interesting summer."

"How do you plan to fight them?"

"Well, not by calling him a lying cheating asshole, even though he has the title locked up," Harlan said.

"That's a non-starter, not going to win any hearts and minds that way. David and I have been talking about a different strategy. The short version is, nothing gets peoples' attention like the use of their own money."

Harlan looked away for a moment, took a deep breath, then looked back at Morrissey. "I'm going to make my case by opening my books – show the homeowners just how much revenue comes from outsiders, and just how little comes from the homeowners themselves. And exactly how much it costs to run all this. Not to mention the assessments to the homeowners association paid by the restaurant, pier, and beach bar – and how much I pay to lease the area we use for outdoor wedding receptions and corporate functions.

"These commercial properties are not viable as a private club, unless all the homeowners are willing to double or triple their own association assessments. If I can get them to see that, I – and David – will be okay. If not, Kagan may be running this place pretty soon."

"Seems like a pretty solid case to me," Morrissey said. "But then, you don't have the luxury of picking your jury. You have to play with what you're dealt."

"Yeah, need to be careful not to underestimate peoples' stupidity. There's an old joke about the wealthy restaurant owner: 'I buy my steaks for $6 a pound and sell them for $18 a pound. That way I make twelve percent.' You don't have to be a genius to be successful financially," Harlan said.

"A lot of these homeowners are nouveau riche, and they got that way by being lucky enough to locate their

116

car dealership or McDonald's franchises on the right street corner or in the right strip mall. Sure, they worked hard, but that doesn't mean they're going to comprehend detailed financial statements and the arguments that go with them.

"Like I said, interesting summer. Life would be a lot easier if that sonofabitch Kagan keeled over while he was working on the warehouse. Sometimes he isn't that bright either – he has a heart condition, and he'll be working down there alone. If he had a problem, he might not be found in time."

Harlan grinned. "From my lips to God's ears," he said. "Instant karma."

Chapter 16

Patricia Dufresne gathered her papers in her K Street office, dropped them in her briefcase, and headed for the door. "Early departure for you, boss," her executive assistant said. "Only 4:30. Good for you – you deserve an evening off. Are you headed for a night on the town or just beating the Washington traffic?"

Dufresne gave her assistant a rueful grin. "No night off, I'm afraid, Sandy. I want to get an early start this evening on a proposal for a new prospect – a Senate campaign in Wisconsin. The tenth of May seems early for next November – 18 months – but we have to get this guy started. I'll work on the proposal from home tomorrow. No distractions. No phone, no email, no meetings – you're my gatekeeper." She smiled. "You ignore those prohibitions at your peril."

Sandy Foster laughed. "God, I love that kind of talk, boss. Don't worry, we won't bother you unless the world is coming to an end."

"Not even then," Pat said. Then she sighed. "Ah … who am I kidding? I can't stay isolated for a whole day. I'll probably check in with you sometime in the afternoon."

"Try to resist that. And good luck. Get those creative juices flowing. See you day after tomorrow."

Dufresne pondered her assistant's last comment as she crossed Key Bridge on her way to her suburban Arlington home. She'd be there only a few minutes before setting out on the road again, hoping her manufactured alibi would hold up. There would be no creative juices flowing tomorrow, she thought, only terminating ones. She was beyond nervous about the next day. She was more frightened than she'd ever been in her life.

She had opened her personal email at home one evening six weeks previous to see a message from a sender calling himself "personalguide." The subject line read, "You killed Richard and Rachel Montgomery … and I can prove it."

Junk mail, she'd thought. Spam. Or a bad joke from some former colleague who supposed she was as gratified at the deaths of the Montgomerys as many other employees of the late Jackson Mansfield. Still a bad joke, though, to have that subject line floating around in cyberspace.

She was about to hit "delete" but the "I can prove it" phrase was unnerving. She opened the email, and along with it the door to a personal purgatory.

"Read this, Ms. Dufresne," the opening line said. *"Read this entire message. If you do not, I will destroy your life. If you try to delete it, print it, copy it, forward it, or otherwise save it, I will know – and I will produce enough evidence implicating you in the Montgomerys' deaths to put you behind bars, or take your house and all your money to pay for a defense against a first-degree*

119

murder charge. And even if you prevail in that, the public suspicion will always follow you. Your ability to make a living in your profession will disappear.

"If you do not cooperate with me, I will provide the police with records I have developed of a trip made by you from Washington to Chicago the week of the crime. Also, I will create photographic evidence that you were in the vicinity of the Montgomerys' residence near the time of the murders. That will directly contradict the accounting of your whereabouts you've given the police. I will also create shots – photoshopped, but realistic – of you in a rundown Chicago neighborhood talking to a known street-corner drug dealer. All that will be enough for the police to proceed with you as their prime suspect. Momentum, and the public pressure to solve the case, will fill in the blanks for them.

"You have an obvious motive – revenge – and the police are keenly aware of it. But unlike the police, I appreciate your motive. You were treated despicably by the Montgomerys and their allies in Jackson Mansfield – hired to rescue a deteriorating practice after the sudden departure of its leadership, and expected to pick up the pieces and spin straw into gold. You were set up to fail. Then you were removed as a partner weeks before the sale of the firm was finalized – cheated out of your partnership share, forced to accept pennies on the dollar in a settlement you can't disclose.

"I am sure you were enraged – and willing, I'm sure, to retaliate against those responsible … if only you could do it without detection.   I can hardly blame you if you *rejoiced at the news of the Montgomerys' deaths. They were well-deserved and, in a sense, long overdue, don't you think?"*

He's right about that, Pat had thought, I wanted to take that "Karma's a Bitch" newspaper headline and frame it. But how did this person know so much? She hadn't been surprised that the Lake Forest police had called and asked about her whereabouts; she was an obvious person of interest – among many, they'd reassured her. Just a matter of routine. This person could have guessed that.

But he knew so much else about her personal circumstances, about confidential firm business, about the settlement and nondisclosure agreement that had followed her lawsuit against the firm for wrongful discharge. Privacy settings and computer firewalls must be next to worthless, she thought. This person had breached them all. He – if it was a 'he' – seemed to know everything.

"You can extricate yourself from the trouble I can cause you," the message had continued, *"by returning the favor I've done you. I rid you of your enemies, now you'll rid me of mine. Do that, and I'll destroy all my manufactured evidence linking you to the Montgomerys.*

"You should acknowledge your reading and understanding of this message by sending an email to journeysend@wrongfoot.com stating 'That sounds good to me.' Your email will bounce back to you with the message 'Fatal error -- undeliverable to this address.' But be assured that I will receive it. I will then send you

121

the 'specifications' of the task I want you to perform and the details of how to do it. On completion of your task – which will be untraceable because no connection exists between you and its object – you will be free of me.

"If you do not respond with your message to journeysend within eight hours of opening this email, I will proceed with my delivery of information to the Lake Forest police. You do not want that, Ms. Dufresne. Cooperating with me will free you and – more important – rid the world of a person every bit as reprehensible as the Montgomerys.

"This email will self-delete one hour after you open it. I await your response."

Pat Dufresne's immediate reaction on reading the email had been to run to her bathroom and vomit. After all she had been through, how could she now be in this situation? How could this have happened to her? The effort to rebuild her life had taken years, and they hadn't been happy ones. Continuing her career as a human resources communications consultant had been foreclosed – she'd been fired as a partner and practice leader, something almost unheard of in the industry. At every firm she'd tried, the conclusion had already been reached: she must be incompetent.

She had finally secured a mid-level position at a political consulting advisory firm, writing campaign ads and producing commercials. The business turned her stomach. Most of the clients were either corrupt incumbents or grasping wannabes, most of their senior staffs cynical, manipulative, and nakedly ambitious.

Utterly distasteful people – but it was a living. She'd been talented enough to learn the ropes, slimy as they were, in short order. Within five years she'd been able to start her own firm and regain her former standard of living. But she didn't enjoy the work nearly as much as her former career, where she'd been mostly – as she thought of it – a force for good.

There was no question that Richard and Rachel Montgomery had almost destroyed her life, and had in fact ruined a good many years of it. She was not a bit upset at their deaths. And if there were others like them – as she was sure there were – maybe she could make the world a slightly better place, and obtain some vicarious satisfaction, by agreeing to personalguide's terms.

In any case, she needed to get his foot off her neck. She had cleaned herself up at the bathroom vanity, then returned to her desk and sent a message to journeysend: "That sounds good to me." If she had to commit murder to end this decade-long nightmare, so be it. She'd force herself to think of it as personalguide apparently did – as justifiable homicide.

A second email waited in the inbox of her personal computer upon her return from work the next day. It catalogued the list of sins of a man named Donald Kagan, a resident of Granite Cliffs Island just offshore of Portland, Maine.

Kagan had multiple character flaws, personalguide told her. He was a liar, a cheat, a betrayer of anyone he

123

dealt with, and a physical bully who enjoyed invading the personal space of those around him and intimidating them. A thoroughly repellent person.

Kagan's business had been real estate development, specializing in rehabilitating and renovating commercial buildings for resale – nothing major, more like house flipping on a larger scale. What Kagan had done in volume was cheat; he left a trail of unpaid creditors and subcontractors behind him after every project. When his creditors tried to collect, he would countersue, alleging shoddy or incomplete work while slandering them in the process. Kagan would then simply outwait them, extending the legal battle until the small-business contractors with whom he dealt had no financial choice but to settle, generally for less than twenty cents on the dollar. He was something of a Donald Trump type writ small, personalguide told her.

Jesus, Dufresne thought as she read, *can you have a more damning indictment than that?*

Kagan was aided in his legal activities by his son-in-law, an ethically challenged one-client attorney who stayed busy prolonging lawsuits when Kagan was the defendant while filing them against anyone who displeased his father-in-law. In one well-publicized case, Kagan had sued a blogger of island life for libel – the man had observed that his subject "wanted to turn Atlantic Estates into Kaganland" – but was forced to drop the suit when it became apparent that the defense would consist of a long parade of witnesses eagerly testifying to Kagan's lack of character. But that was only a minor setback.

124

Kagan and his son-in-law did quite well paying creditors with fractional dollars, and settling with those he sued when the opposition became willing to pay something – anything reasonable – to make them go away.

Kagan was now maneuvering, both in court and by subterfuge, personalguide said, to bankrupt or simply wear out the Atlantic Estates developer and the island's restaurateur. As he did so, he was creating bitter divisions within the community. The island would be far better off with Kagan gone, personalguide told her.

"Think of the situation this way," he wrote to Dufresne. *"The Montgomerys had a total lack of empathy for others and were motivated entirely by greed. They were arrogant snobs who thought themselves better than everyone else. In contrast, Kagan is closer to real evil – a destructive, poisonous force, a cancer that should be excised. You should feel no remorse, no pangs of conscience after dispatching him."*

Personalguide concluded with, *"This email will self-delete one hour after you open it. As before, signify receipt and agreement by sending, "I see your point" to journeysend@wrongfoot.com. You will be given instructions on how to proceed in tomorrow's email."*

The next day's message came in two parts. The first was the usual self-deleting email; it outlined how Kagan was to be dealt with, what weapon Dufresne should use and how to obtain it, when and where she was to carry out her task, and how she should dispose of her weapon and disappear from the scene.

The second part of the message, which personalguide allowed Dufresne to print out for reference, read like a handbook describing how to travel undetected and leave no trace that you were anywhere but where you said you were – in Pat Dufresne's case, working at home.

"You will drive from Washington to Portland," the message said. *"Do not travel on any toll roads. The toll barriers photograph every vehicle passing through in order to catch toll evaders. Use toll-free interstates or – better yet – secondary highways."* Personalguide suggested a number of routes for her to take, depending on the traffic she might encounter.

"The night before you leave Arlington, switch license plates with a neighbor you know to be away for a time. This is in case a motel requires you to record your plate number. Do this. Details matter.

"Stay in single-owner motels on country roads, not in chain motels. Pay in cash. Do not eat in restaurants or visit supermarkets or convenience stores to purchase your food. Video cameras are everywhere – even McDonald's has cameras to help police identify which teenager started the fistfight. Get your food at fast-food restaurant drive-thrus – despite what Joe Pesci says about drive-thrus."

Huh, Dufresne thought. Even though she was filled with fear and inner turmoil about all this, she almost smiled. The guy has a sense of humor, she thought. He's trying to help me be more comfortable with this.

126

Personalguide then specified the date for her journey – early May, just after the new spring ferry schedule increased the frequency of boat trips to the islands. *"If you leave your home in Arlington before six p.m.,"* personalguide wrote, *"you will be in southern Vermont shortly after midnight. Leave your motel"* – he specified three small motels on Vermont's historic Route 7A – *"shortly after six a.m. and you will catch the 10:00 a.m. boat with time to spare. It will be filled with freight and sightseers, and you will blend in easily. Disembark at the pier on the private side of Granite Cliffs Island to avoid the crowd at the Atlantic Estates pier. Leave from the private side pier to return to Portland on the 12:15 p.m. boat.*

"You should arrive at your home in Arlington between 1:00 and 2:00 a.m. A long day, but worth it to have this behind you."

Chapter 17

As her predecessor had three months before, Pat Dufresne parked in the Top of the Old Port lot overlooking the Portland waterfront. She was clad in running shorts, tights, and a tank top, along with a thin windbreaker to ward off the early May chill of the ocean. After jogging down to the Casco Bay Lines ferry terminal, she purchased a ticket on the 10:00 a.m. ferry, careful not to dislodge or reveal any items as she removed her cash from her fanny pack

The boat – the Mohegan II – was the largest in the Bay Lines fleet, designed to carry the bulk of the day's heavy freight to all the islands down the bay. "The Mailboat Run" was also each day's major attraction for sightseers – an opportunity to view all the islands in a three-hour round trip.

This early in the season, the boat was not nearly as crowded as it would be on a summer day. Pat found a place on the after deck to do some solitary pre-jog stretching and hopefully be left alone as the boat steamed toward Granite Cliffs Island.

"Not planning to run laps around the boat deck, are you?" asked an older gentleman standing at the rail.

Just what I don't need, Pat thought. A conversation so I'll be remembered.

"No," she smiled. "I'm training for the Maine Marathon in October, and I'm sampling the islands to find the best one for long training runs. City streets with pollution aren't the best running routes, and the path around Back Cove has too many people."

"Good idea," the old fellow said. "Running is a solitary sport. You'll have plenty of privacy out here on the islands, plus beautiful scenery. Where are you running today?"

"Granite Cliffs today. Young Island tomorrow. Charbonne on Friday."

"I think you'll like Charbonne. Bigger island, more possible routes – long as you want. Of course I'm a little biased, living there. Granite Cliffs" – he shrugged – "beautiful island with the fort and all, but some of the Atlantic Estates people can be a little prickly. Try to stay away from them."

The ferry was pulling in to the Granite Cliffs pier, and Pat turned to position herself at the head of the gangplank the boat crew was wrestling into position.

"Thanks for the advice," she said to the old gent. "Maybe I'll see you on Charbonne Island."

"Maybe. Good luck with the marathon."

She stepped off the boat along with two Granite Cliffs islanders, who carried their L.L. Bean bags filled with groceries to a golf cart, then wheeled up the pier and connecting causeway. She was left alone on the pier as the ferry pulled away.

Thank God for no more conversations, she thought. Please don't let him remember me that well – hopefully he's just an old guy who enjoys chatting up younger women. Washington was full of them.

Pat was grateful for personalguide's instruction to adopt a simple disguise. She'd worn a blonde wig over her auburn hair; it was tied back in a ponytail and pulled through the back strap of a baseball cap. Her fair complexion was covered with a bronze toner, and her running tights and windbreaker hid the skin of her legs and arms. If anyone did remember her, it would be as a blonde with an early summer tan, not a pale redhead.

Her watch read 10:40. She had just over 90 minutes to find Donald Kagan, dispatch him from this world, dispose of her tools, and return to the pier for the 12:15 return trip to Portland. And to be as invisible as possible in the process.

She jogged up the long bridge that connected land and pier – a staple of all the islands, to account for the huge tides in the Gulf of Maine. Then she crossed the narrow land causeway to the island proper.

All dirt roads, she saw, and deserted now at mid-morning. Island kids in school, people busy with fishing, lobstering, or chores. Just as personalguide had promised.

Pat veered off the principal island road that led to the Atlantic Estates main gate and made her way down to a road that paralleled the shoreline and led to the back gate of the old fort.

The gate functioned as what the more snobbish residents of Atlantic Estates called "the servants' entrance." The dirt road opened onto a wide field that held the development's infrastructure: the broad expanse of David Borman's sewage treatment facility, an old coal storage warehouse, and an area filled with trash dumpsters the City barge took away each week. Predictably, Don Kagan was already making noises about forcing the City to move the barge landing farther away from his planned residence at the construction building.

Pat Dufresne stopped a hundred feet short of Kagan's building, opened her fanny pack, and extracted and put on some latex gloves. She then removed a police strength taser – obtained through some Washington security contacts after she'd told them "I'm a single woman living alone; I'm afraid of handguns, but I want protection that's more than a stun gun. Those actually have to touch your target, and I don't want to have to be that close."

She loaded a taser module into the device frame, took a quick survey of her surroundings to make certain she was unobserved, and walked through the truck entrance door into the construction building.

Donald Kagan was standing on a scaffold eight feet above ground level, working with a large power drill to secure a 2" x 8" ledger board to the interior wall. He was as unfriendly and unpleasant as personalguide had predicted.

"Who the hell are you? Get your ass off my property!"

Pat smiled at him as she reached inside the fanny pack. "Good morning to you too, Mr. Kagan. I just wanted a look at your last house."

"What the hell is that supposed to mean? How do you know my name? I don't know you! Get out of here or I'll come down there and kick your ass!" He moved to the edge of the scaffolding, still holding the drill.

She pulled the taser out and leveled it at him. At that distance she supposed it looked like a black handgun, and it stopped him.

She'd had a large enough sample of Kagan's bullying hyper-agressiveness. Personalguide was right; the world would be a better place ...

"This isn't the movies, Mr. Kagan. I'm not going to waste a lot of time talking. I couldn't care less if you don't realize what this is about."

And she squeezed the taser's trigger. Two wires shot out of the module and covered the ten feet that separated her from Kagan. The barbs on the wires' ends pierced Kagan's thin t-shirt and embedded themselves in the skin of his chest. A charge of two million volts coursed through his nervous system.

Dufresne was – well, "shocked" was a good word, she thought later – at the effect on Kagan. Her victim's body went into spasm – convulsed – everywhere, and his legs gave way. He pitched off the scaffolding, hands and arms useless, impossible for him to reach forward and try to break his fall. His head hit the cement floor, and blood immediately started to pool around what had to be a fractured skull. His body still twitched from the massive electric shock.

He has to be dead, Dufresne thought. If the electric charge hadn't stopped his weakened heart, the fractured skull and cranial bleeding surely had. Even so, she carried out personalguide's next instructions. She removed the barbed leads from Kagan's chest, pulled them through the fabric of his shirt, and unclipped the used taser module from the device. She reached into her fanny pack, took out another module, clipped it into place, and hit Kagan with a second taser charge, this time in the neck.

His body convulsed again, not as violently this time, only as an inert mass jolted by a large electric charge. Dufresne extracted these barbs too, removed the second module from the taser, and wrapped the spent wires around the entire package of device and modules.

She looked up to Kagan's scaffolding to see his power drill hanging by its cord, dangling, with the drill itself four feet off the floor near Kagan's body. Perfect. The scaffolding had been a dividend. The scene couldn't have been staged better: Kagan had suffered a heart attack, collapsed, fallen from the scaffolding, and died from the combination of the seizure and a fractured skull. An autopsy would reveal the two twin pinpricks in his chest and neck from the taser charges, and likely show heart damage attributable to the electric charges but unrelated to his heart condition. All well and good – personalguide had his reasons, he'd said, for the police and public to realize ultimately that Kagan had been murdered.

Dufresne left the premises with her wrapped taser package in hand. She walked past the side of the building fronting the shore, then down two hundred yards of shoreline to a sheer cliff dropping into a deep hole in the ocean floor. She threw her package, still wrapped in the lead wires, as far as she could into the deep. The package sank immediately. The latex gloves she was wearing would go into a distant trash can somewhere on a secondary road on her way home.

She returned to the construction building and, after another quick look to verify no one was in the vicinity, she re-entered the structure. Kagan was undeniably dead, his body noticeably cooler than normal body temperature. He couldn't be seen from the dirt road that passed by, and he was so unpleasant no one would drop in to see him. Only by chance would he be found before the end of the day.

The initial conclusion would be heart attack and tragic fall. More than a few people would fault Kagan himself. The damn fool had a serious heart condition, but insisted on living on an island that put him an hour away by boat and ambulance from a hospital's cardiac care unit. He worked alone at the construction building to boot. A fair amount of Forrest Gump's "stupid is as stupid does" would pass among Kagan's neighbors.

Dufresne stripped off her latex gloves and put them in her fanny pack, then resumed her run, retracing her steps to the back gate of Atlantic Estates. She continued on nearly deserted private side back roads, waving once to a passerby some distance away on an intersecting road, and arrived at the ferry pier at 12:10p.m., in time to be doing some cool-down stretching as the boat docked.

She felt numb on the boat, but thankfully made no new friends on the ride back to Portland. She disembarked, passed alongside the terminal on an outside walkway, and jogged to the Top of the Old Port parking lot. Then, as her predecessor had done, she drove past the turnoff for the Maine Turnpike tolls and settled onto old Route 1 for the start of the long drive home.

Once she was certain her voice was steady, she completed one last task from personalguide's handbook. She stopped at a rest area on New Hampshire's Route 9, pulled out a burner phone she'd purchased two days earlier, and called her office. Don't use your own cell phone, personalguide had said. The location could be traced, even after the fact.

Sandy Foster answered. "Dufresne Consulting Services. How may I help you?"

"Hi Sandy, it's me," Dufresne said. "I knew I couldn't stay incommunicado all day. What's shaking?"

"You're fine, boss. Nothing major at all has come up. But … this is a strange number you're calling from."

Dufresne laughed. "Temporary, Sandy. Somehow I let my cell phone battery run down completely. It's charging right now. I had my land line here at the house taken out a month ago – I never use it – so I had to run out and buy this toy phone at a convenience store to call you. Now I guess it's a spare.

"So ... if we're good and the world is still turning, I'll get back to work. See you tomorrow, Sandy."

And back on the road. As personalguide had predicted, she arrived at her Arlington home at 1:45 a.m. She retrieved her license plates from her neighbor's car, put her neighbor's plates back in place, and fell into bed for a few hours sleep.

She explained her lack of a proposal in hand to Sandy the next morning. "Our prospective Senate candidate got a sudden case of cold feet last night. Apparently the people of Wisconsin will forgive anything but being caught in bed with a dead girl, a live boy, or bad brandy. Nothing these guys do surprises me any more – he had two out of three. He'll try to manage a quiet divorce and restart his political career later. But not now – no way his behavior stands up to opposition research in a primary and a general election.

"So I spent a day writing pretty good boilerplate for future proposals. I'll just put this in my personal background files. Every day's another adventure, isn't it?"

Chapter 18

Donald Kagan's body was not discovered until just after 5:00 p.m. on the day of his death. His wife Sally finished her day's work at a real estate office in Portland and caught the 4:30 p.m. ferry to Granite Cliffs Island. The Atlantic Estates service vehicle was waiting for her. It was charged with carrying Estates residents across the island after Russ Bannerman's war had forbade their golf carts on the private side.

As Joel Easton, the vehicle's driver, pulled up in front of the Kagans' parade ground residence, Sally noticed that her husband's golf cart was missing. He usually beat her home by a few minutes each afternoon.

"I see Mr. Kagan's not home yet," Joel said. "Would you like me to check on him? I worry about him a little working down there all alone."

"He probably wants to finish up something he's in the middle of before he knocks off," Sally said. "But thank you, Joel, I'd appreciate it if you did check on him."

Easton drove the service vehicle down to the construction building's shorefront lot, spotted Kagan's golf cart, and walked into the building callIng Kagan's name.

He turned and walked right back out at what he saw. Easton had an application in to the police academy and already was familiar enough with procedure to know not to touch anything.

He called Tom Warren on his cell phone. "Tom, it's Joel Easton. Sally Kagan asked me to check on Don down here at his shorefront building. I just got here, and he's lying dead on the floor. No doubt about it – huge pool of blood around his head, looks like he fell from his scaffolding. I'm guessing maybe a heart attack? He had a heart condition. But I figured I should call you first … no, I haven't touched anything."

He listened to Tom for a moment, then said, "Okay, if you'll call the fire department, I'll wait here for the rescue boat with the EMTs. You'll be here shortly? Who's going to tell Mrs. Kagan?"

He listened again and said, "I don't think Mr. Borman is on the island today. Maybe Jeff should break the news? He's head of security. Okay, I'll call him and let him handle it … yeah, I understand, even if she rushes down here she's not to touch anything … but you'll be here before she is anyway, right? Okay, I'll keep anyone else away in the meantime. See you in a few minutes."

Easton ended his call, then dialed Jeff Fielding, the Estates head of security. Two minutes later Fielding was in motion. Easton then considered his situation. He wanted to be out of it as soon as possible. He knew enough about island politics to understand that there would be some smiles of grim satisfaction around Atlantic Estates this evening, and he would much prefer not to be part of the story. Let Tom Warren and Jeff Fielding handle it, then the fire department, then David Borman.

Which reminded him – he'd better call Borman and update him as well. This would probably make his day.

Tom Warren arrived within minutes, took one look at Kagan, and turned to Joel Easton. "You're right. Deader than hell. Good job securing the scene and leaving it undisturbed." He turned and looked up the road from the parade ground. "Here comes Jeff with Sally Kagan. Let's deal with her as gently as possible."

Kagan's wife was shaken but philosophical. "I was afraid this would happen, with his heart condition. I had such reservations about moving out here, an hour's worth of elapsed time by boat and ambulance to get to a hospital. But he really thought Atlantic Estates could be his ship coming in."

I'll bet he did, Tom thought. *The backstabbing sonofabitch.* But what he said was, "Sally, if it's any consolation, I think it happened very fast. Heart attack and then the fall. Looks like he didn't even reach his hands out to break his fall. I doubt he felt a thing."

He looked down the shoreline to see the fire and rescue boat pulling into the barge landing. He turned back to Kagan's wife. "Sally, can we make you more comfortable at home? Someone can help you with phone calls there. Joel can give you a ride up. This will take a while with the EMTs, and they'll have to take him to the hospital. All unattended deaths require a coroner's review."

"All right. Thank you, Tom – and Joel – for looking after him." She shook her head. "Damn it, I knew this

139

would happen. I knew it, I knew it ..." Then she walked away.

The EMTs walked up from the barge landing, Dave MacKenzie and the boat captain following. Warren gave MacKenzie a quick update, and they stood and watched the technicians at work.

One EMT did something of a double-take, then stood and came over to MacKenzie. "Captain, I think we might have a problem. Tom, you should take a look at this, I'd like your take too."

The three men walked over to Kagan's body, and the tech knelt and lifted the collar of Kagan's t-shirt away from his neck. "See that?" he pointed. Two small pinpricks were visible on the side of Don Kagan's neck, barely the size of the mark a mosquito bite would leave before the swelling started.

"That could be the signature of two taser barbs, I think. Tom, what do you say?"

Warren looked at MacKenzie. "I'd say you're right – we have a problem. Déjà vu all over again, Dave, just like Presidents Day. Looks like something tragic but innocent, except it isn't. If it was a taser, that jolt would probably have been enough to kill him, what with his heart condition. The fall from the scaffolding might not even have been planned. I don't think a killer would have made him climb the scaffolding and then shocked him – the drill wouldn't be dangling the way it is.

"We need to tell the coroner about this, Dave. See if he wants to come out here himself, or wait. Probably also need the cops to look at the scene before we move him."

"I agree," MacKenzie said. "You call the coroner's office. I'll call PPD."

MacKenzie did not call Kate Harwood directly. Go through the proper channels on this, he thought. Don't want anyone to hear me calling Kate directly. Besides, this is the right way to do it.

"Good afternoon, this is Captain Dave MacKenzie of the Portland Fire Department. Can you connect me with the day watch commander at RHD? Thank you ..." He waited a moment, then said, "Hi Fred" when Lieutenant Fred Dayton answered. "I'm on Granite Cliffs Island, and I'm afraid we may have another homicide out here – somewhat similar to February, looks like something unfortunate but innocent, except it's really something else ..."

He filled Dayton in on a few details, then listened and said, "You'll send Sam Chapman and Kate Harwood? Yeah, good idea, they handled the last one, they know the people out here. Tell the police boat to skip the pier and come to the barge landing on the western side. We're right at the old construction building ... Thanks, Fred. I'm sure we'll talk again later."

As the EMTs continued their examination of Don Kagan's body, not moving or otherwise disturbing it, the tech who'd discovered the suspicious marks raised his hand and turned to look at MacKenzie. "Captain, I don't think there's any doubt any longer. There are two pinprick holes in this guy's t-shirt, and if I raise the shirt a

141

little off his chest, I can see two more barb marks. This guy was tasered twice. Pretty far-fetched to think the first might have been an accident, but no doubt now. You have to detach and replace a taser module to jolt somebody twice — somebody seriously meant to do this guy in."

"Where's the taser now, do you think?" MacKenzie asked

"In the ocean, I imagine," the EMT said. "Who's going to carry it around or even hide it in the house and possibly get caught with it? Besides, it wouldn't do you any good to find it — it wouldn't be recorded or registered, it's not considered a firearm."

Sam Chapman and Kate Harwood arrived 20 minutes later, having ridden the police boat on a high-speed trip to the island. A two-man forensics team and a rep from the coroner's office were aboard with them, and they quickly took measurements and photos. Chapman listened to a summary from MacKenzie and Warren, and within a half hour said to the fire department EMTs, "Okay, you can take him." He turned to the coroner's rep and said, "Ask your boss if he can let us know when he'll do the autopsy. I'd like to be there."

He gave Kate Harwood a rueful smile. "We'll have to cover all the bases on this one, and that still won't be enough. Langdon will go bananas, two island murders unsolved by two incompetent detectives. I'm sure the first order of business will be to ascertain John Morrissey's whereabouts today."

Tom Warren was taken aback at Chapman's remark. "What?? What the hell are you talking about, Sam?"

Chapman grimaced. "Relax, Tom. I don't think John is responsible for this any more than you do. I'm sure Langdon doesn't think he is either. But he'd *like* to think John guilty, or at least be able to cast enough suspicion on him to sully his reputation. That's how small a man Langdon is. He'd make pond scum look like a higher form of life."

"Sam ... Sam ..." Kate Harwood spoke in a quiet voice. "Maybe better to keep those opinions to ourselves, don't you think?"

"Yeah, you're right, Kate, it just pisses me off, this jihad of his because John is so revered by everyone. It's a waste of our time, it's totally unprofessional, it's —"

"Sam ... you're doing it again ..."

Tom Warren laughed. MacKenzie smiled. "Don't worry," Warren said. "Your secret is safe with us. Not much of a secret anyway. Pretty common knowledge that Robert Langdon is hopeless. Apparently the only person who doesn't know that is Armand Anthony."

Warren looked at the two detectives. "If Langdon is going to go apeshit about this, maybe you'd better start your investigation right now, on the pretty safe assumption that it's a homicide. Why don't you come over to the house and we'll get a hamburger or some mac and cheese into you ... you're going to miss dinner otherwise. I can give you background on Don Kagan to start you off."

143

"What's that mean?" Kate asked. "Do you think there are people here who'd have liked to see him dead?"

"Line forms to the right, Kate. Winds all the way around the island. I have lots to tell you. Come on, let's get you fed and started up."

"Looks like the EMTs are ready with Kagan," Dave MacKenzie said. He nodded to Warren. "Thanks for all your help, Tom. I think we're out of here."

A brief "see you later" look passed between MacKenzie and Harwood. No one else saw it. Never a dull moment, they both thought.

Chapter 19

Warren led Chapman and Harwood to the enclosed porch he was building at the rear of his house. He had yet to begin his finish work, so the porch was plywood subfloor, unfinished sheetrock, and untrimmed windows. "This will have a great view down to the water if I ever get it done," Warren said. "Anyway, here's my alibi – I was all day working at this, and the air's still blue from my swearing."

"The work didn't go well today?" Harwood asked.

"Oh, it went fine," Warren laughed. "But you can't do carpentry work without swearing, Kate. It's an island rule." He moved toward the kitchen and said, "I suppose it's a PPD rule that you can't have anything to drink while you're still on duty, even after shift change. But I won't tell."

"Better not," Chapman said. "We need to keep our wits about us on this."

"Okay," Warren said. He slid a casserole dish of macaroni and cheese into the oven, fixed himself a gin and tonic, and poured tonic water over ice for Harwood and Chapman. "You can pretend this is gin and tonic."

His new porch had an old table and chairs set up at one end of the room, and Warren settled into a chair. "Have a seat, and I'll tell you just how popular Don Kagan was."

145

"You suggested a few minutes ago that he had a lot of enemies," Kate said.

"I don't know if I'd call them actual enemies, with all that implies. I guess that's why I think the possibility of this murder by an islander is pretty remote. That's not to say murder out here is inconceivable. In some respects the islands are still the wild frontier, and it's not unheard of to have shootings at sea because of guys poaching other men's lobster traps or lines. And of course there was the suspected murder a few years ago when the dock master at the Estates who was supposedly fooling around with the wife of an islander disappeared."

"What??" Kate asked. She looked at Chapman. "I never heard of that. What happened?"

"Not enough evidence, Kate. Couldn't even definitively say murder. Never turned up a body."

"Back to Kagan," Tom Warren said. "Enemies or no, he was sure as hell thoroughly disliked by a lot of folks. Even the people who took his side in battles about the restaurant or the covenants weren't really followers loyal to him, it was just that their interests aligned. For example, a good many of them didn't want a restaurant at all, and he wanted to run Jack Harlan out of here and possibly take it over himself. Strange bedfellows.

"Anyway -- when I think of the people you could say really hated him, I still have a problem. I guess you're thinking about motive, but I'm not sure there were many – or any – people who loathed him enough to seriously consider murder and then carry it out. He made life difficult and burdensome for several people, and they were vocal about it and about what they thought of him, but that doesn't make them murderers.

"For example – me. He tried raising hell about my fuel oil deliveries, making noises about licenses and permits, which I had, and wanting oil deliveries at the Estates put out to bid. You might say you could cheerfully strangle a guy like that, but you wouldn't really do it.

"And then there's the blogger – Jed Stashun – who said 'Kaganland' and got himself sued for libel. Kagan finally folded his tent when people started lining up to testify about what a shit he was, but it cost Stashun a few thousand dollars in legal fees before that happened. Stashun might *wish* him dead after that, but I don't think he'd *make* him dead."

"All the same, it's people who might have motives like that who we have to check out," Harwood said. "Are you comfortable talking about your neighbors in that context?"

"You already know the few people who Kagan caused the most significant problems for, so I don't think I'm giving anybody up. I can talk about them and in the same breath tell you why I don't think they should be persons of interest."

Warren held up his hand and ticked one finger. "So here we go. David Borman, and all the trouble Kagan caused him. But Borman will tell you that's par for the course for a developer. They always have to fight battles like that. Kagan hadn't really succeeded in court, or with the Portland planning board, or with any other authorities in his shenanigans with Borman. He was just

147

a giant pain in the ass. I can't see Borman as a guy who would resort to murder in the first place, and very likely not the way things stand now. And most important ... he wasn't on the island today."

Warren continued, ticking a second finger. "Jack Harlan. Kagan was trying to restrict his activities; Jack thought he might be trying to turn the restaurant into a private club for homeowners and take over the running of it. But it's the same deal as with Borman – it's the nature of the business to have to deal with people who don't like your restaurant. I'm sure Jack's used to it – and besides, Kagan's death doesn't end that fight, there are still people here who are anti-restaurant, and they're not going away. The big thing is, Jack doesn't own that place, he leases it – he can always start another restaurant somewhere else. He wouldn't have to murder Kagan to maintain his livelihood or keep from being ruined financially."

"Yeah, but he's an ex-Marine," Chapman said. "I imagine he was down at the restaurant all day today getting organized for his season's opening ... but I also imagine he doesn't have a lot of patience for people screwing with him. He might be just the kind of guy, with his background, who could call some old service buddy and arrange a hit to make his problems go away."

He looked at Harwood. "I keep thinking about that mystery woman who we're sure was responsible for Bannerman. Like maybe we're now dealing with a series of hits by professionals. Whether they're arranged by Jack Harlan or somebody else ..." – he nodded to Warren

148

– "I understand Tom thinks it's not Jack, but perhaps someone out here or in Portland …"

Harwood chimed in, on the same wavelength. "First thing tomorrow we have to canvass the boat crews and any regulars coming out from Portland on the morning boats to see if anyone remembers any strangers getting off at Granite Cliffs. We're not at summer population yet, maybe somebody remembers something."

"That's a thought," Warren said. "Two things to think about, though. It would be awfully brazen for a hit man – or woman – to come out here in broad daylight, in the middle of the day, on the busiest boat, to pull this off. A pro is a pro, of course, prepared for anything, but why do it that way? Wouldn't a hitter be more likely to put a bullet in Kagan's head sometime during the night, or even walking down a dark street in Portland?"

Warren continued. "The other thing is, I don't really think anyone out here would have a clue about how to contact a hit man. Yeah, there's some rough trade on that waterfront, and I know of some pretty unsavory characters – but even I wouldn't know how to go about contacting and conspiring with someone to do a murder.

"If Bannerman was a hit, and Kagan was a hit – and we haven't even established a stranger on the island yesterday – I don't think they were local arrangements. Nobody knows how to go about it – they'd be just as likely to get caught up in a sting by an undercover cop."

149

"So if they were hits, you think it's more likely they were a pro or pros from away?" Chapman said. "You may be right. There are people here with money, and some of them are serious people in cutthroat businesses … I guess I can imagine someone with badass contacts out in the big wide world away from Granite Cliffs … but now I'm back to asking why?"

"Maybe it's not related to the Granite Cliffs battles at all," Warren said. "Maybe someone had brutal experiences with both Bannerman and Kagan sometime in the past, and this is revenge."

Harwood looked at Chapman. "We're back to what John Morrissey theorized and suggested we look into."

"And now you have two murders out here," Warren said. "As an added bonus, having the hits take place on Granite Cliffs raises the possibility of islander involvement. That would be a great red herring — really muddies the waters for you."

Harwood pondered that, and turned to Chapman. "That's worth looking at, Sam. We can use the computer to find Bannerman's and Kagan's histories of legal filings, trials, or contested foreclosures — see if there's anything in common that's serious enough to drive someone to this. That and the canvass tomorrow should keep Langdon satisfied."

"Except we'll have to check on Morrissey's whereabouts," Chapman nodded. He looked at Warren. "I'm not kidding. First thing that sonofabitch Langdon is going to ask."

Warren stood. "Mac and cheese should be ready. I'm sure you want to start drafting your report of your day – you can work at this table while I get dinner out of the oven and get the dining table set. After we eat I'll run you back to Portland on my boat."

Chapter 20

Chapman and Harwood stopped in the Bay Lines office at the ferry terminal after Tom Warren dropped them off, but the office staff had all left for the day. The night operations manager told them the first morning boat to the inner Casco Bay islands left at 7:45 a.m. If they arrived at the office by 7:30, they could learn who had crewed the morning boats the day before.

At 7:30 they were told that the crews who had manned the 7:45 and 10:00 a.m. boats the previous day were assigned to them again. They could take the 7:45 inner bay trip, return in time for the 10 o'clock run, and speak to both crews. The earlier boat was called the "work boat" – it carried construction crews and other workers out to their daily jobs on the inner bay islands.

"Fairly big crowd for the Atlantic Estates stop," one deckhand said. "The carpenters and trades for the new construction and rehabs, plus the Estates staff, plus the early shift restaurant workers. But everybody on this boat knows everybody else; it's like a commuter train."

The crew members didn't recall any previously unknown people disembarking at either the Granite Cliffs private side pier or the Atlantic Estates pier. Neither did the commuting regulars, and while they seemed convivial enough, they struck Harwood as a closed community of workers who would notice anyone new.

"That doesn't mean a hit man couldn't have ridden this boat," Chapman said. "Easy enough on a boat this size to keep to yourself, not talk to anyone."

"Yeah, Sam, but my money's on the 10 o'clock boat, if we actually had a hitter ride out here. The EMTs said that Kagan's body temperature indicated that he died late morning. Why would a hit man ride the 7:45 boat and then have to make himself scarce – hide – till doing the hit just before noon?"

"Good thought. Let's see what we can find on the 10 o'clock boat."

The mail boat run was again filled with freight on the after deck, but didn't have as many riders as the work boat. "That will change after Memorial Day," Sam told Harwood as they boarded. "The boat will be packed with sightseers, people going out to the islands for a long walk or a lunch on one of the outer islands … but with not too many people right now, maybe someone got noticed yesterday."

"Who's coming out to the islands at this hour?" Harwood asked him. "The workers have already taken the 7:45 boat."

"Some of the islanders like to take the early morning commuter boat in, arriving in town at 7:30. They can get their grocery shopping or other errands done early. In fact, for groceries, the supermarket packs their stuff in those big boxes bananas come in, for a buck a box, and then runs them down to the terminal. Easy

153

way to handle your shopping if you live on an island, and you're home before noon."

After boarding, Harwood and Chapman made the rounds of the boat crew. One deckhand, lashing large items fast on the after deck, stopped and thought a moment. "You know, there was a woman back here, dressed in a running outfit – shorts, tights, windbreaker – doing stretching exercises."

A woman. The lights went on for the two detectives; they were immediately alert. "Can you describe her?"

"I really only glanced at her. Blonde, I think, wearing a baseball cap. Tall, slender, looked like a runner. Maybe late 30's, early 40's." Then he brightened. "I think I saw her talking for a bit with Jim Finzz, who lives on Charbonne Island. I'm sure he's on the boat, he comes in early every day to get his mail and run his errands."

They thanked the deckhand and asked another inside the cabin to point out Jim Finzz. They were congratulating themselves on their good luck when they ran out of it.

Finzz was a genial, portly man in his mid-70's, wearing wraparound dark glasses. He returned their hello and said he'd be glad to try to help. He acknowledged meeting and talking to a woman – who said she was a runner – on the after deck the previous morning.

"Can you tell us what she looked like, Mr. Finzz?"

"Not really, I'm afraid. I have cataracts, and everything is blurry and foggy to me. I can make out enough to get around familiar territory on Commercial Street in Portland, and of course I know my island well. But as far as distinguishing details or physical characteristics, I can't be much help. All I saw was tall and slender and a baseball cap. Oh – blonde hair, I believe."

Crap, Harwood thought. "Can you tell us anything else about her? The deckhand said you had a brief conversation with her."

"Oh, sure," Finzz said. "Nothing wrong with my hearing. She didn't have any trace of a Down East accent, or a Boston accent either. Pleasant voice, bit more of a flat Midwestern tone.

"I could make out her doing stretching exercises and asked if she was a runner. She said she was training for the Maine Marathon and sampling the islands for good routes for her training runs. Good idea – little traffic, not a lot of people."

"Did you happen to see – remember – where she disembarked?"

"Oh, yes. She got off on the pier on Granite Cliffs. Not Atlantic Estates, but what they call the private side. Only a couple of other people got off there."

The detectives looked at each other. Bingo. And then another bingo. "You know," Finzz said, "she told me she was going to run on Granite Cliffs, then run today on Young Island, then tomorrow on Charbonne. But I don't think she's on this boat today." He smiled. "As much as I can look, I kinda looked for her this morning."

"Mr. Finzz, thank you so much, you've been a great help," Harwood said. "You seem to have had much more interaction with her than anyone else. Would you be willing to work with a police sketch artist to help us get a better idea of what she looked like?"

"Detectives, I think I've given you all I can. I really can't see details. She could have had a nose the size of Jimmy Durante and I wouldn't know it. Ask around the boat – although I think she stayed on the after deck the whole time, so maybe the only other person who saw her was the freight deckhand."

As they thanked Finzz again and made their way aft to ask the deckhand to work with the sketch artist, Harwood looked at Chapman and said, "Who the hell is Jimmy Durante?"

Chapman laughed. "Well, there's a generational divide for you, Kate! The deckhand probably won't know either. We'll just have to ask if she had a big nose."

The deckhand agreed to work with the police artist – it made him feel important, and the ferry line would pay for his time – but said again that he'd only had a glance at the person Chapman and Harwood were already thinking of as "Mystery Woman 2." Or maybe, just possibly, Mystery Woman 1 in disguise.

"You said blonde hair," Chapman said. "Could it have been a wig?"

"Geez, I don't know," the deckhand said. "I think she wore it in a pony tail. Can you pull a wig back into a pony tail?"

"Yes," Harwood said, smiling. "No end to the devious tricks that women can employ." Then another thought hit her. "What about her coloring? Did you notice? Can you remember?"

"Now that you mention it, she had the beginnings of a pretty nice tan. Must come from running a lot."

"Could she have been Latina?" Harwood asked. "Hispanic?"

"Look, all I can tell you for sure is she wasn't pale. Not sure I could tell the difference between tan and Latina. You're asking maybe olive skin? Don't think so, it wasn't a dark tan, but not olive either, I don't think." He paused a moment. "Hey, Detectives, don't reach any conclusions based on what I say. I only noticed her for a few seconds."

Harwood thanked the deckhand and told him they'd call the police artist and make arrangements for the two to meet. Then they made the rounds of the boat, checking to see if anyone resembling Mystery Woman was aboard or if anyone else remembered her from the previous day. No on both counts.

They left the mail boat on its Atlantic Estates stop and called the police boat to fetch them back to Portland. As pleasant as the sightseeing run was, they needed to return to PPD and report to Fred Dayton – and Robert Langdon.

157

Lt. Dayton was encouraged by their progress and intrigued – but somewhat disheartened – with the possibility of another mystery woman. "If this is another professional hitter – or the same one in a broad daylight disguise – it's possible, maybe probable, that she's left the Portland area already," he said. "I hate to think it, but she might be in the wind too."

"You didn't move fast enough, Detectives," Langdon said. "Speed is the essence of the successful resolution of murder cases."

Chapman looked at Langdon in disgust. *Second-guessing asshole. I wonder what preschool detective primer he read that in,* he thought. What he said was, "Captain, if that was a professional hitter who had done her work by noon, she was long gone from Portland by the time we got the phone call just after 6:00 yesterday evening. We're pretty good, but we don't do time travel." His sarcasm was obvious; Dayton turned away, hiding a smile.

"Never mind that. There's another thing I'll bet you haven't done, and that's establish Morrissey's whereabouts yesterday."

"On the contrary, Captain." Chapman almost sneered. "I called John this morning, very early, and he saw right through my cover story."

"What was your so-called story?"

Chapman was close to gleeful in responding to Langdon. "I told him we were checking to see which residents of Granite Cliffs were present there yesterday and might have noticed anyone unfamiliar on the island.

He said, 'Bullshit, Sam, you're checking to see if I was on-island yesterday because Robert Langdon is telling you to.'

"Morrissey had a doctor's appointment yesterday, Captain. Complete physical, tests most of the day. He went into Portland on the 8:30 a.m. departure of the work boat from Atlantic Estates, returned on the 2:45 boat from Portland. I'll confirm that with the doctor's office today. But unless he and the doc are conspiring to kill people out on Granite Cliffs and be each other's alibis, I'd say Morrissey is in the clear for yesterday.

"Now if you'll give us leave, sir, we have an appointment with a Bay Lines deckhand and the sketch artist to try to get a better picture of this woman. And we're still using the computer to see if there are any commonalities in Bannerman's and Kagan's histories, if there might have been someone harmed enough by both of them that they'd hire someone to hit them."

Langdon dismissed them – reluctantly, but he couldn't think of anything else to criticize them for. That was apparently his idea of good management. Fred Dayton gave both detectives a quick wink as they left Langdon's office. On their way to the first floor and the sketch artist, Chapman said to Harwood, "I really feel for Fred Dayton, having to deal with him every day. The guy is really getting intolerable. He keeps this up, he'll be lucky if John doesn't file suit for harassment."

Chapter 21

Harwood and Chapman spent the first part of each of the next two mornings at the Casco Bay Lines terminal, distributing the artist's sketch of the woman who had spoken with Jim Finzz, asking if anyone else had met her or remembered her, if anyone could refine the sketch they had. No one could. It appeared that the woman had spoken only with the freight deckhand and Finzz, and no one at all remembered her on what must have been her return trip to Portland at noon the same day.

Late the first morning, Chapman attended the medical examiner's autopsy of Donald Kagan, then returned to join Harwood at RHD. "Anything?" she asked, looking up from her desk.

"Nothing unexpected. The violent blow to his head when he hit the floor is what killed him, but he fell because he was going into cardiac arrest from the first taser round to his chest. That would have been enough to kill him by itself. The hit to his neck was the second taser round, and it was basically insurance. Someone really wanted him dead."

They returned to work, spending both afternoons exploring past legal proceedings involving their two victims. They found several large foreclosures and resales for Bannerman, nothing of similar magnitude for Kagan – he made up for small dollar settlements with the

160

sheer volume of the lawsuits he initiated. "A small-time chiseler," Chapman said, "whereas Bannerman was a vulture feasting on big transactions." There seemed to be no overlap, no opponents or victims common to the men's activities.

Harwood reached the end of the second day frustrated, convinced that she and Chapman were floundering. "You know what we need?" she said. "A skull session. We need to sit and talk through all the possibilities we have floating around in our heads, see if we can eliminate some of them, or at least get them in some order so we can focus on the most promising ones first.

"And I know just the guy who can help us – he's already offered to brainstorm with us if we need it. Thing is, we'll have to do it under the radar; Langdon would go nuts if he knew we were consulting with John Morrissey."

They called Morrissey to ask if he was willing to be an unpaid consultant to PPD. He laughed when they told him why. "Of course," he said. "Always good to feel needed. I feel like an admiral again. Come out first thing Monday morning. I'll make you an island breakfast and we can talk. Get your ducks in a row so we can go through your possibilities in a logical way. I'll see you when the boat docks."

Morrissey met them at the Estates pier at 8:30 Monday morning. "I've been experimenting with preparing various breakfasts," he said, "because I've been pestering Jack Harlan to open for breakfast for all the

161

island geezers. He says if I get any better I'll have to be the cook!"

John had prepared bacon, ham, and cheese omelets; English muffins and bagels; juice; coffee; and assorted fruit. "Hey, this looks great, John," Chapman said. "No end to your talents."

Kate cast a critical eye at Morrissey. "You'd better eat a good part of this, John," she said. "You're getting awfully skinny."

"Lean and mean," Morrissey laughed. "Combine the physical labor of getting this place in shape with laying off the donuts in the cop shop, and you get skinny in no time. I feel great."

Breakfast finished, they repaired to Morrissey's back deck and seated themselves at a circular picnic table overlooking the Estates pier and protected cove. "What do you have?" Morrissey asked.

"A lot of possibilities," Kate said. "What we'd like to do is run them by you and ask your help in ranking them in some order of probability to give us some focus. We don't necessarily want to eliminate anything entirely for fear of throwing out the actual solution by mistake, but we'd like to proceed from here by dealing with the likeliest possibilities first.

"Here goes, our possibilities essentially in the order we considered them.

"First scenario is one island native committing both murders, Bannerman and Kagan. The question is, why go to all the trouble with the theatrics of arson and tasers? Why stage them to initially look like accidents, knowing that we would shortly figure out the real cause of death? Why not just shoot them? This island is sparsely populated and very dark at night. The way these have been done – somebody went to a lot of trouble. Besides, we have these two female suspects for these murders. How do you explain them? They were here one moment, gone the next. I really doubt that it was someone native to the island acting all by himself.

"Second possibility is a bit of a reach, but maybe the first is some kind of revenge murder, and the second is a copycat? That could explain the difficulty we're having imagining someone with a revenge motive for both Bannerman and Kagan. Maybe someone saw the first murder and thought, I'll do an unusual one of my own, muddy the waters, make it look like a serial killer when there isn't one."

"Okay, let's think this through," Morrissey said. "I see your point about a low probability of one islander as a double murderer. Nobody not in the murder business is likely to go to that much trouble, certainly not going to dress things up as artistically as has been done here.

"And the idea of a copycat – or somebody doing something along the lines of 'First let's kill all the lawyers' – good thinking, good imagination, guys, but I think that's pretty remote. What else have you been thinking about?"

Chapman and Harwood shifted to reviewing their examination of the Bannerman and Kagan financial and legal histories, noting that they'd found no commonalities, that the two men had played in different leagues: Bannerman in the big time, Kagan in Class D ball.

"That suggests the murders weren't one person out for revenge," Chapman said. "But we're still wrestling with the issue of one murderer or two. One would mean a paid assassin doing both murders - or we could have one person making arrangements with two different 'contractors.' But if we're going to conclude these are paid hits, and it's one person who's the driving force – the employer – what's the motivation?"

"Let's get back to the notion of one paid hitter or two," Morrissey said, "and deal with that first. Where's your thinking on that?"

"The woman – or women – we've heard about were tall and slender, and very attractive," Harwood said. "One seemed to be Latina – black hair, dark and dusky; the other fair – a blonde with a tan.

"But you can take care of the hair with a wig, and you can cover an olive complexion with a bronze toner. Could have been one woman, in disguise the second time, especially if in broad daylight last week she wanted to take care not to be recognized as the mystery woman in February. So just on looks, I don't think we can conclude either one or two."

Morrissey nodded. "What other impressions of them do you have from the people you've talked to?"

"The woman last week seemed to strike people as a professional of some kind. I don't mean pro assassin, I mean professional as in white collar, office worker, lawyer, vice president, consultant, that sort of job. Just the way she carried herself, one man said. He's almost legally blind, but his other senses are attuned to that kind of thing.

"We've heard that the mystery woman at Harlan's restaurant in February seemed comfortable as a single woman in a bar. I don't mean a drunk or a hooker, more like she'd been in that ambience before – maybe as a bar or restaurant worker. Hard to get a handle on that from people – remember, most everyone thought she was Seth Toomey's date, not an unaccompanied woman."

"That's all pretty thin," Morrissey frowned. "What would it tell you if you knew for sure it was two different women?"

"I think that increases the probability that we're dealing with paid assassins," Harwood said. "But if it's one paid hitter or two, the question is, who's paying her or them? We're back to our question of motivation.

"We had a long talk with Tom Warren about Kagan's possible enemies, and Tom doesn't think the enmity rises to the level that anyone here would actually commit murder or even hire it done. Borman and Harlan might be possibilities, but Warren says they have to deal with headaches like Kagan all the time. Plenty of people hated Bannerman as a toxic guy, but neither Borman nor Harlan had any real business beef with him. So it's hard to see either of them with a motive for both Bannerman and Kagan."

Harwood took a long look out to sea, then turned to Morrissey. "We're considering one other possibility if it's one person," she said. "Kind of out of left field, but here goes. If it's not an islander out for revenge, and it's not an assassin paid by an islander – and Warren argues that he doesn't think anyone out here would know how to go about that – then there's this.

"Suppose it's someone who thinks of himself – herself – as an avenging angel, dispatching people she thinks need – deserve – to be dead. Remember Charles Bronson in 'Death Wish'? He tracks down and kills the guys who invaded his home and killed his wife. But once he does that he acquires a taste for it – he keeps on killing bad guys. Judge, jury, and executioner.

"But Bronson's character does it in a big city. Why start your avenging angel business on a small island? Unless the small island isn't the only place you've done it? Are there other high-profile murders out there, with hated people as the victims? Could that motivation explain why the deaths are theatrical – the murderer is acting out in a self-righteous rage?"

Kate paused, looked out to sea again, shook her head.

"John, that about covers where we are. I guess all our thinking gets us to two primary lines of investigation. We look for two things: a paid hitter hired by someone – maybe a wealthy homeowner protecting his real estate interests? – or an avenging angel eliminating people who he – probably she? – thinks need to be eliminated."

Morrissey smiled. "I don't think you two are out in left field at all," he said. "I like your two main possibilities. I don't think I'd pursue those two to the exclusion of everything else, but they're certainly worth a look. I like the idea of somebody wealthy, either here as a homeowner or possibly thinking about development in all that open land on the private side – acting not out of revenge, but in protection of his financial self-interest, hiring an assassin or assassins who happen to be female.

"And as for the avenging angel – well, stranger things have happened. You have to find other similar visible murders of despised people elsewhere, and then see if they had anything in common with Bannerman and Kagan, or Granite Cliffs, or Maine. And hey, maybe they don't. Maybe your person is just reading the newspaper and reacting to stories about some really horrible people.

"They're good roads to follow. And both you guys are a rare combination: logical and intuitive. I'm proud of you. Also, your timing is great, you got me at just the right time, because I'm taking off in a few days to go fishing."

"Oh?" Chapman said. "Where are you going?"

"Pulaski, New York," Morrissey said. "To a fishing camp I'm renting on the eastern shore of Lake Ontario. Lake trout fishing."

"I didn't know you were a fisherman," Chapman said. "I don't think you ever went fishing on your summer vacation, did you?"

"Nope. But I've always loved to fish. Dottie and I tried lake trout fishing in the spring one year, and had a great time. The water's really cold right up to the surface, and the trout come up to feed. They stay very deep in mid-summer, and you can't catch them with a spinning rig. But in the spring – wow, one of the great

167

game fish in the world. Really looking forward to it, I know Dottie will be right there with me."

"Will you come back with a freezer full of lake trout to add to your breakfast menu?" Kate asked.

"No. I'm strictly a catch and release guy. They're such magnificent creatures, they fight like hell, they deserve to go back to their lives. I couldn't bring myself to kill 'em.

"So – I probably *won't* be thinking of you," he laughed. "But keep up the good work. I'm sure you'll get this. Call me again if I can help."

Chapter 22

Harwood walked into RHD spaces the next morning shaking her head, bleary-eyed. "Sleepless night?" Chapman asked. "It happens to me. Case runs in circles inside your head all night long."

"You got it, Sam. But at least I came to a conclusion about which way we should go."

"Oh? That's progress. What are you thinking?"

"An assassin who was paid by a powerful businessman protecting his financial interests – like a guy contemplating development on the island … that might hold water in theory, but how do you check it out? The preparation and business research for something like that would be very hush-hush, something known only to Mr. Big and his closest associates. How do we determine that was coming into play? Who do we ask? Where do we start? I have no idea."

Kate smiled. "So … process of elimination, let's go the avenging angel route first. I lay awake thinking of how to look for murders with the right characteristics, and came up with several filters for our computer search."

"Okay," Chapman said. "What are we going to search?"

"Newspapers. Not just big-city newspapers, but all the papers we can access. In the time before the

Bannerman killing, and especially the time between Bannerman and Kagan. For starters, I think we should limit the search to the Eastern part of the country and the Northeast and Middle Atlantic states. Maybe other Eastern seaboard cities too – Miami, Atlanta, Charlotte. Think about it – if an avenging angel did two murders here, I can't imagine he or she would be flitting off to L.A. or Phoenix or Seattle in between."

"Makes sense for starters. What else?"

"Key words," Harwood said. "I really tossed and turned on this. I need your thinking on it too. We want circumstances similar to Bannerman and Kagan, but phrases like 'everybody hated the bastard' aren't going to work. Of course I'm thinking 'murder' but also trying to link wording in initial stories like 'accidental death' or 'tragic death' to words later on like 'apparent homicide' to get at the artistic 'things-weren't-as-they-first-seemed' angle that we have."

"That's good," Chapman said. "Now how do we say 'everybody hated the bastard' in a nice way?"

"Well put," Kate smiled. "I don't think newspapers, whatever we may think of the press sometimes, are going to be especially vicious in writing about the very recently dead. I'm thinking key words like 'prominent', 'well-known', 'controversial', 'high-profile', 'stirred passions' – words like that."

"It's a start," Chapman said. "Teach this dumb old dinosaur how to turn the computer loose and we'll both look."

By noon the next day Harwood had a list of nine murders in their geographic search area between January 1 and May 1 that included both 'unpleasant' people and flamboyant means of dispatch.

"Incredible how quickly we were able to narrow this down," Chapman said.

"Yeah," Harwood replied. "Amazing the percentage of all homicides that can be eliminated quickly because they involved handguns. We are one trigger-happy country. And a lot of the rest certainly weren't staged to be deceptive – stabbings, bludgeoning with a baseball bat – in your face stuff. And even the people who were hated and were offed in a showy way – hell, the perps were indentified and apprehended right away. Some did it in front of multiple witnesses. Not an avenging angel mentality. Say what you will about them, serial killers' minds are a little more organized than that."

"Okay, how many do we have left?" Chapman asked, reaching for Harwood's list.

"Nine, but I think we can eliminate most of them. This bad guy with the long record who was found in the Cuyahoga River in Cleveland with his feet encased in cement – that's a mob hit, an informer or someone trying to muscle in on another gang's turf. Doesn't fit our narrative."

"What about this martial arts black belt who liked to bully people in his favorite bar?" Chapman asked. "Picked fights so he'd have a self-defense excuse after he beat the shit out of somebody."

Harwood smiled. "Oh yeah, that guy. Turns out a black belt is worthless against a shotgun blast to the face. I found the follow-up story to that. The guy who pulled the trigger – one of his victims – did it in the parking lot in front of a dozen people."

She smiled. "My favorite is the 'controversial' sociology professor with the vaguely white supremacist polygamy theories who was whacked with a machete while he was in bed with a coed. Pretty clear it was his umpteenth coed, and his views were really hateful replacement theory stuff, but the police in Atlanta are zeroing in on the wife, who apparently isn't the least bit upset that the guy is dead."

Harwood gave Chapman an evil smile. "So let that be a lesson to all you married men!" Chapman chuckled in response. Homicide detective gallows humor – one of the lesser-known benefits of police work.

Chapman looked over the list once more. "I now have a top two. What about you?"

"Same here. My first is the hedge fund private equity guy in Charlotte who targeted small companies to move offshore and threw hundreds of people out of work in the process. And then the husband-wife consulting pair who stole their partners blind while they ran their company into the ground."

"Same as mine," Chapman said. "But I'm inclined to agree with where the Charlotte police are heading. They have a business rival as a person of interest – every bit as sleazy as the guy who was killed – and the police think this other guy was tired of being beat by the victim

172

in buying and selling companies. Doesn't exactly sound like an avenging angel motivation to me – besides, if this other private equity guy goes down, society will be rid of both of these assholes. So I say concentrate on the husband-wife pair."

"The Montgomerys," Kate said. "Richard and Rachel. Lake Forest, Illinois. Okay, let's get all the news reports we can find, see if more similarities line up, then maybe call the Lake Forest police and compare notes."

Chapman and Harwood had seen enough by the next morning that Harwood was ready to call Lake Forest. She identified herself and asked to speak to the homicide detective in charge of the Montgomery investigation. His name, she was told, was Lt. Joe Plesnar.

"Plesnar." He sounded like a man who didn't have a lot of time to waste.

"Lt. Plesnar," Kate said. "My name is Kate Harwood, and I'm a homicide detective with the Portland Maine police department. I think we may have something in common, aside from being homicide detectives. We have active cases with some remarkable similarities, and I'm wondering if there might be a connection between my two cases and your Montgomery case."

"I'm grateful for any new idea," Plesnar said. "Frankly, we're kind of stalled here. We've run down dozens of alibis, motives, histories in the last two months and can't get close to identifying a likely suspect. What do you have?"

"Two separate murders on a small resort island off the Portland coast involving high-profile people – very unpopular, ethically challenged people – who were killed in unusual ways. Theatrical, almost. Staged to look like accidents, but not too carefully. Like the killer knew we'd discover – even wanted us to discover – the real cause. Almost sending a message that these people deserved it. That sounds very similar to your case of Richard and Rachel Montgomery."

"It sure does, Detective. What's your theory? Paid hit men?"

"No sir, we've considered that, and don't believe the people on the island had the connections – or shall we say, the expertise – to go about arranging a hit. Possible, but unlikely. And even though many people on the island really loathed the victims – few if any people cried themselves to sleep over their deaths – we don't think the animosity rose to the level where the relatively genteel people on this resort island would commit murder."

"So do you have something else?"

"Yes sir, we're wondering if we're dealing with an avenging angel type – like Charles Bronson in 'Death Wish' – who's dispatching people he or she believes need to be dead. People who have hurt so many others so much that the world is better off without them. And our killer sees himself or herself as just the person to carry that out."

Plesnar was taken aback. He hadn't expected this. Was this woman a crackpot, a loose cannon in her own department?

"Whoa, Detective. That's pretty far out. I mean, I'm intrigued, but my instincts are saying, no way, that's movie stuff, not real life."

"Yes sir, I'll admit it seems pretty remote on the first take, but my dad, who's a captain and deputy chief in the Boston police department, always reminded me of the Sherlock Holmes theorem ..."

Plesnar interrupted. "Yeah, I know that one. You eliminate everything else, and what's left, no matter how crazy it may sound, has to be the solution."

Harwood laughed. "Great minds think alike, Lieutenant. Look, I'm sure you don't have time to kick this around on the phone all morning. What I'd like to propose is that I come out there to see you when it's convenient – hoping 'as soon as possible' is convenient ..." She laughed again. "We could compare notes in some detail. Maybe we find something else in common, maybe something with your victims and mine, that helps us narrow this down."

"Detective Harwood, if you're willing to come out here to try out this theory, we'll make time to do it. When would you plan to come?"

"I need to run this by my captain, who may not be as agreeable as you are, but I should do it as a matter of form. But even if he says no, I'm coming anyway – my own time and my own money."

175

Plesnar straightened in his chair. Wow. This young woman was not a loose cannon. She was a storm trooper, charging straight ahead. A family pedigree in the Boston Police Department, bright, articulate, respectful of others' time. Her stock with Plesnar rose thirty points in as many seconds.

"Okay. Listen, Detective, if your captain needs more persuasion, as in the form of an endorsement from here, I'll be glad to call him. Hell, I'll have my captain or chief call him. We need to get off dead center here, and we'd be glad to have some other heads working on this."

"I'm glad you're so receptive, sir. I'll let you know what my captain says."

"Fine. Oh, and one more thing, Detective. We're colleagues on this, different departments working together. No need for rank. You're Kate, I'm Joe. That okay with you?"

"That's fine, Joe. Thank you, I'm flattered. I'll call you back as soon as I talk to my captain."

She knocked on Robert Langdon's office door moments later. "Captain, if you have some time later today, I'd like to talk to you about a possible next step Sam and I have come up with in the Bannerman and Kagan investigations."

"Well, Harwood, if you've made any progress at all, I'd certainly like to hear it. Let's do it now."

"Fine, sir." She sat and briefly covered the recap they'd gone through with John Morrissey – without mentioning Morrissey. She stressed what they saw as the

176

diminishing possibility of an islander committing the murders, or of an islander contracting with paid assassins.

"What we're down to, sir, are two possibilities. Both could tie in to the mystery woman or women whose presence we've documented on the island. The first possibility is an assassin retained by some financial heavyweight protecting some existing or potential interest on the island – ridding the place of divisive people who could harm its reputation and put our man's investment at risk. But if that's the case, the business activity is extremely confidential at this point, and very difficult to uncover.

"So what we'd like to do is pursue the second possibility – that our murders might be committed by a person who sees himself or herself as some sort of avenging angel, dispatching people who are perceived as deserving of this person's justice."

Langdon – for once – looked thoughtful. "That's an interesting possibility, Detective. But why would your avenging angel start his ... crusade, I guess you'd call it ... on a small island? Unless he or she were an islander? Which possibility you seem to be discounting in favor of this homicidal mystery woman of yours."

This homicidal mystery woman of yours. *God, he's condescending,* Harwood thought. *And sexist.* But she smiled, and appealed to his vanity.

"Exactly what we first thought, sir. But then it occurred to us that the island might not be the only place this person is meting out his brand of justice. So we looked for murders with similar circumstances – well-known but unpopular people, bad reputations, killed in unusual or theatrical means. We've researched several such murders on the Eastern seaboard and in the Midwest, and we've come up with one in Chicago that's remarkably similar."

She reviewed the basics of the Montgomery case, her conversation with Joe Plesnar, and his willingness to compare notes to develop new leads if she would travel to Lake Forest.

"So I'd like your approval for me to go out there for a day, sir, to see if both departments can latch on to something worth pursuing."

Langdon looked pained. "Here I had my hopes up that you were actually making some progress, Detective, but you end up with this crackpot theory."

"I admit it might sound far-fetched, sir, but when you've eliminated everything else …"

"Yes, yes, Sherlock Holmes," Langdon interrupted. "But you're not there yet, Harwood. You haven't completely eliminated all the possibilities."

"Agreed, sir. But I think we've established that the other possibilities we've looked at are remote enough that this one deserves a look."

She decided on another appeal, this time to this little man's self-interest. Their work was still all about him.

"Captain, this is not only to try to solve these cases, it's for the department's protection too. If the possibility of a connection to those well-publicized murders out there occurs to some savvy reporter, and he asks if we're exploring that possibility – and we're not – well, that could be awkward."

Langdon, always attuned to how events might reflect on him, said, "Detective, be careful. If you're suggesting you might leak this if I don't approve your trip …"

"Captain, leaks are not my style. They're dishonest and unprofessional. I'd be more likely to take some vacation time, pay my own way, and go out there and see if there's any connection. If there were and it broke the case, I'm sure the press would be curious as to how it was done. I suppose you could order me to be silent, but you couldn't silence Lake Forest PD. The word would get out eventually, one way or another. This department would look bad, and there would be a lot of explaining to do."

By you, asshole, she thought. *You can't be so stupid you don't realize that.*

"Hmmm. You may have a point. I still think it's probably a wild goose chase, but if some smartass reporter asks if we've ever considered the possibility, we can truthfully say 'yes.' Would you be the one to go out there?"

"Yes, sir. Just me, just for a day."

"Good decision. They're more likely to cooperate and share information with a pretty girl."

She remembered Tom Warren's comment about cheerfully strangling somebody. What a jerk. Incredibly sexist, and insulting to her competence and Lake Forest PD's to boot. This guy was really something special.

"Yes, sir. Thank you, sir. I'll call them right now and go out there tomorrow."

Chapter 23

Harwood boarded a 5:30 a.m. flight out of Portland the next morning and landed at Chicago's O'Hare Airport at 7:00. She was met by the driver Lake Forest PD had sent so she could avoid the rental car gauntlet, and arrived at the upscale suburb's police station thirty minutes later. Joe Plesnar was waiting for her in a conference room, murder book and forensics reports spread out on the table. They reviewed the material for 90 minutes, then Harwood pulled out the copious notes from her own murder books and outlined the corresponding details in the Portland homicides.

Plesnar thought for a minute. "Clearly a number of things in common," he said, "not least unpopular people. A high profile mortgage predator, a thief who essentially stole from his own partners while his firm went to hell, and a small time chiseler. And unusual means of dispatching all of them. 'Unusual means' doesn't necessarily mean some rage-driven desire for torture, more likely a desire to make sure the exits of these people were noticed."

"My thought as well," Harwood said. "Like someone wants to make sure we appreciate his art work. Where do you think I should I go from here?"

"We've talked to virtually everyone associated with the old firm Jackson Mansfield – the people the

Montgomerys hurt so much. I'd suggest as a next step that you talk with Hank Reynolds," he said.

"I didn't see his name here anywhere," Harwood said, looking at the array of papers on the conference room table. "Who's Hank Reynolds?"

"Long story," Plesnar said. "He was a superstar consultant at Montgomery's firm ten years ago, decided Montgomery was full of shit, and bolted the firm with four of his partners. Founded a very successful retirement planning company targeted to middle class people, not the executive suite. Lake Forest PD is one of their clients. We love the guy, he's really done right by us.

"Anyway, he might have some good insights about peoples' motivations or feelings about the Montgomerys way back when – maybe you can get a better sense of whether this is strictly local or if something more sinister is at work."

"You say your department is their client?" Harwood asked. "Are their offices close by?"

"They're in Libertyville, just north of here. But he's in Georgian Bay, Ontario – cottage country north of Toronto. He's their chairman, and kind of their oracle and chief strategy officer. He doesn't involve himself in day-to-day operations. I can call Libertyville if you like and I'm sure they'll set you up for an encrypted Zoom session with him."

"I think I'd prefer to meet him in person. I'll fly to Toronto right away if you can set it up."

Plesnar laughed. "You're all street cop, aren't you, Kate? Nothing better than being up close and personal, even if it ain't that convenient. Good on you, kid."

Harwood laughed too. "The Harwoods go a long way back in the Boston PD. They'd revoke my birthright if I took short cuts."

"I'll call Libertyville and see if they can get him to agree to see you. I'm sure he will, he's a great guy," Plesnar said. "They'll set up a time for you to meet, and Annie out front can help you with airline tickets to Toronto and car reservations once you get there.

Good luck, Kate. Let me know if you find anything."

"Will do, Joe. Thanks so much for your time."

Harwood arrived in Toronto, flashed her badge through Customs, assured them she wasn't in Canada to try to arrest anyone, and picked up her car. The drive to Reynolds' town of Diamond Cove was scenic; the drive through his waterfront neighborhood – called Dreamscape by the locals, she learned when asking directions – even more so.

She was 35 minutes early for her appointment with Reynolds, so she killed some time driving through the village and his waterside locale. Finally she figured it might not hurt to have him a little off balance – he might reveal something that he wouldn't otherwise – and she pulled into his driveway at 2:40 p.m..

The house was beyond arresting – all glass, native stone, and light polished oak in a colonial contemporary design. Not a gargantuan trophy home, but far from a

modest cottage.   Tasteful and imaginative.   An
understated showplace.

She knocked on the door and shortly found herself
to be the one a little off balance. She was greeted by a
stunningly beautiful woman who looked to be in her early
30's, although Harwood knew from her last conversation
with Plesnar she was ten years older. Nevertheless, drop-
dead gorgeous.   Flawless face, Katharine Hepburn
cheekbones, sun-bleached brown hair, dark eyes.   Her
shorts and tank top revealed enough to know there was a
swimsuit model's figure underneath.

"Ma'am? Dr. Reynolds?" she said. "I'm Detective
Kate Harwood of the Portland Maine Police Department.
I hope I'm expected. The Lake Forest PD was going to call
ahead to set up an appointment with Mr. Reynolds."

"Yes, of course," the woman smiled. "Please come
in, Detective. You're a few minutes early, but that's fine.
Hank's still out on his afternoon run, but I expect him any
minute. I think he planned a quick shower before your
meeting at 3:00."

I'll bet he figured I might show up early, Harwood
thought. *She doesn't seem surprised either. They're not
fools. They probably don't have anything to hide, they
just want me to know they're not fools. Duly noted.*

"Dr. Reynolds, I can drive around and sight-see for a
while – it's beautiful here – and come back at 3:00 o'clock
..."

"Don't be silly. Come on back to my office and we'll
wait for Hank there. And please call me Arianna. I can't

abide physicians who insist on being called 'Doctor' in non-medical settings. Way too much ego."

They walked to the back of the house to an office off the large gourmet kitchen. A wall of glass overlooking Georgian Bay dominated the room, fronting an oversize table top desk and executive chair. Two large Eames chairs, a glass coffee table, a glass-fronted lawyer's file cabinet, and a Persian rug completed the picture.

"This is my fantasy escape," the woman said. "Always wanted an office like this. Hank and our daughter designed most of the house with a little help from an architect. They were nice enough to ask my opinions and give me right of approval."

"Wow. How can you go wrong?" Harwood asked.

"Well, that's an interesting question," Arianna Reynolds said. "I love the view, and it's not a distraction, because I just grind away every Wednesday and Friday afternoon catching up on paperwork in here — forms, medical reports, patient notes — nothing very demanding. But Hank and our daughter both prefer a blank wall in front of them — they're both incredibly visionary, and they see things no one else does. They don't need a view for inspiration. It actually detracts from their imagining whatever it is they see."

She paused. "Can I get you anything while we wait for Hank? Soft drink? Coffee? Police live on coffee, do they not?" She smiled.

Harwood laughed. "Yes, we do. But not me, not at 3:00 in the afternoon anyway. Thank you, I'm fine."

185

They heard the front door open, and a voice called out. "I'm back, I'm still alive, Rini, no thanks to the intervals you laid out for me!"

The woman chuckled. "I'm blessed with a professional athlete's genes, but he's determined to keep up with me when we run together. I'm setting up some interval training for him to improve his pace."

"Will it work?"

Arianna Reynolds gave her a huge smile. "Will it work?" She laughed. "Yeah, it'll work. You look up 'irresistible force' in the dictionary and his picture is there. He can do anything he sets his mind to."

A tall man appeared in the office doorway – six-one, 180 pounds, dark hair with a touch of gray at the temples. Movie star looks and bedroom blue eyes.

He looked at his wife. "Hi, gorgeous," he said. "Hi, handsome," she replied.

Holy shit, Harwood thought. *They might be the best-looking couple on the planet. Life is not fair.*

The tall man looked at Harwood. "You must be Detective Harwood. I'm Hank Reynolds." He started to glance at his watch. "Sorry if I'm late."

"No sir, you're fine. I should apologize, I'm a little early."

Reynolds looked at his wife. "Can we get Detective Harwood something to drink?"

"Dr. Reynolds already offered, sir, thank you. I'm fine."

The woman laughed. "I told you, Detective – 'Arianna.' And don't call him 'sir.' He was 'sir' when he was a naval officer, but now he's ferociously egalitarian. Easy position to take when your leadership style is 'hero.'"

Wow, Harwood thought. *This woman is crazy about this guy. He hasn't been in here a minute and the place reeks of sexual tension. I wonder if they'd be doing it right now if I weren't here.*

"Give me a minute," Reynolds said to her. "I'm sure you're on a tight schedule, so I can go without a shower right now. I'll change out of this sweaty t-shirt and grab a bottle of water, then we can sit in the living room." He turned and left the office.

His wife's gaze followed him out of the room. "I kind of liked the sweaty t-shirt …" she murmured.

Harwood was completely disarmed. She looked at Arianna Reynolds and said, "I'm not jealous, I swear to God I'm not jealous. Honest, I know the feeling. I have a guy like that myself."

"Good for you, Detective. Take good care of him. There aren't many of them around. They break the mold after they make them."

Hank Reynolds appeared in the doorway again, chugging water from a bottle. He gestured to Harwood to come with him. "Shall we? It's this way."

They had just settled in their seats, he in a leather chair, she on a matching leather couch at right angles to it, when the front door opened and a girl in her early 20's came through the foyer. She had obviously come from the beach – cropped t-shirt over her bikini, ratty white

187

beach sneakers. Medium-length brown hair tied back in two pigtails, her mother's supermodel face and figure, deep brown eyes, killer cheekbones. A dazzling smile probably shared only with her father.

"Oops. Sorry, Dad. Didn't know you had company, or I would have sneaked in through the walkout." She looked down at herself, her hands spread in a curtsy pose. "Sorry again. I'm a little underdressed." A bubbly infectious laugh.

Reynolds introduced them. "Detective, this is my daughter Logan Hutchinson, the most beautiful lifeguard in Georgian Bay. On her last footloose and fancy free summer before starting her life's work. Logan, meet Detective Harwood of the Portland Maine Police Department."

The girl, entirely self-possessed, had already walked over to Harwood's chair and extended her hand. "Detective. I'm pleased to meet you."

Harwood took her hand. "Likewise, Logan."

"Don't pay any attention to Dad's attempts at suave lines. My mom says they're really weak. I agree with her."

Reynolds protested. "Hey, I may be clumsy, but I'm sincere. And it's not always over-the-top compliments. That t-shirt of yours fairly screams 'geek.'"

The t-shirt was a modern-day classic. Solid black with white lettering. 'You matter. Unless you multiply yourself by the speed of light squared. Then you energy.'

Now it was the girl's turn to protest. "It doesn't necessarily say 'geek,' Dad. It says sophisticated sense of humor. An aura of mystery – why's an otherwise normal-looking girl wearing a geek t-shirt?"

Harwood laughed. "Why *are* you wearing it?"

Logan Hutchinson laughed too. "Because I *am* a geek. I'm attending Cal Tech, majoring in cosmology – the study of the entire universe. Math, physics, astronomy, astrophysics, a little chemistry and astrobiology thrown in. Doesn't get any geekier than that. But I love it."

Her father looked at her, drinking her in. "Logan's going to hold dark energy and dark matter in her hands and win the Nobel Prize of the millennium."

The girl spoke to Harwood. "I want to see what the expansion of space caused by dark energy does to the distribution of dark matter throughout the universe. I think the large-scale structure and fate of the whole works depends on that. And the key to that is buried way back in the very first sliver of the first second of creation."

She smiled. "It's the ultimate puzzle. The last big mystery." She looked at her father. "And it won't be easy to solve. So can we dial back the expectations a little, Dad? No more holding dark energy and dark matter in my hands?"

"Okay," her father said. "Dialing it back. Logan's going to *figure out* dark energy and dark matter and win the Nobel Prize *of the century*."

The girl laughed, looked resigned, and shook her head. "He's hopeless," she said. Then her expression grew more serious. She didn't want to overstay her welcome, and she was a little concerned about a police detective sitting in her living room talking to her father. She glanced at Reynolds, then back at Harwood. "I'll leave you two to your business. Pleasure meeting you, Detective. Later, Dad." And she was gone.

Harwood watched her leave. "She is spectacular, Mr. Reynolds. She lights up the whole room. She's the poster girl for charisma. Beautiful, brilliant, funny – if the position of rock star cosmologist doesn't already exist, she'll invent it."

She looked at Reynolds. "This impresses me as a very happy home."

"It is. Logan is just like her mother. 'Spectacular' is a good word. I'm a very lucky guy. Now, what can I help you with?"

"The police in Lake Forest steered me to you for this conversation. I'm sure they mentioned the deaths of Richard and Rachel Montgomery when they called to set this up. Obviously I'm out of my jurisdiction both here and in Chicago, but we're wondering if there's a connection between the Montgomerys and some homicides we've had in Portland. While the Montgomerys' deaths were initially thought to result from accidental overdoses of cocaine – we know they had long-standing cocaine habits – Lt. Joe Plesnar of the Lake Forest PD now knows it was premeditated murder, dressed up to look like an accident. After reviewing the files with him, I agree – it was murder.

"We've had two similar – we're calling them 'unusual means' – murders in Portland, of high profile individuals who had earned their unpopularity ... they were hated, really. Similar to the Montogmerys. So we're wondering about possible connections – are we dealing with a serial killer, or some sort of vigilante avenging angel ranging far afield? Or is this just coincidence?

"You left the firm Mr. Montgomery headed to start your own. From what we hear, your old firm was at that time – unlike this house – a very unhappy place. So we're wondering about possible motivations within that firm."

Reynolds' face was unreadable. "What makes you conclude premeditated murder? And am I a suspect, or a person of interest? Should I call my lawyer?"

"You're definitely not a suspect. You're in the clear, Mr. Reynolds. Lake Forest PD has already established your presence here in Georgian Bay the entire week of the murders, and besides, we think any motivation on your part would be nonexistent. 'Living well is the best revenge' and all that. You won. They lost. You left when they wouldn't listen to you and founded an incredibly successful firm that's empowered millions of people. They ran your old firm into a forced fire sale and became objects of derision and ridicule. You have nothing to get even for. I'm just here to see what insights you may have."

"Well, Lake Forest PD is one of our oldest and most loved clients," Reynolds said. "I'm happy to help them – and you – however I can. Can you give me some more background?"

"Lt. Plesnar started considering murder because the Montgomery scene looked a little too pat. Almost like it

191

was staged. The autopsies established tetrodotoxin poisoning, with the poison mixed into the Montgomerys' weekly cocaine binge. Again, unusual means. But the strongest connection is what's common to our homicides: the ill will of so many people. The Montgomerys hurt a lot of people, undermined the careers of many young consultants. So we're wondering who might have hated them enough to do this, and go to the trouble of making it look the way it did. Who were their worst enemies? Do you have any thoughts?"

Reynolds was pensive, his focus on the middle distance. Finally he seemed to get his thoughts in order. "I don't know that they still had sworn enemies after all this time. 'Enemies' implies action, either overt or clandestine. Shooting war or cold war. Hostility, animosity, anger, resentment, even wishes for bad fortune – that I can understand. Enemies, I'm not so sure. Ten years is a long time to hold a grudge that could lead to murder. My friends in Libertyville tell me most everyone holds them in contempt. Wouldn't that be enough?

"I think you may be looking for a connection within the firm where there isn't one. Yes, their selfishness hurt a good many people, damaged a lot of careers. But the partners all realized a payout from the sale of the company – not as large as it might have been a few years earlier, but still sizable. As for the younger people – yeah, there might have been significant anger among people who had their career paths set back or short-circuited. But enough to commit murder all these years later?

Wouldn't any retribution have been far more likely in the immediate aftermath? All those people have had time to rebuild their careers, regain their footing. Why risk all the progress you've made with murder at this point?"

A faint smile crossed Harwood's face. "The Sicilians say, 'Revenge is a dish best served cold.' Lt. Plesnar and I were talking this morning about Patricia Dufresne."

Reynolds' demeanor changed to a faint scowl. "Detective, don't ask me to throw Pat Dufresne under the bus. I don't even know her. She was hired to run the communications practice after the two top people there came with me. I know her story. She was a partner, and they fired her a month before the sale of the firm was announced. So for some reason they wanted to leave her out in the cold – not that her holdings would have enriched anyone, split among the remaining 35 partners. Anyway, she sued, and they reached some sort of confidential settlement."

"It seems to us that she might have had the most passionate – and most justified – hatred," Harwood said.

"Hey, come on. I imagine walking into a case like this is like walking into a highly charged consulting situation. You do it with a preconceived notion and it can be a prescription for disaster. Pat Dufresne has landed on her feet too. She's now a successful political advertising consultant. She's like the rest – why would she risk what she has now?"

He held up his hand to forestall any objection from Harwood. "Look, before you decide I'm defending everyone at that firm because of the old school tie, I'll tell you this. I'm not that fond of any of the people my partners and I left behind. We wouldn't hire any of them for our company because we thought they lacked the integrity to stand up to those sociopaths and their suck-ups. So I'm not going to reflexively come to their defense and try to steer you away from them. I just don't think there's anything there."

Harwood nodded in agreement, surprising him. "Just between us, Mr. Reynolds, I think you're right. But we have to touch all the bases, and your old firm is one of them. I feel as you do, though – there's likely nothing there. I believe there's a connection to our murders, although it may look far-fetched. As I said, all the deaths initially looked like accidents, but the staging – if that's what it was – wasn't perfect. Almost like the perp wanted us to realize eventually that it was murder, and that those people deserved it. But if there is a connection between these murders, we don't know why, and we don't know how the murderer chooses his victims."

Reynolds grimaced. "I see. I think you have a lot of possibilities. I'm discounting the idea of people in the firm, but still, Rick and Rachel Montgomery must have alienated a lot of people in many walks of life. Equal opportunity shits. I don't envy you the process of elimination you're facing – here or in Portland."

Harwood smiled. "Maybe we should enlist your daughter. If she can solve the mysteries of the universe, this one should be easy."

Reynolds chuckled. "Wear your darkest sunglasses, Detective. When she turns up the wattage, the light is blinding."

He stood. She realized that, as personable as he was, he was a busy man. From his perspective, the interview was over. "Come," he said, "I'll show you out. Please call me if something comes up and you think I can help further."

She handed him her card. "Thank you for your time. And please call me if anything else occurs to you or jogs your memory."

When Harwood arrived at the airport, she used her phone to email both Chapman and Plesnar. "Reynolds doesn't think there's anything there with the people in his former firm. I agree with him. He has a lot of insights into human behavior – would have made a good cop. Surprising coming from an actuary – but it turns out he's a very rare bird. He was a psychology major; I saw his college diploma on the wall. Explains a lot. More for you when I get back home."

Chapter 24

Harwood arrived at the Portland airport at 9:00 p.m. and was back at her apartment a half hour later. It had been a long day. She'd met some extremely nice, extremely impressive people, but she didn't have much to show for it in the way of new leads. A little discouraged, she walked in the front door to find Dave MacKenzie seated at the desk in the kitchen nook.

Her spirits lifted. Arianna Reynolds was right. With a very few men, they threw away the mold.

"Nice of you to come over and welcome me home. Thank you. You're working late," she said. "What on?"

"Laying the groundwork for some volunteer fire departments on each of the islands. We don't maintain any stations out there, only some old equipment and hoses. Fire is such a horrendous danger on an island, they need to be able to do something before we arrive in the fireboats. They wouldn't have been able to save Russell Bannerman on Granite Cliffs, but they can at least get the fire engine and pumper to the scene, start hosing down neighboring buildings, buy us some time. As it was, we were lucky that Bannerman's fire didn't spread to other houses. We have to do better than that."

"How's it going? Seems to me the Granite Cliffs people would want to help with an island fire, especially since they just had such a close call."

McKenzie shook his head, gave a rueful laugh. "The guys who say they want to help are mostly fighting over who gets to drive the trucks. But that's the least of the problems. You'd be surprised at the number of people who aren't willing to pitch in at all. Don't quote me on this, but islanders can be really self-absorbed people. I can count on guys like Tom Warren and Joel Easton, but a lot of them just want to stand and watch the fire. Those upscale Atlantic Estates people are really entitled – only a handful willing to take responsibility."

"Is my friend John Morrissey helping you? I can't believe he wouldn't."

"The retired detective, the guy you call the admiral? Restored the old guardhouse at the fort? Yeah, he's an ace. I can understand why you guys respect him so. Low key, but real presence. I'd officially deputize him as Granite Cliffs commander if I could, but he still wouldn't have much to work with. A lot of his neighbors are so wrapped up in themselves they're worthless."

"Well, Dave, most of them are 'from away.' Massholes, most likely. Too much money, not enough sense. As we like to say in Maine, you can't carve rotten wood."

"Yeah, you'd think I could do something about their indifference – that being a fire captain would carry a lot of power. It really doesn't. I can't order people to do this – they have to volunteer. Most of this job is getting people to do what they should already be doing in the first place."

197

He paused. "Enough of that. How was your trip? Are you hungry? Can I get you something?"

"I had the paltry airline snack on the plane. Before that I had the good sense to get a sandwich at the airport. So, no – I don't need a meal this late."

He smiled at her. "A really long day for you. You look like a girl who's ready for bed. Maybe a little exercise first to help send you to dreamland."

Harwood burst out laughing. "You're incorrigible. And about to get lucky too. Today I met with a guy who's incredibly successful, an empire builder, but his top priority is his wife and daughter. I want some of that. Top priority. Take me to bed, Captain."

Their lovemaking had been desultory of late, both of them stretched thin, and both tired from work. But this evening they needed each other more. They undressed each other like expensive Christmas gifts, each one's eyes locked on the other's the entire time.

Dave was always gentle and attentive, but tonight he seemed to savor her, and she surrendered. She felt secure and safe, and her arousal increased exponentially. Her reaction spurred his, and when he came, he exploded inside her, a half gasp half groan escaping him.

Her orgasm came at the same time, and it was a tidal wave crashing over her, her world a billion diamond shards of light. She cried out oh my God oh Dave and held him tight, her legs wrapped around his, pulling him ever deeper into her.

As they both recovered their breath, he said, "Wow. Hit that one out of the park, didn't we?"

"Grand slam, sweetie. God, I needed that. Every once in a while you have a really good idea, Dave."

He turned on his side, arm bent at the elbow, hand supporting his head, his other hand tracing lines around and between her breasts.

"Tell me about this empire builder you talked to. I'm starting in the empire building business myself. Maybe I can learn something."

Harwood's brow furrowed, her gaze off in the distance. "He's a brilliant guy, really visionary. An actuary. Started his company about ten years ago with a handful of his former partners from his old firm, and they've built it into a huge retirement planning business. Middle class clientele, for the masses, not the executive suite. He seems pretty laid back, but the people who know him well say he has the passion of a revolutionary priest. Which I guess is what he is – he thinks of his practice as a crusade.

"You'd think he'd be all business, no-nonsense, totally focused on work. But his family is what's most important to him, by far. They clearly come first. His wife and daughter are both gorgeous, and crazy about him too. His wife is a former touring tennis pro, now a sports medicine physician. The daughter – get this – supermodel looks, but majoring in cosmology, the study of the universe. Off the charts brilliant.

"He seems like such a gentle guy, but I really wonder what he'd do if someone hurt them, or even threatened to. I don't think it would be pretty."

Harwood turned her face up to MacKenzie's and smiled. "He's got the world by the ass, Dave, and we're just working stiffs. But we should remember his priorities. Busy as we are, you come first with me, I come first with you."

"That's a deal. Can't build an empire if it doesn't have a capital. Now go to sleep, Kate. Time enough for that tomorrow."

She curled herself into his side, inside his arm, and was gone within seconds.

The next morning Harwood's phone rang in the kitchen and MacKenzie answered. The male voice confused Hank Reynolds.

"Good morning, my name is Hank Reynolds, and I'm trying to reach Kate Harwood. I'm afraid I may have dialed the wrong number."

"No, Mr. Reynolds, you dialed correctly. This is Dave MacKenzie; I'm Kate's boyfriend. Doing my Saturday morning cooking breakfast thing. I think I just heard her stirring, so I picked up her phone."

"Oh yes," Reynolds laughed. "Apparently my wife and your girlfriend were comparing notes yesterday on what terrific guys we are."

"Good to know. Actually, I think we're pretty lucky ourselves." MacKenzie looked up to see Harwood stumbling into the kitchen. "Here she is, Mr. Reynolds. A little bleary-eyed from her long day yesterday, but present and accounted for."

He handed the phone to Harwood. "Hank Reynolds for you."

Reynolds sounded a little uncomfortable. "Detective, I hope I didn't overstep any bounds or violate some sort of confidentiality standards by talking to my daughter about this, but ... I shared what we talked about in relation to possible connections. Not the specifics of the Montgomery case, but about the unusual means and ill will similarities and how the murderer might choose his victims.

"She sat around with this thousand-yard stare of hers for an hour or so last night and ... well, I told you about the wattage when she turns it up. I have my darkest sunglasses on this morning!

"She's excited about talking to you about her ideas, and would like to do it via Zoom."

"Well, okay, I guess, Mr. Reynolds. Can you give me a few minutes? It was a really long day yesterday, and I just got up. I look a sight, and I need to get some coffee into me to get my motor running. Particularly if I'm going to try to keep up with Logan!"

Reynolds laughed. "Sure. Why don't I email you the Zoom link, and you two can talk in an hour or so."

They linked with Zoom in an hour's time. *Life is still not fair,* Harwood thought. *Who looks that good first thing in the morning?* Harwood could see what Logan's father had said about the light being blinding. The girl was bubbling; the charisma Harwood had mentioned to her father was radiating off her.

201

Harwood spoke first. "Hi, Logan. Do you have a solution already?"

"Morning, Detective. Don't know if I have a solution. Just an idea. If it's a crazy idea, it's just another possibility you can eliminate. If not, maybe you can run with it. But all puzzle solutions start with an idea, you know?

"There's an old movie called 'Strangers on a Train.' Farley Granger, Robert Walker, 1951. Ever seen it? These two men meet by chance on a train and start talking about their troubles. One of them is the black sheep of a very wealthy family, and his father is about to cut him off and disinherit him. The other is being sued for divorce by a vicious gold digger determined to take him to the cleaners. They hatch an idea where each will take care of the other's problem.

"Pretty intriguing scenario, huh? Each of them can establish an ironclad alibi for the time of his own enemy's murder, and no connection at all exists between each victim and the actual murderer. And except for this chance meeting in a train compartment, there's no evidence that the two men know each other.

"The movie's set in the greater New York area, but I think this approach might work even better if the reciprocal killings took place in widely separated parts of the country.

"What do you think? Could your murders have happened that way? Different individuals murdering people totally unrelated to them?"

"Okay," Harwood said. "I get the evidentiary problems with that scenario. The whole traditional opportunity-alibi applecart gets upset. But the setup of two men on a train sounds random, and the similarities in our cases don't seem random. Besides, where's the train in our case?"

"The train – their meeting place – is the internet. And you're right, I'm thinking it's not random. You told Dad you can see the similarities of unusual means and ill will, but you're stuck on how the connection gets made, and how a single perpetrator might choose his victims.

"You can research anything on the internet. I'm thinking along the lines of an orchestra conductor or – maybe better – a puppet master who's choosing victims and recruiting people to help him do them in. As to how he chooses -- ever read Lawrence Sanders' Deadly Sins books? The hero is a police detective so obsessed with delivering justice that his wife calls him 'God's surrogate on Earth.' Maybe we're dealing with a twisted version of that, a person meting out his version of justice where he thinks society has failed. He's using the internet to pick out victims – people he thinks need to be dead – like the two in Portland and the couple in Chicago.

"He could be anywhere, choosing victims by surfing the internet, maybe mixing in the settling of old scores. But I think your puppet master is probably working from the Portland area, committing 'away' murders of peoples' enemies and then getting those people to reciprocate by committing murders on your island. He might even use encrypted emails to coach his recruits through the murders he wants them to commit.

"But to make this hang together, the Montgomerys have to be the second murders he's committed. The first one would predate your first, somewhere else in the country. He then contacted and coached his first recruit through the first island murder, then he killed the Montgomerys a short time later, then recruited an enemy of the Montgomerys to commit the murder you just had in Portland. See how the dominos are falling?"

"I do," Kate said. "You may be on to something. The difficulty is changing 'may' to 'probably.'"

"I think the key is to this Strangers on a Train scenario is the first murder. Have to find that one, because otherwise all you have is coincidence – murders in Chicago that look a lot like your two murders in Portland."

"I agree that's key." Harwood said. "But the other big requirement is that the puppet master has to recruit people to reciprocate and commit the 'home' murders in Portland. You say he finds these recruits from his internet research. But what if the new recruit, the one who's supposed to reciprocate, says no, he or she won't do it?"

"Then they're threatened with exposure," the girl replied. "Evidence will be produced linking them to a crime for which – face it – they're already a person of interest because of a revenge motive. Maybe evidence that undermines whatever alibi they may have – after all, they didn't know their enemy was going to be murdered, how strong could their alibi be for the time of the killing? They get help from the puppet master in strengthening their alibi if they co-operate, they get thrown under the bus if they don't."

Harwood considered this for a moment. "Yeah, Logan, but the big risk is what if they still say 'no' and say they'll go to the police? They now know about the reciprocal murder mechanism – they're really dangerous. The puppet master can't absolutely count on the police dismissing that possibility. After all, I'm not dismissing it."

Logan nodded. "I understand the danger to the puppet master. This is where it gets ugly to think about. Mark Twain said it best: 'Two people can keep a secret, as long as one of them is dead.' Our puppet master has already committed murder at least once; he wouldn't have any compunction about doing it again. He'd have to start over with another recruit, but so what? It's not like he's never done it before."

Harwood was amazed. The girl had absorbed all the evidence, all the possible connections, all the implications – in one evening's time. She had even found a way to marry Kate's idea of an avenging angel with a larger theory that might explain the murders better. *She's playing a game the rest of us are not familiar with,* Harwood thought. *This must be how the minds of chess grandmasters work.*

"You've persuaded me that this is a real possibility," she said. "I agree the key to pulling the whole theory together is finding the first murder. Let's say we're really lucky and we've correctly identified the Montgomerys as the second one. How do we find the first?"

"We're thinking he used the internet to bring this off," the girl said. "Wouldn't it be ironic if the internet was his Achilles heel? Everything's on the internet, you can find anything if you know how and where to look. I think maybe his mistake was 'unusual means.' I'm betting most murders are committed with guns, knives, baseball bats, strangling … but death by arson, adulterated cocaine, taser … probably not so much. Maybe the first murder was unusual means too. That would narrow our search considerably, wouldn't it?"

Ohmygod, Harwood thought. *She said "our search." Is she offering to help?*

She decided that was a question to take up on another day. For the moment, she said, "You'd make a great detective, Logan. You're intuitive and imaginative, with a very impressive grasp of detail. Mark of a great detective, rather than just a good one."

"Ooh, don't say that. Dad's already freaking out that I'll punt cosmology and become a detective – just when he has a place picked out on the mantel for a Nobel Prize."

"I wouldn't deprive the world of the person who's going to solve the last mystery of the universe. But I would like to be able to call you and pick your brain if need be."

The girl gave her a dazzling smile. She was clearly flattered. "Feel free to call, Detective. Any time. Except for the subject matter, this puzzle is fun. Have a great day!"

And she was off. God, she's not only gorgeous and brilliant, Harwood thought, she's nice. Really likeable. She's probably the most popular girl at Cal Tech. In all of Pasadena. Wherever. Life is definitely not fair.

Chapter 25

Kate walked into RHD spaces on Monday morning to find Chapman hunched over his computer, employing his newfound skills in computer research. He glanced up at her and said, "I'm still looking for more avenging angel victims besides Chicago. Don't want to have all our eggs in one basket, especially with Langdon looking over our shoulders. How was your trip? Find out anything?"

"The same similarities we already had," Kate said. "A few more details that line up pretty well, but we still can't tie the cases together for sure."

She took a deep breath. "Except … well, here's something that might be a reach, but the person who suggested it said if it's easily shown to be a screwy idea, you just discard it as one more thing that's been eliminated. If it looks like it might hang together we could run with it."

Chapman turned to face her. "What's the idea?"

"There's an old movie called 'Strangers on a Train.' Ever seen it?"

"Yeah, I think so. Two guys meet by chance, decide each will do in the other's worst enemy? Alibis all set, no connection between victim and killer, no connection between the two guys except the chance meeting no one else knows about."

"That's the one. Maybe that's what's going on here," Harwood said. "Except the meeting on the train is meeting on the internet."

Chapman exploded. "Kate, for Godsake, that's silly. How do you advertise on the internet? 'I'm looking for someone to kill the worst person in my life, and in return I'll kill the worst person in yours.' Even on what they call the dark web that would be suicidal."

"Nope, my friend said it could be just one person orchestrating this – he finds a really bad character, kills him, and then contacts the guy's enemy and says, 'I did yours, now you do mine – or I'll frame you for this one.' That would explain murders of passionately hated people, different parts of the country, not separated by very much in time ... it kind of resonates with me.

"Besides, we've about eliminated every other scenario. Same argument I used with Langdon to let me go to Chicago. And this seems more plausible to me than the idea of a lone serial killer prowling around the country dispensing his brand of justice, like Charles Bronson in 'Death Wish.'"

"Who's the genius who came up with this?"

Another deep breath. This wouldn't sit well with Chapman. "A young woman, a Cal Tech coed named Logan Hutchinson. She's the daughter of Hank Reynolds, the guy I interviewed in Georgian Bay about the Montgomery murders. After our conversation, he filled Logan in on our idea of a Charles Bronson avenging angel or whatever, and she came up with this – in detail."

Chapman reacted as she'd thought he would. "Kate. Jesus Christ. You can't involve this kid in an active investigation. That's police business. Langdon will go ballistic."

"Langdon doesn't have to know, Sam. The idea is to solve these cases, not worship at Langdon's feet. Don't stand on ceremony. Police forces have hired technical consultants since forever. She's just an unpaid consultant flying under the radar."

"Yeah, but this is all speculation, Kate. You won't find many fans of speculation in police departments – conventional wisdom says it's too wide-ranging, unfocused – a distraction."

Harwood smiled, remembering a long-ago conversation. "My dad once told me if enough people speculate, someone's bound to get it right. He said not to discount conjecture as an investigative tool. Besides, you could just ask Logan Hutchinson to let her imagination run free, and she could easily come to the right answer in any number of cases."

"You talk about her as if she's otherworldly."

"She is, kinda. She's studying cosmology – the science of the whole universe. And she's a puzzle master. She sees interrelationships faster than the rest of us could ever hope to. She thinks about the structure of the entire universe, how it works, what's going to become of it, and what started it all. Having to imagine who could have orchestrated a series of murders is probably child's play for her."

Chapman grimaced. "God, we're playing with fire here, Kate. What would you plan to have her do?"

"Well, as you might expect, she's a computer wizard too. She thinks – and I agree with her – that the key to the Strangers on a Train idea is the first murder, the one that set the whole chain of events in motion. The guy orchestrating this – she calls him the 'puppet master' – is probably here in Maine, since we've had two murders here. To have this hang together, we have to find the first murder, the one that triggered Bannerman. Otherwise we're just dealing with coincidences."

"Find your first murder out of all the murders in the country? Good frickin' luck, Kate. Even with an internet expert."

"I've seen her mind at work, Sam. Listen to me. A little over three weeks passed between Bannerman and the Montgomerys, then eight weeks between the Montgomerys and Kagan. That three week interval between Bannerman and the Montgomerys suggests the puppet master did the Montgomerys himself. If he did, he wouldn't have needed to spend time recruiting and coaching someone else after Bannerman. But he did need extra time, the whole eight weeks, between the Montgomerys and Kagan, because he had to recruit and coach someone to do Kagan.

"So that helps narrow it down. If we let her help us, Logan could look in a precise time frame before Bannerman for the first murder. Centered on, say, eight weeks before, because he'd need that time to recruit and coach someone to do Bannerman. So she could use an interval of six to ten weeks before Bannerman for that search. And she could also look for unusual or theatrical means – we've had roofies, arson, poisoned cocaine, and a taser. Not likely the first one was just plugging a guy with a handgun in a dark alley."

"Why do you two think the first one would be theatrical? No real need for that, is there?"

"She thinks there is. So do I. At first glance Bannerman and Kagan looked like accidents, but it became apparent pretty quickly it was murder. We think her puppet master is making a statement – 'These people need to be dead, they deserve it.' If the first one was theatrical too, it would make it easier to convince the first recruit to go along – 'See, I know your pain, I understand how this terrible person wronged you. Now do this, to another person just as terrible.'"

Chapman gave her a thin smile. Grudging acceptance. *Boy, she's bright. Let's see where this goes.*

"What do we do if this Logan thinks she's found something?"

"We'll know if the local police, wherever they are, have closed the case or whether the investigation is continuing. This is where it gets a little dicey. If I'd made an arrest, I wouldn't appreciate some detective from God knows where calling and asking, 'Are you sure you got the right guy?' Maybe we can't do that and just have to keep looking. The case is a much better candidate if it's still open. We can call and say, 'Hey, we have this idea that might help you. Can we talk?' Same way I did with Joe Plesnar and the Lake Forest police."

"What would we do as she's scouting around the internet?"

"We could expand our alibi checks," Harwood said. "We've been determining people's whereabouts at the specific times of the Bannerman and Kagan murders, maybe we can try to find where those same people were during the time interval Logan would use. Six to ten weeks before Bannerman is the first ten days of December to the first ten days of January. Eight weeks is the week before Christmas."

"Ugh. That's a lot of time to track down, Kate. Especially over the holidays, when people might be traveling. Holiday travel could be a good way to explain being out of town, especially if you're planning on a side trip to commit murder. How do you track those people?"

"Obviously a problem. That's why for starters Logan would focus much more closely on eight weeks, just before Christmas. And remember, we may have several days or a week we have to look at, but this doesn't involve many people. Borman, Harlan, three or four people whose lives Bannerman really ruined – they could all prove they weren't on Granite Cliffs for the island murder, but we haven't looked at eight weeks before."

"Your idea is growing on me, Kate," Chapman said. "This might actually come together."

"And we can also look at where those people were at the time of the Montgomery murders. That will make Langdon happy that we're doing something, and we don't have to tell him about the Strangers scenario. Looking at

213

those people for that time fits into what he calls my 'crazy-ass serial killer' idea."

Chapman laughed. "First thing he'll want to know is where Morrissey was when the Montgomerys were killed."

Harwood smiled. "He's already asked, Sam, just before I went to Chicago on Friday. John was at Sunday River, it was his condo week that whole week in March, and he was teaching skiing. In fact, he was also up there for twelve straight days last December, assimilating into ski school at the start of the season. As much as Langdon may want to hurt him, John's in the clear."

Chapman sat slumped in his chair, looking glum. "I feel a little obtuse, Kate. You're going so fast. Hard for me to keep up. Maybe I'm losing my edge."

Harwood smiled. "No, Sam, you definitely are not. Or if you are, I'm losing my edge too. You've just had a crash course in Logan Hutchinson's mind working at warp speed. It is definitely a challenge to keep up. I had pretty much the same questions for her as you just had for me. I'm not leaving you behind."

Chapman brightened a little, then sobered. "Maybe. You know, I just had another thought, and it's not a happy one. Kagan was killed almost two weeks ago. If your Strangers scenario is right, and three weeks is the interval between a Granite Cliffs murder and the next 'trigger' murder, we're due for another killing sometime in the next week or ten days. Except we don't know where, or who, or how. Or even if we'll be able to find it after the fact."

"Shit. You're right," Harwood said. "And maybe another Granite Cliffs murder eight weeks after that, near the end of July. Once these guys start – lone serial killer or puppet master – they tend not to stop. Is there any way we can prevent these from happening?"

Chapman communed with himself for a moment, then said, "I suppose we could theoretically send a bulletin to the state police in all 50 states, asking them to let us know if any unusual or theatrical murders take place in the June 1 to June 15 interval coming up. But there are some big problems with that. State police aren't necessarily called in on all murders. Here in Maine, homicides are local jurisdiction unless the locals ask for help or are a real small department. So it's possible the staties wouldn't even know about it after it happened.

"Second, they'd probably think we're nuts if we send out a bulletin like that. Can you imagine the reaction? 'Who do these lunatics think they are – do they have a pipeline to God or something?' Most state police would very likely ignore any bulletin we send and toss it in the circular file.

"And third ..." – he smiled at Kate – "we'd have to get Langdon to authorize the bulletin, which he is definitely not going to do if it makes him look nuts. And we'd have to let him in on our Strangers scenario and probably how we came up with it – which I'm sure you don't want to do.

"As a practical matter, we can't stop one murder over a 50-state area in a 15-day interval. If it happens, it will likely be committed by someone who's gotten pretty good at it. All we can do is rely on the guy's penchant for theatrics and look just as hard for that murder as your friend Logan would be looking for the first one."

"And if we find it?" Harwood asked.

"We check the whereabouts of our persons of interest for that time. And I guess we start the eight-week clock ticking down to the next Granite Cliffs murder. I don't even want to think about what we'll have to tell Langdon or Chief Anthony, to say nothing of the residents of Granite Cliffs."

Harwood sighed. "Well, at least we're not stuck in a blind alley any more, are we, Sam? We have plenty to keep us busy."

Chapter 26

The first thing Jerome Darlan did on the last morning of his life was what he did most mornings. He screamed at his wife.

"Liza! What the hell is this duffel bag doing by the front door?"

In the kitchen of their Lost River, West Virginia home, Eliza Darlan cringed. Another day in paradise, just like every other day. If she could only get out of here without being hit this morning, she'd be ahead of the game.

"I'm going to my sister's in Clarksburg for two or three days. We talked about this, Dar. She just had surgery and she gets home from the hospital today. You know she needs help; Ed is so lame he can barely get around himself. I'll be home as soon as I can – as soon as they can manage by themselves."

"Jee-zus Christ! Will I need to put up with this shit every time she has surgery?"

That wasn't a joke, Liza Darlan thought. *He's not being flippant, he means it. He must be the most self-centered man on the planet.*

"You'll be fine, Dar. I've left sandwich makings – ham, roast beef, cheese, lettuce – in the fridge, along with three evening meals. All you have to do is pop them in the microwave. I left the cook times and stirring

217

instructions on Post-It notes on the top of each dish."
God, how helpless can you get, she thought.

"Yeah, but I'll bet you forgot beer!" *Stupid bitch*, he thought.

"No, there's a case in the basement, along with the bottles already in the fridge up here."

"How the hell is that supposed to last me three days?"

Good Lord, she thought. *Aren't almost 30 bottles enough for three days? And if they aren't, are your arms and legs broken? You can't go and get more yourself?*

But she didn't say that. Early in their marriage, 23 years before, she would have snapped back at him, but he'd snapped bones and loosened teeth too many times since then for her to continue that practice.

Now she just shrugged. "Sorry if that doesn't turn out to be enough. I'll pick some up on my way back this weekend."

She walked out of her kitchen through the small dining area to the front door, where her packed duffel bag and handbag sat. Her husband stood there glaring at her. *Give me strength*, she thought. *Just get me out of here away from him for a few days.*

"What are you planning while I'm gone?" she asked. *It would be nice if you looked for a job, you lazy bastard. We're still paying off your legal fees from the trial.*

"Hunt coyotes," he said, a wiseass grin in his face. *Like hell you are,* she thought. He'd be poaching deer in the national forest again. That was his idea of putting

218

food on the table. Buying food with money paid to him for honest work – that was beneath him. An insult to his manhood.

The only way Jerome and Liza Darlan kept body and soul together was her doing. They lived in the house her parents had left her, after she and Dar had lived in rat-trap apartments for fifteen years. What little cash they had came from her wages cleaning houses, taking in wash, and making sewing repairs to peoples' wardrobes. Dar had been fired from his job shortly after his manslaughter trial the year before – he'd been acquitted by a friendly jury, but he hadn't fooled the owner of the gravel pit where he'd operated heavy equipment.

The owner knew Dar was guilty as hell, and he simply waited for the slightest transgression on Dar's part to fire him for cause. Given Darlan's volatile nature, it hadn't taken long. And of course Dar, grievously wronged in his own mind, had refused to look for work after such an injustice. He'd adopted a steady diet of guns and beer instead.

He shouldn't have been allowed to own a gun at all, much less hunt with one. But he'd beaten the manslaughter rap – the accidental shooting of a young man sitting with his uncle in a deer blind in the woods. Darlan had seen movement and a flash of color just before he pulled the trigger, but that didn't stop him – the deer was more important. Once it had been determined that the young man had been gay, the shooting was even less important in Darlan's mind. No

219

remorse. "On less fag in the world," he'd said to friends. "Shit happens."

The prosecuting attorney had been outraged. Darlan gave guns, hunting, and West Virginians a bad name. There was a solid case for manslaughter, the prosecutor thought. He didn't settle for an indictment for negligent homicide – he wanted substantial jail time for this Neanderthal. In fact, his fifteen minutes of fame had come from a memorable line in his summation to the jury. "You fire a gun, you own the bullet." The gun magazines had approved; it buttressed their safety argument.

But the jury hadn't seen it that way. A combination of gun culture and homophobia ruled in that corner of West Virginia, and Darlan walked free. The victim's family had been so upset they had left the area and moved to Minnesota. "I never believed you could find twelve people in this state with that much hatred," the boy's uncle said. "But I guess it wasn't that difficult. I can't even stand to look at these people anymore."

But all that was in the past. Although he owed thousands in legal fees, Darlan was confident his defense attorney would eventually give up and write off the remaining amount. *Can't get blood from a stone*, he thought. He had no assets for the attorney to attach. Liza's parents had made sure the house was in her name alone. Darlan had been furious about that at the time, but it had worked out well for him.

After clearing and washing Darlan's breakfast dishes – *God forbid he'd do this himself,* she thought, *I'll be looking at a mountain of dishes when I get back* – she carried her bag to the car and started her drive to Clarksburg. Darlan watched her go, walked to the refrigerator, and grabbed a beer. *Sun's over the yardarm somewhere in the world,* he thought. A beer wouldn't hurt, this should be easy. Out of season, the deer weren't hiding in the deep woods, spooked by hunters. And school wasn't out yet, so there would be few if any hikers in the national forest on a weekday.

Their home bordered the national forest boundary, so Darlan walked directly into his hunting territory. He was unaware he was being stalked for the entire half mile his pursuer trailed him. And he never heard the snap of the crossbow from sixty yards away.

The arrow entered Darlan's neck, slicing through his carotid artery, nicking the spine, staying lodged in the neck. Darlan collapsed as dead weight, his clawing at the arrow quickly becoming less frantic as blood poured out of him.

The man who appeared in his fading vision was shaking his head. *Damn it,* he thought. *I had the sights lined up for a center mass heart shot. The crossbow must be more powerful than I thought. I should have practiced more; I don't want to have to shoot him again to finish the job. At least initially this should look like a hunting accident.*

He dropped to one knee to speak to his prey. "Mr. Darlan. Can you hear me?" Darlan blinked, tried to form the words *help me.* "There's no help coming, Mr. Darlan. You brought this on yourself. You fire a gun, you own the

221

bullet." The man smiled. "Tell you what, sport. You can keep my arrow."

The man, who would introduce himself to Liza Darlan as "personalguide" in an encrypted email ten days later, stood and watched the life ebb out of Jerome Darlan. Killed by a wayward arrow, left to die by a panicked hunter who'd likely been after coyotes too. At least coyotes are what Liza Darlan would tell the authorities her husband had been hunting. All in all, an ironic twist of fate, although few tears would be shed for Jerome Darlan.

Liza Darlan might come under suspicion, personalguide thought, but likely wouldn't be arrested. Her travel time and arrival in Clarksburg would be documented, and an autopsy would reveal alcohol in Darlan's system, consumed before going hunting. Not enough time for Liza Darlan to do what she'd possibly fantasized but never put into action. There should be little need to threaten her with falsified evidence to have her do his bidding – he thought she'd be so grateful she wouldn't need much persuading to become his recruit. Especially since her target was every bit as ugly a person as Jerome Darlan.

Mission accomplished, personalguide walked back through the woods to a hiking trial that led to a trailhead parking lot on the highway. He tossed his crossbow and remaining arrows in a bag and put the bag in the well for his spare tire, covered by the carpeting in his SUV's cargo area. The small donut spare tire was hidden beneath the lowered rear seat. He'd put it back in its proper place once he'd found a permanent resting place for the crossbow -- some secondary road trash can hundreds of miles away.

A quick ride up Rt. 259 from Lost River and the George Washington National Forest, then east on Rt. 48 into Virginia, then on to his favorite highway, Interstate 81. No tolls, no cameras, little traffic. Perfect for moving about the country undetected.

Chapter 27

On the Monday following the 4th of July weekend, Harwood and Chapman were tidying up their final reports of cases from the previous week. Breaking and entering plus aggravated assault against a woman who'd thrown her boyfriend out of the house. A game of pool gone bad in the Commercial Street Pub – pool cue, fractured skull, felony assault. "The hot-weather blues," Chapman called them.

As they organized their paperwork, Robert Langdon called them into his office. "You two need to get moving," he said. "You're way low on straight-line achievement."

The two detectives ignored Langdon's cheap shot. They had cleared a number of violent cases in the past month, and provided ADA Garfield Levenson with additional evidence on two of "Morrissey's unsolved cases" that Langdon had foisted on them. More important, they'd spent six full weeks researching and following every lead, no matter how tenuous, arising from the sordid personal histories of Russell Bannerman and Donald Kagan.

Langdon continued. "I want you to treat John Morrissey as a person of interest in the two Granite Cliffs homicides," he said.

"Yes, sir, exactly how do we do that?" Chapman asked. "He has solid alibis that he was elsewhere at the time of each crime."

"You've been looking at revenge motives in the Bannerman and Kagan murders," Langdon said. "And you've also been considering the possibility of contract killers being hired because of those same motives. But in the latter search you've skipped Morrissey. I want you to include him in your list of people who might have hired a paid killer."

Kate was shocked. This was ridiculous, even for Langdon. She'd thought his hatred for Morrissey might diminish once John had retired, but it seemed to have intensified. Maybe because John looked better and better in the rear view mirror, she thought, and Langdon looked ever worse.

"Sir, as we've looked at the detailed histories of Bannerman and Kagan, Morrissey hasn't shown up in them, even tangentially. Not surprising, that litigation and those financial transactions were civil, not criminal. So what's your thinking on Morrissey's possible motive?"

"I have it on good authority that Morrissey spent a substantial amount of time last summer making inquiries about his neighbors, about who was considered a good citizen and who was not."

"Making a list and checking it twice?" The sarcasm was evident in Chapman's voice.

"Not funny, Chapman," Langdon snapped. "Start thinking. He could have decided some people needed to

225

be eliminated, and he would certainly have underworld connections who could do it."

"Yes, sir, while I think that may be a little remote, we'll check into it," Kate said. "You entertained my theory, we're certainly obliged to follow up on yours. No stone left unturned."

Outside Langdon's office, Chapman glared at Kate. "What the hell was that about? 'Oh yes sir, we'll check it out, yes indeedy sir.' What are you smoking?"

Kate gave him a grim smile. "I wanted to get out of there. Of course it's ridiculous, Sam. It's nuts. He's blinded by his hatred for John. But it's clear to me that he has a mole on the island, keeping him informed of John's activities, and that mole is an enemy of John Morrissey. I want to find out who it is — it could be someone trying to deflect suspicion from himself by throwing it on John."

"How do we find that out?"

"Well, this may be bending the rules, but if Langdon wants John to be treated as a person of interest, we'll do that, except we'll also tell John we're doing it. And tell him there's a mole on the island feeding information about him to Langdon, and see where he thinks that might lead.

"I think we should forgo a ferry or rescue boat trip to the Atlantic Estates pier, being met by John, walking up to his house, all of that. Too visible. Let's call him and Tom Warren and arrange to meet him at Tom's, under the radar, on the private side of the island."

226

Ten minutes later, two phone calls made, Kate permitted herself a smile. "All set, Sam. Stealth conversation at Tom Warren's house. Tom even said he'll pick us up in his boat at the public pier in town to keep our visit low profile."

The next morning Tom Warren sat Harwood, Chapman, and Morrissey at the table on his back porch, fortified with coffee. "I shouldn't be here for this," he said, starting to leave the porch.

"Why not?" Morrissey said. "I don't mind. And if there's a mole out here who considers me an enemy, we could use your ideas about who it might be and why."

Warren looked at Harwood and Chapman. "Stick around," Chapman said. He went on to repeat what Langdon had said about Morrissey's research into his neighbors and his contacts within Portland's criminal element.

Morrissey burst out laughing. "You said, 'Making a list and checking it twice?' That's rich. You'll give him a stroke yet."

Then he turned serious. "Look, guys, on the face of it this is ridiculous. I spent my life putting crooks behind bars. I'm not the most popular guy in that set. If I tried to contract with anyone in Portland, they'd be on the phone to Chief Anthony or Langdon in a heartbeat, giving me up for conspiracy to commit murder. They'd want a favor or an IOU, of course, but mostly they'd want to screw me. And if I tried to contract with anyone outside

Portland, they'd immediately contact someone in Portland to check me out. Same result."

"Besides," he said, "from what you've told me this morning I'm fairly sure I know who your mole – Langdon's informant – probably is. I doubt he's a murderer, and certainly not contracting with paid killers. Just acting out of personal animosity, I would think."

"I'm all ears," Chapman said.

"Me too," said Warren.

"Judge James Cooper – my neighbor across the parade ground." He looked at Harwood and Chapman. "You probably don't know him, he's a municipal court judge. Traffic court."

Morrissey sighed. "I've never engaged in the cop habit of bitching about judges, about some of them being stupid or soft on crime or whatever. I made it a practice not to talk about them, except very occasionally to note when a judge was particularly wise – fair, sensible, even-handed about what he'd allow or not allow in court, what he'd hand down in sentencing.

"Judge Cooper isn't in that category. I've never bad-mouthed him, but plenty of people have. He's a stiff-necked, moralistic prig on a power trip. You ever read about 'Maximum John' Sirica in the Watergate trials? Sirica used sentencing as leverage to get people to reveal criminal information. Cooper is 'Maximum James' in traffic court with his fines and suspensions – not for any higher purpose, but because he's a self-righteous sanctimonious bastard. I'm sure he knows, or at least surmises, what I think of him – so he's keeping what tabs

228

he can and conveying them to Langdon. Langdon's probably the horse he's betting on as the next chief of police – Cooper thinks that kind of connection will help his career.

"Anyway, I'm sure he's your mole, and while he may be an asshole, he's not the type to murder someone or try to contract to have it done. So relax. I don't care what he thinks or says about me, or to whom."

"John, thanks for the reasoning about how implausible it would be for you to contract with a paid killer," Chapman said. "We can toss that back in Langdon's face when he asks if we've made any progress in making that connection." Chapman paused. "I think we're set now. Thanks for your time."

"On a lighter note," Kate said, "how was your fishing trip to Lake Ontario?"

"Fabulous," Morrissey said. "I love lake trout fishing. I was really fortunate my old Holy Cross buddy Ev Drayman was willing to rent his cottage to me. And I'm going fishing again in a couple of weeks, on Sebago Lake, with a friend from ski school, Rollie Merron. We're looking to take some northern pike out of there – someone introduced the species a while ago, and the pike are raising hell with the food chain, endangering the trout in Sebago."

"Mighty nice of you," Tom Warren said. "Fishing as a public service."

"Always glad to do my part," Morrissey laughed. He nodded to Harwood and Chapman as they rose to start their trip back to Portland. "Call me if you think an old flatfoot might have some ideas. Always glad to help you two as well. I don't envy you having to put up with Langdon wringing his hands about how all this reflects on him."

On their return to RHD, Chapman prepared for an afternoon date in court to testify on an assault case. After he left the office, Kate debated with herself on a possible next move. Risky but necessary, she thought. They were stuck. They needed help.

Arianna Reynolds answered the phone in her Georgian Bay home. "Hello, Dr. Reynolds, this is Kate Harwood in the Portland Police Department. I was hoping to reach Logan."

"Kate, first of all, I've asked you to call me Arianna. And second, Logan's on the beach lifeguarding this afternoon. She'll be back here just after 5:00. Should I have her call you? We have your number."

"Yes, please … Arianna." Kate laughed. "There, I said it. Police are so used to being formal with people, first names can come a little hard. But I promise, 'Arianna' from now on. Looking forward to Logan's call. Thanks."

Logan Hutchinson's call came through at 5:15 p.m. She was understandably curious. "Did you break the case, Kate? Tell me all about it!"

Kate sighed. "No, Logan, the reason I called is because we haven't broken the case. Not for lack of trying, but now I think we're stuck. We need a fresh set of eyes. I was hoping that could be you. I think we need some more technical computer skills for our searches, maybe even some creative ideas about what searches to conduct.

"I think that might be difficult to do with Zoom. Could you by any chance come to Portland this weekend? We could hole up in a hotel suite so we wouldn't be interrupted. Brainstorm like we did before."

"I would love that, Kate! Dad will have a fit that I'm playing detective again, worrying that I'll give up cosmology. No chance of that, but I would love a little more intellectual stimulation than I get sitting on a lifeguard tower."

"Listen," Kate said. "I'll be glad to pay your air fare, but it'll take me a couple of months to budget it out. Is that okay?"

Logan laughed. "Kate, don't be silly. Dad has 80 kazillion airline miles, and I have about 60 kazillion myself. Not a problem. Let me make arrangements to take Friday afternoon off and figure out a flight arrival time. Call you tonight?"

"Fine," Kate said. "And … umm … Logan, you're my cousin, visiting, okay? I'm kinda bending the rules on this, involving you in a police investigation. No one else knows about this, not even my partner on the force."

"I love it, Kate! What's a puzzle without a little intrigue? I'll call you tonight with my flight info." And she was off.

Chapter 28

Logan flew from Toronto to Portland on Friday afternoon, arriving at 4:50 p.m. She cleared Customs and walked out of the security area to find a tall good-looking man holding a sign with her name on it.

As he reached to take her bag, she said, "Hi, I'm Logan Hutchinson. You're my driver?"

The man smiled. Cute smile. "No, I'm Kate's boyfriend, Dave MacKenzie, sent to pick you up. Full-time boyfriend, part-time chauffeur."

Logan was instantly on guard. No one was supposed to know what she was doing with Kate. "Nice to meet you. I'm Kate's cousin."

"No you're not." He saw the look on her face. "Hey, relax. It's okay. Kate and I are a secret, just as you and she are. She asked me to give you this." He handed Logan a handwritten note.

Logan, he's legit. And just so you know this note is legit too, and it's from me ... Dave is my dark energy.

Logan looked up, her face changing from suspicion to brilliant smile. "Dark energy. Well, I guess that establishes your bona fides. Let's go."

They walked out of the terminal into short-term parking. Dave had what looked to be a brand new pickup truck. "Nice ride," Logan said as she opened the door to

232

get in. "My dad would like this – his taste runs to trucks and oversize SUVs."

"Yup, man needs a truck," Dave said. "But isn't your dad the chairman of the board? I would have thought limousines and sports cars."

The girl laughed. "You don't know my dad. Outdoorsy. Action hero type." She giggled a little at a long-distant memory. "A long time ago I named him 'Hank the hunk.'"

She looked over at him, flashed another smile. "Kate's done well. You're not bad yourself."

MacKenzie burst out laughing. "Aren't you sweet? Would you say that if I weren't?"

She laughed too. "No. Definitely not. You're a genuine hottie, Dave MacKenzie."

"And you are an outrageous flirt, Logan Hutchinson."

She smiled, settling back in her seat. "I try for excellence in all things, Dave."

When they reached the Portland Regency Hotel, MacKenzie pulled under the portico, opened his door, pulled her bag from the back seat, and came round to her door to open it. "Chauffeur to the end. And from this point on you're Kate's cousin. Let's get you checked in. Kate will be along in about a half hour. I'll wait with you in the lobby."

Kate arrived from PPD thirty minutes later. Logan noticed the flash between her friend and MacKenzie. "Hey Cousin, I made dinner reservations just up the street," Kate said. Then in a lower tone so she wouldn't be overheard, "No shop talk tonight, just us girls. If we're going to be informal police partners, we need to know each other better."

Kate turned to MacKenzie. "Thanks, Dave. You're the best."

"My pleasure. Enjoy yourselves," he said. That flash between them again, then he turned to the girl. "Great meeting you, Logan. Hope we can do it again sometime."

"I hope so too. Thanks for giving up your afternoon for me, Dave."

As Kate watched MacKenzie leave, Logan reached for her handbag and laughed. "Stop staring, Kate. You two won't be a secret for long if you keep those lightning flashes going."

Kate flushed. "Oh my God, is it that obvious?"

Logan smiled. "Yeah, it kinda is. And you don't even have to be an official detective to see it!"

As they settled into their seats at Portland's upscale Grille 36, Kate said, "I'm sorry I couldn't get off work to come pick you up. Everything go okay with Dave?"

"Uh-huh. I think I might be in love. He's a keeper, Kate. You're lucky."

"Yes, I am. How about you? Do you have anybody special?"

"Oh, I date some, but the pickings at Cal Tech are a little slim. Wonderful brains to work with, but no real candidates for The Guy."

"Who's The Guy?"

"You know," Logan said. "You feel an electric charge go through you when he takes your hand in his. You start to melt when he looks into your eyes. You want to surrender when he kisses you. That guy." She smiled. "Still waiting for him."

"You seem to know a lot about him already."

Logan laughed. "Well, I read a lot on my own. And I'm not exactly oblivious to the 24/7 lovefest my parents have going."

"Yes, I caught a bit of that," Kate said. "I'm sure it will happen with you. Be patient. Keep the faith."

"Oh, I will. If there's one thing I've figured out ... if you want it to happen, stop looking."

The girl turned serious. "So ... what are we going to do tomorrow?"

"I thought we could work here. That's the reason I reserved a suite for you, so we'd be away from any interruptions or any emergency call-outs for me. Now, enough shop talk."

"Time out," Logan said. "My money was no good when I checked in. That suite is expensive, Kate. You shouldn't cover that by yourself."

"You're a consultant on this case, Logan. An unpaid consultant. The least I can do is pay for your room."

"Yeah, but the police department isn't paying the bill. You are. Not right. Can't let you do it, Kate."

"Logan ..."

"Kate," the girl interrupted. "My mother was a professional athlete who saved her money. My father is the board chairman and principal owner of a very successful consulting firm. And I ..." – she smiled – "I am a lifeguard, getting paid to get a great tan. It's no big deal for me to pay my own way, and besides, I'm excited about the puzzle. I'd almost be willing to pay you to let me be in on it."

She fixed Kate with a cool stare. "End of discussion, Kate."

Wow, Kate thought. *Tempered steel beneath that smile. There is no end to the surprises with this girl.*

She steered Logan away from her first Maine lobster. "You can have lobster here anytime. This is the height of the fishing season, so see what an upscale chef can do with halibut or, better yet, ahi tuna if they have it. You'll thank me later."

They worked their way through the meal, sharing entrees, and Logan said, "Wow. Georgian Bay game fish are great, but this is something else. Here's the thanks you predicted."

Kate laughed, then turned more serious over profiteroles and coffee. "Tell me something. You've made all these allusions to various old novels and movies. How is it you came to be so well versed in them?"

The girl cast her eyes down and murmured, "The first ten years of my life were pretty sheltered. I didn't get out much – no after-school activities, no cruising around the neighborhood with other kids – because my mom was hiding from someone she was sure would hurt us. So I spent a lot of time alone, locked in my castle tower, with books and movies."

She smiled. "Then Hank – my dad – came into my life and turned me on to puzzles and the mysteries of the universe."

"I wondered how you made such a specialized career choice so early. It was your dad, huh? He steered you?"

"Oh no, he'd never push me into anything. He just liberated me. He freed me – freed all of us, me, my mom, my gramma. I'd like to say he was riding a white horse, wearing a suit of shining armor, but he was barefoot, with a clipboard and a Sudoku puzzle in his hand." She smiled. "I guess the hero shows up when he's most needed. Doesn't matter what he's wearing."

Kate caught the look on the girl's face as she talked about her father. "I think The Guy is going to have a very high standard to meet."

Logan laughed. "Oh, The Guy is out there. And I'm sure he'll meet the standard. It'll happen. Only a matter of time."

"So you believe in Fate?"

The girl frowned a little. "Not exactly. I'm a scientist, remember? On large scales and over billions of years, the evolution of the universe looks kind of inevitable, but that doesn't mean it was preordained. It just happened in the way it happened, and it allowed us to develop and be here. But on smaller scales, what we can relate to personally, I think the way life unfolds is pretty random."

She brightened. "I'll give you a summary of a hot debate within the scientific community. We know a lot of the constant values in the physical laws of the universe. We also know that, if any of them were the slightest bit different, the universe wouldn't be the way it is – might not exist at all – and we wouldn't be here.

"Some cosmologists theorize a multiverse – a bunch of universes, all with different physical laws and constants, and they say we just happen to be in one that allows atoms and stars and galaxies – and us – to exist. We call that reasoning the anthropic principle."

Logan shrugged. "Maybe. One universe is enough for me to figure out right now. But here's the screwy thing about what people think of as Fate. I guess you'd call it a perversion of the anthropic principle. Some other people say that, if different values for those constants would mean we couldn't exist, then somebody had to fine-tune the dials at the beginning."

She laughed. "Which is a classic circular argument. It's like discovering that Lou Gehrig died of Lou Gehrig's disease and saying, 'What are the odds of that?'" She shook her head. "Besides, even if the fine-tuning argument were true, how could you explain us? We'd be a miniscule afterthought. Atomic matter – all the stuff we can see – is only four percent of the universe. All the complex elements – above helium in the periodic table, the stuff we and our planet are made of – make up only one percent of that four percent. Nobody fine-tuned the dials for us to be here. How self-centered can you get?"

She smiled. "I'll get off my soapbox now."

Kate was enthralled. The girl's father was right. Her intensity was spellbinding. "No," Kate said, "It's fascinating. And the way you explain is so clear … I told your dad when I was in Georgian Bay that you were going to be a rock star cosmologist. You are."

Logan smiled. "Well, right now I'm a detective. And I'll tell you this. On smaller scales, with shorter time frames, life may look random, but it isn't always. On these cases of yours, somebody's fine-tuning the dials. I'm sure of it. We just have to find the dials and read what they say."

"Okay," Kate said. "That's the subject for tomorrow. "I'll see you here at 8:00, and we'll play dueling computers."

Chapter 29

Kate knocked on Logan's door at the Regency Saturday morning to find a room service breakfast spread out in the suite. "I figured if we're doing stealth detecting," Logan said, "you'd want to stay out of the public eye as much as we can."

"Good thought," Kate said. Over breakfast, she gave Logan a bird's-eye view of their persons of interest and possible motivations. She included John Morrissey, then explained she hated to do it, but her boss would be all over her and her partner if they skipped over John.

"He sounds like a terrific guy." Logan said. "Your friend John. Your captain, not so much."

"John's a legend – the greatest detective ever in this city," Kate said. "He's already helped us think through a lot of issues. And this is the thanks he gets."

"Life isn't fair," Logan said. *Sure isn't,* Kate thought. *Every time I look at you, kid, the same thought crosses my mind.*

"I was thinking," Logan said. "Instead of trying to find the first murder with the whole country as our search area, and then checking peoples' whereabouts against that if we find anything, let's come at it from the opposite direction. Assume the first murder did take place when we think it did – we don't know where – and see if we can determine peoples' whereabouts at that time. That'll limit the number of places we have to look. It'll also reduce the chance of our missing something. Didn't you say you'd restricted your search to east of the Mississippi when you happened to find the Montgomerys?"

"I did," Kate said. "If the Montgomerys are really the second murder, we got lucky. So … good idea, Logan. We have a limited number of people whose whereabouts we have to try to determine. Lots easier than looking all over the country for a murder similar to ours."

"Okay then," Logan said. "Let's get to work. I'm psyched!"

Two hours later, sitting at her laptop, Logan said, "Huh. Whaddaya know. Bet no one knows about this."

"What?" Kate asked.

"I'm afraid you may be upset at this, Kate. I'm looking at your friend John Morrissey. He was in New Mexico for a week last December."

"Not possible," Kate said. "I remember just after the Bannerman murder, Jack Harlan told me that John had been at Sunday River that whole week in February. In fact, he said John had been up there the better part of the winter already. He told me John was there most of December, assimilating into ski school. John even asked Jack to walk past the guardhouse every couple of days just to check that everything was all right." She paused. "Why do you think he was in New Mexico?"

"I've been looking at Sunday River's hotel occupancy records for their quarter share owners," Logan

241

said. "Owners can use their week however they want – stay in their condo, rent it, even leave it vacant I suppose. They can also trade it with a vacation exchange clearinghouse to get a week somewhere else. That's what John Morrissey did. Traded his December Sunday River week for a week at Angel Fire ski resort in New Mexico. Fits our time frame for our assumed first murder – although it's way outside the original search boundary you used for the Montgomerys."

Logan was right. Kate was upset. She took a deep breath. "What's next?"

"I want to see how long he had the vacation exchange in place. This could be completely innocent. Maybe his trip was a spur of the moment thing; he originally planned to go to Sunday River but this exchange came through. John had already asked Jack Harlan to keep tabs on his house; maybe he didn't tell Jack about his change in plans since he was going to be gone anyway.

"But if he'd had the exchange for a good while, Kate, we need to start looking for a first trigger murder somewhere in the Southwest during that time period."

"I'm almost afraid to ask, Logan. How did you get this information?"

The girl gave her a wicked grin. "Kate, Big Brother is here, and he has mischievous kids. Some are about 15 years old, others are my age or even a little older. None of your private information is absolutely safe if it's sitting in a computer data base somewhere. Remember the movie War Games? Matthew Broderick hacks into a

242

supercomputer and starts playing 'global thermonuclear war'? The authorities are chasing him all over creation and his girlfriend asks him, 'Are you in all this trouble because you changed my grade?' Because he started their adventure by changing her grade on their school's computer.

"And that movie was – what? – 1983? How much better do you think kids are now at hacking into computers? Hotel occupancy records, a vacation exchange firm's records – that's pretty easy."

Logan paused. "Actually, it *was* pretty easy."

Kate was horrified. "My god, Logan, doing that could make that evidence inadmissible at trial!"

"I don't see how, Kate. I'm just a girl hacking into computers. I'm not a police officer, I'm not even a paid consultant to the police. You can get those same records either by asking, or if you need to, with a subpoena. Only difference is you'll know in advance what you'll be seeing."

Kate felt herself standing on shifting sands. She didn't know how to react to Logan's story. She could either be bowled over by her brilliance – again – or devastated at its implications. But in the next moment, she decided she was a detective, an officer of the law, bound to follow the evidence wherever it led her.

"Keep going on the vacation exchange, and look at Southwest murders regardless of how long he had the exchange reservation. And, Logan – this is our secret, you don't tell *anyone*. Don't leave tracks, because we might

243

eventually have to retrace your steps and get all this information with proper police procedure."

"Will do." Logan looked at Harwood. Sympathetic. "I'm sorry if I ruined your day, Kate."

"Well, you haven't, not quite. To have Morrissey involved in these trigger murders, we'd have to place him in Chicago for the Montgomerys, and we can't. We have all kinds of records that he was at Sunday River for his March quarter share week when the Montgomerys were killed. Captain Langdon put me through the wringer on that as soon as I suggested there might be a connection between those murders and ours.

"Besides," Kate continued, "John would have had to get to Illinois. We've already checked air and train manifests for all our persons of interest. Nothing. The bus doesn't seem plausible, and for all three our perp would have needed to get around Chicago once he got there."

"Your Montgomery killer could have driven," Logan said. "Long drive, but doable."

"We checked turnpike records – photos at toll plazas – none of our people passed through any state turnpike barrier. Nobody's car left Maine. And we checked rental cars too – rental car records in Portland, and near the airport, train station, and bus terminal in Chicago. Video records at rental car offices don't show anyone looking like any of our persons of interest around the days a rental would have been taken out. We've been pretty thorough, Logan."

"Could have driven out there on secondary roads," Logan said. She saw the look on Kate's face. "Hey, Kate, I'm not bent on trying to prove John Morrissey guilty of anything. Remember we're trying to eliminate possibilities, and eliminate means proving it couldn't have happened. I'm just trying to imagine if something *could* have happened, despite appearances."

"I know," Kate said. "I'm just hoping the ski school and lift records are tamper-proof and show beyond doubt that John was at Sunday River that week in February. And that there's an innocent explanation for the vacation exchange."

She knew Kate wouldn't like it, but Logan spent the rest of the weekend, until she had to leave for her return flight Sunday afternoon, looking at John Morrissey. At noon on Sunday, she said to Kate, "The vacation exchange transaction records were a little hard to get into, but I finally did it. This is kinda discouraging, Kate. Morrissey's vacation exchange with Angel Fire ski resort was in place for six months before he went out there. Could be coincidence, the records show he's made December ski trips before, but I think we're obliged to look in the Southwest for our kind of murder during that week."

Kate shuddered. "Can you keep working on this in your spare time at home?"

"Sure, I'd be glad to. Lifeguard night life doesn't really interest me that much, and … well, The Guy hasn't shown up yet, you know?"

In spite of her darkened mood, Kate laughed. "Okay. Thank you. Let me know if you find anything in the Southwest. And if you really have time, you might check all our persons' whereabouts starting about two or three weeks after the Kagan murder. The Montgomerys were three weeks after Bannerman, and if the timing for trigger murders holds true, this one could have happened sometime near the first of June."

"Will do, Kate. I'll be in touch. Thanks for the great Maine meals. But next time I want lobster, whether that marks me as a tourist or not!"

Chapter 30

Kate had just checked in to RHD on the Thursday morning after Logan's visit when her phone chimed with a text. "Leaving the house for lifeguard duty shortly. Can we Zoom this evening? Text me with a good time – Logan"

She wondered all day what her young genius had found and posed the question as soon as Logan's face appeared at 7:30 p.m. "Hi, Logan. Did you find something in the Southwest?"

Logan shook her head. "No, and I looked for two nights running. Then I started rethinking our search criteria. We've been looking at *murders* – unusual means, sure, but still murders. But, Kate, our murders didn't start out that way. At first they all looked like *accidents* – fell asleep smoking, cocaine overdose, heart attack. Then you and the Lake Forest police did your due diligence, and you established pretty quickly that they were murders dressed up *to look like accidents*.

"So I asked myself, 'What if there were deaths that looked like accidents and the local police weren't as astute or observant as Kate and Lt. Plesnar?' Maybe the police considered murder, maybe not, but if they concluded accident, those cases might be closed now and put to bed."

"How did you change the search criteria?" Kate asked. "If you opened the search to all but natural causes, you'd have too many cases to count."

"I searched on the combination of accidents and unusual means, and gradually got better at defining unusual means," Logan said. "For example, first thing you think of is accidental falls, but if it were murder, there might be signs of a struggle, or someone might have seen the victim and the murderer together beforehand. Trial and error -- after a while I got more efficient making my list.

"Anyway, long story short, I found something. Not in the Southwest in December, but in West Virginia on the second of June. That's the right timing after Kagan, isn't it?"

Kate sat up straight. Logan had her full attention. "What was the unusual means? And have the local authorities concluded it was an accident?"

"Ostensibly a hunting accident. A man with a rifle was found dead in the woods with a crossbow arrow in his neck. It had sliced his carotid artery in two and he'd bled out. Nobody reported it when it happened, and they haven't found the other hunter."

Oh my God, Kate thought. *Crossbow. We may have missed something. Overlooked someone. We have someone new to look at.*

She tried to still her alarm and hide it from Logan. "Have you had a chance to look at follow-up news accounts? Did the police consider murder?"

"The sheriff is quoted as saying both hunters may have been poaching – deer are out of season. Maybe the crossbow hunter didn't know he'd hit anyone, or he did know and he panicked and ran because he knew he was already in serious trouble for poaching. I haven't seen anything to suggest the police believe it was murder.

"But here's where it gets more interesting for us. There have been some comments on social media – I know, it's a swamp, but it can be useful – along the lines of 'good riddance.' The victim was apparently an all-around horror: racist, sexist, homophobic, some people think he beat up his wife pretty regularly. And here's the kicker. He was arrested and tried last year for manslaughter after he accidentally killed another hunter in the woods, but a gun-friendly jury let him off. Very unpopular verdict – the guy's victim was gay, and the accused showed no remorse, even made some anti-gay comments along the way. Total jerk."

"Logan, that's great work, very thorough given the length of time you've had this. Do you have contact info for the sheriff?"

"Sure do." She read off the name and phone number of the sheriff in Lost River, West Virginia. "So all that fits, right? Unusual means, the right timing, a really awful person for a victim?"

"It does fit, Logan, and it also suggests someone new I need to look at. I want to call the sheriff in Lost River – I have to be tactful, tread softly, not look like I'm second-guessing him, but the more background I can get, the better off we'll be. Can you keep looking for the first trigger murder in the Southwest?"

"Sure, glad to. Hey, tell me something. This new person you have to look at. Is it someone other than Mr. Morrissey?"

"Yes … yes it is."

"Well, that's good, I guess. Now I don't feel quite so bad about upsetting you last weekend. I'll let you know right away if I find anything in the Southwest."

They ended the Zoom call and Kate sat in her living room, her emotions swirling. *Oh, dear Lord*, she thought. *Seth Toomey.* The island's most eligible bachelor. They'd never even given him a first look, to say nothing of a second. But now some pieces began to fall into place.

Seth Toomey was an accomplished crossbow hunter. He conducted a winter-long depredation hunt each year to thin the Granite Cliffs deer herd, which had no natural predators on the island. He donated all the venison to Portland homeless shelters, and he used a crossbow instead of a rifle to put island minds at ease about stray rifle shots.

Everyone thought Seth was a model citizen because of what he did. Now there was this crossbow death in West Virginia. And there was the mystery woman in February they'd connected to Russ Bannerman's death. Everyone at Jack Harlan's party had thought she was Seth's date *until Seth said she wasn't*.

And maybe that was the truth. Maybe instead she was his accomplice. Had Toomey still been at the restaurant at the time of Bannerman's death – or had he left? How did he feel about Bannerman? How did he feel about Donald Kagan?

Kate's mind was a jumble. It was conceivable that Toomey was the Strangers puppet master. It was also conceivable that he was a Charles Bronson vigilante, roaming the country dispensing his brand of justice. The focus of her case had suddenly become very blurry.

She and Sam had a lot of work to do, and little time to do it. They were more than six weeks out from June 2. If this fit their theory, and the timing held, they were due for another Granite Cliffs murder in less than two weeks.

For this evening, though, Kate needed to talk to the Lost River sheriff, Buford Blood. She steeled herself, imagining a West Virginia sheriff less than thrilled to field a phone call from a female detective in the liberal Northeast. Particularly one who, he might surmise, was second-guessing his work.

Kate was pleasantly surprised. Sheriff Blood was courtly and charming on the phone. The gravel in his voice put him in his late 50's or early 60's. "Always glad to help a fellow officer of the law. What's on your mind, Kate?"

First name basis right off the bat, Kate thought. *What a smoothie. Probably wins his elections with 80% of the female vote.*

As diplomatically as she could, Kate outlined her reciprocal killing theory, and how Blood's case might fit. Blood chuckled. "Kinda like 'Strangers on a Train,' isn't it? One of my favorites. Except real life is usually messier."

251

"Sheriff, have you definitely concluded your case was an accident?"

"You mean did we consider the possibility of murder? Yes, we did, but not for long. The obvious suspects – the family of Jerome Darlan's victim last year, and Darlan's wife, whose life he made miserable – all have pretty solid alibis. Not ironclad, but persuasive. The other thing is, everyone knows everyone else around here, and we don't have any crossbow hunters. This is a rifle and shotgun town.

"So we think it was probably another poacher, and we're chalking it up to a case of karma's a bitch who loves irony. Darlan took a life by accident and died the same way. And just between you and me, very few people around here would have cared much if we didn't look too hard anyway."

"Sheriff, thank you for your time – and candor. I appreciate it. I'll let you know if we find anything – like a confession out of the blue."

Blood laughed. "You do that. Nice talking to you, Kate. Hey, if your theory is right, who's going to play me in the movie?"

Kate walked into the squad room the next morning and said to Sam, "I bit the bullet and asked Logan Hutchinson to help us by searching the internet for trigger murders for the Strangers scenario. She hasn't found the first one yet, still looking, but she did find a death in West Virginia that might be a third trigger

252

murder. Timing is right – three weeks after the Kagan murder, on June 2.

"The bad news is this: if our theory is right, we're only about ten days out from a reciprocal killing in the Portland area or maybe Granite Cliffs again. Further bad news is, we may have overlooked someone."

"Oh shit," Chapman said. "Fill me in on that second piece of bad news."

"The death in West Virginia looked like a hunting accident – a hunter, probably poaching, was found dead in the woods with a crossbow arrow through his neck." Kate paused. "Sam, Seth Toomey out on Granite Cliffs is a crossbow hunter. He conducts a depredation hunt every winter to thin the deer herd."

"Oh shit, again," Sam said. "Seth is a private side resident of ten or fifteen years' standing. How does he feel about island politics? How did he feel about Bannerman and Kagan? Was he ever vocal in any dislike for them?"

"First thoughts that occurred to me, Sam. We have to determine that as soon as we can, as discreetly as we can. I don't want to pit neighbor against neighbor more than they already are. Right now the rumor mill has the residents believing – as we do – in our two mystery women. If they suspect the killer is in their midst, all hell's going to break loose."

Chapman's brow was furrowed; he was performing some mental gymnastics. "Wait a minute. You said the West Virginia death, what might be our third trigger murder, took place on June 2? Wasn't June 2 a Thursday?"

"Yes and yes. The victim's body – he was a really awful guy, by the way, so that fits – was discovered about Friday noon, dead 24 hours according to the coroner. Why?"

Chapman grinned. "I think Seth Toomey is home free. He couldn't have done it. Thursday is his biggest and busiest day of the week. He's on the waterfront all day – he does all the weekend seafood buying for eight or ten fine dining restaurants, including Jack Harlan's. Jack says Seth calls Thursday his 'Fiscal Friday.' He can't afford to miss Thursdays – that's half his weekly commission. Somebody would have raised hell if he'd been missing on June 2. He didn't do this."

"That's a relief," Kate said. "I was having some suspicious thoughts that maybe his relationship with mystery woman number one the night of Bannerman's murder wasn't as non-existent as Seth had said. I guess we can discard that idea too."

"Right," Chapman said. "But back to your first piece of bad news – that we might be ten days or two weeks out from another murder here. You said the crossbow death looked like a hunting accident – is that what the local police think, or are they thinking murder?"

"I talked to the sheriff last night," Kate said. "Right now he's thinking a hunting accident involving two poachers, and the crossbow guy panicked and ran. He's not hostile to our Strangers theory, but he thinks it's far-fetched, and we'd probably need some pretty compelling evidence to make him change his mind."

"So that may very well *not* be another trigger murder, and no need to sound general quarters on Granite Cliffs Island for the next two weeks."

"I suppose not," Kate said, "But it *could* be a trigger murder, despite what Sheriff Blood thinks, in which case we're sitting on a time bomb."

"What do we do in the meantime?" Sam asked. "Just wait it out?"

"Keep looking. I'll have Logan continue her search for the first trigger murder and we'll keep looking at the unsavory pasts of Messrs. Bannerman and Kagan to see if there's anything there."

"One more thing," Chapman said. "Langdon is sure to ask about Morrissey's whereabouts on June 2. We should probably verify that for our own peace of mind."

"First of all," Kate said, "I don't think we need to tell Langdon about the West Virginia death, at least for the moment. If Sheriff Blood says – for now – that it's a hunting accident, it doesn't enter into our equation.

"As for Morrissey, I believe that week was the stretch of time he was planning to be lake trout fishing. Pulaski, New York, he said. Lake Ontario. Remember ?"

"Yeah," Chapman said. "Let's check turnpike records to make sure we can put him there for certain, without having to ask him directly and embarrass all of us. That way, if this surfaces at some point, and Langdon starts tilting at windmills, we'll already have checked."

Chapter 31

Liza Darlan hadn't needed much persuading from personalguide to sign on to the idea of reciprocal murder in Portland, Maine. Once she read the email that said, "I solved the worst problem in your life, now I want you to do the same for me," she was on board. She knew at least one kindred spirit, she thought.

Liza was an angry woman. Not because Jerome Darlan was dead; her reaction to that news had been a mixture of relief and exhilaration. And not because Sheriff Blood and the police had asked cursory questions about her whereabouts and alibi for Thursday June 2. She knew the spouse automatically became a person of interest, and her presence at her sister's home in Clarksburg was unquestionable.

She was angry at her neighbors, her supposed friends and supporters, who had been virtually no help to her over the years. With Dar's death, they surfaced with faux sympathy and some veiled comments about mixed blessings and silver linings, but they had been missing in action during her years of misery. One person, years ago, had said, "You could leave him and go to the women's shelter in Morgantown. They could keep you safe until the divorce was final and then you could disappear."

But that had been no help at all. "How do I do that?" Liza had asked. "The house is all I have. He'd let

256

the fire insurance lapse and burn the house down, just for spite. And he'd come after me no matter where I went. I need a better plan than that."

But no better plan was forthcoming, and no further help ever came – until personalguide had put an arrow through Jerome Darlan's neck. For that she was – would be – eternally grateful; and if her savior wanted a favor in return, by God Eliza Darlan was happy to provide it.

She followed to the last detail the instructions he'd given her in follow-up emails. Cross from Lost River to Interstate 81 in Virginia, then north to Interstate 88 in New York State – both toll-free, no cameras – then secondary roads around Albany to avoid the New York Thruway. Route 7 to Bennington, on to a night's rest in a small family-owned motel on Vermont Route 7A. Cash only, non-chain gas stations, drive-thru meals at fast food restaurants. Sleep in, then over to Portland in an easy drive the next day.

Liza arrived in Portland at 3:30 p.m., parked in the Top of the Old Port lot, and walked to the ferry terminal. The midsummer ferry schedule was at its most frequent, and she caught the 5:00 p.m. boat to Atlantic Estates – Jack Harlan's "early seating" run.

But she was not going to the restaurant, where she would have needed a reservation, or where she might be remembered for sitting alone in the lounge. Instead, she blended in to the large crowd making its way to the beach bar, past the restaurant, near the pond that had supplied the fort with fresh water in years past.

The beach bar was not the crown jewel in Jack Harlan's fine dining empire; it was the flashy trinket. The large circular covered structure featured a grille that served hot dogs, hamburgers, grilled fish, and lobster rolls. The balance of the circle was a bar, where patrons enjoyed their drinks or danced on the beach to live music every Friday night. "The most fun you can have on this island with your clothes on," Harlan had declared. Naturally, the fun police – led by Thalia Sandberg and her allies – were determined to eradicate it.

Liza ordered a wine spritzer in a plastic cup and mixed with the crowd walking the perimeter of the fresh water pond. This was Harlan's prime venue for corporate functions and wedding receptions; a large tent sat on the far side of the pond on a broad expanse of grass next to the woods. It was an easy matter for Liza to slip into the trees as the other sightseers took in the beauty of their surroundings.

Following the path personalguide had told her would be there, Liza emerged from the woods at the Atlantic Estates gate separating the old fort from the private side of the island. There, taped to the bottom of one of the brick pedestals from which the gate hung, she found an ordinary house key.

The key was a duplicate from the set Atlantic Estates security stored with the island fire trucks in a barn near the restaurant. A key for every historic dwelling was kept there in case of fire or health emergency. It had been simple for personalguide, a member of the volunteer force, to borrow the key to Thalia Sandberg's condo for a couple of hours to make a copy and then return the original.

It was now 6:30 p.m. Thalia Sandberg was attending what personalguide called the weekly "Friday night bitch session" of her unhappy group, plotting and scheming how to rid the island of the restaurant and beach bar, how to force their fellow homeowners to conform to their standards of décor and landscaping, how to make life for others as miserable as their own lives were. Sandberg would be gone until 8:00 or 8:30 p.m., personalguide had promised.

Liza let herself in the back door of Sandberg's condo, one of eight in a restored 109-man barracks facing the parade ground. She took a quick look around and noticed the sturdy 8" x 8" timber that supported the second floor above the large expanse of the living room. She moved the dining table under the beam, climbed up, and used pliers to screw a sturdy self-tapping hook through the covering sheetrock and into the timber.

She hung a hemp rope over the hook and secured it at one end to the newel post in the railing that led up the stairs to the second floor. The other end of the rope was a hangman's noose. It hung directly in front of Sandberg's large living room window facing the parade ground.

Liza moved the dining table until its edge sat just under the noose. Now all she had to do was wait.

At 8:25 p.m. Liza heard footsteps on the front porch, a good-night call to some others walking away, and the sound of a key in the front door lock. She stood behind the front door with a policeman's sap in her hand. She had practiced on a sandbag – "sandberg," she thought with a smile – to perfect the wrist action needed to deliver a knockout blow.

Thalia Sandberg entered her living room, reaching for the light switch in the dimming summer twilight. As she did, she noticed the noose hanging in front of her living room window.

It was the last image that would ever register in her brain.

Liza Darlan stepped out from behind the door and struck Sandberg with the sap behind the right ear. Sandberg collapsed immediately, unconscious. "There is no sense debating the issues or explaining why this is deserved," personalguide had written in an email. "That's for the movies. This is real life, and it's serious business. Get it done."

Wiry but strong from more than two decades of West Virginia housework with few modern conveniences, Liza Darlan heaved Sandberg's inert form on to the dining table and looped the hangman's noose around her neck. The correct way. The efficient way. The professional hangman's way.

There is a common misconception, viewed after the fact at innumerable suicides and lynchings, that the hangman's knot is positioned at the back of the victim's head. But all this does is doom the person to an agonizing death by choking and strangling. The professional executioner places the noose's knot to the *side* of the person's head; when the condemned drops from the scaffold, the force of his or her weight causes the noose to break the neck. Death is instantaneous.

Liza Darlan moved the knot to the side, put her hands under Sandberg's arms, and lifted the woman to a standing position. *She certainly weighs enough to make this work,* Liza thought. She looped the slack in the rope over the hook several times, then kicked the dining table out from under both of them and jumped free.

Sandberg's body dropped – it didn't have to drop very far – and there was an audible crack as her neck broke. Death, and the final indignity: the bowels and bladder of the victim evacuate at that moment.

Liza wondered if personalguide had considered Sandberg worthy of this last insult. She supposed he had. He had planned everything else in painstaking detail.

Liza shoved the dining table back into place, lifted Sandberg's body so the table supported it, unlooped the extra rope from the hook, and adjusted the noose so the knot was now at the back of Sandberg's head. She kicked the dining table over again; now the hanging would look like suicide, at least until someone knowledgeable took a clear look.

Taking a strain on the other end of the rope, still tied to the railing's newel post, Liza hauled Sandberg's body into the air and secured it to hang in full view in front of the living room window. With the interior lights off, the scene would not be visible from the road that encircled the parade ground. Sandberg would hang undiscovered until the next morning, when the rising sun

261

would backlight the condo and her body through the unit's rear windows.

Liza put her latex gloves, the policeman's sap, and the duplicate key to the unit in the small backpack that had held her noose. The items would find a permanent home in a trash can somewhere on a New Hampshire roadway later that night.

Liza Darlan caught the 10:30 p.m. boat from the Atlantic Estates pier with a crowd of happy diners from the restaurant. She stood at the rail of the ferry's main deck gazing at the sky, clearly a person who wanted to be alone with her thoughts. No one approached or tried to make conversation with her. No one would remember her either.

Once in Portland, she walked past the ferry terminal, up the hill from the waterfront to the Top of the Old Port lot, and said goodbye to Portland by way of old Route 1 rather than the turnpike. She would sleep in a small New Hampshire motel that night and be home to Lost River, and a new life, by dinnertime the next evening.

Saturday morning arrived, and with it a woman named Jean Louise Ellis. She was a person given to high drama. A Southern belle on the far side of middle age, Jean Louise was prone to swooning at the slightest provocation, particularly if events struck her delicate sensibilities as unseemly. So when, on her morning constitutional around the parade ground at 8:00 a.m., she saw the body of Thalia Sandberg hanging in the front window of her historic dwelling, the result was predictable.

Jean Louise became hysterical, at full shrieking Southern belle volume. She collapsed to her knees, her face in her hands, sobbing, declaring, "I'm a good Christian woman, a gentle person, I shouldn't have to witness this, I'll never be able to unsee what I've just seen!"

A fellow early morning walker, seeking her distress, asked after her. "Jean Louise, what's the matter?" She keened some more and pointed to the window. Her acquaintance, a more grounded soul named Harmon Jones, took one look and called Jeff Fielding, the Atlantic Estates security chief, along with Tom Warren, in Harmon Jones' estimation the most level-headed man on the island.

Fielding arrived first, duplicate key to Sandberg's condo in hand. Warren arrived seconds later and shouted to Fielding, now on his way inside, "Don't touch anything around her, but see if you can find a sheet in a linen closet or something. Maybe we can hang it from the second story porch and shield this from the ghouls in the neighborhood." Warren then called Captain Dave Mackenzie of the Portland Fire Department.

"I don't think this is a rescue, Dave, it looks like transport of a deceased. But either way, she's going to the hospital. Not the ER, the morgue. I'm calling PPD next."

Kate Harwood and Sam Chapman had the weekend duty, and they hopped on the PFD rescue boat with MacKenzie and the coroner's assistant.

"What do you know about this?" Chapman asked MacKenzie.

"Warren said it's Thalia Sandberg, a hanging. Meant to be seen by the looks, hanging in the front window. Exhibitionism if it's a suicide, artistic expression if it's not."

Once at the Sandberg dwelling, MacKenzie, Harwood, and Chapman all stepped inside. All three had an immediate reaction: "Murder."

Harmon Jones, on premises because he had reported the death, asked why they thought so. "Look at her position," Chapman said. "Her head is hanging at an angle from the side. Her neck is broken. But the noose's knot is behind the head – usually the work of an amateur or a suicide without know-how. Can't break the neck with the knot behind, all you have is slow choking and strangulation. Someone either broke her neck and strung her up, or hung her twice and did it right the first time."

The EMTs were finished with the body, the coroner's assistant with his preliminary examination and photos, and Harwood and Chapman with their photos and measurements. They all headed back to the mainland with the body on the afterdeck.

"Shit's gonna hit the fan with this one, isn't it?" Chapman said to Harwood.

"Undoubtedly. First thing Langdon will want to know is where Morrissey was."

"Actually, he's fishing on Sebago Lake with a ski school buddy of his. But you're right, Kate. Three things inevitable in life, not two. Death, taxes, and Langdon wanting to know where Morrissey was."

"So Morrissey's clear," Kate said. "So are Borman and Harlan. Tom Warren told me Borman was off-island, and Harlan was at the restaurant past midnight. The coroner said Sandberg had been dead for twelve hours when she was found this morning."

"I know he's clear for the crossbow death in West Virginia, but what about Seth Toomey? Where was he?" Chapman asked.

Kate laughed. "Tom said Seth had company last night. New girl, named Karen. Tom thinks Seth really likes her. So he's clear too."

She frowned a little. "I think the timing puts us back on track with the Strangers scenario. The time intervals line up perfectly. Let's spend tomorrow, before we have to meet with Langdon, checking on the whereabouts of Sheriff Blood's possibles. I think he may be back in the game, whether he's thinking murder down there or not."

Chapter 32

Robert Langdon wanted to see Harwood and Chapman immediately when he arrived at RHD on Monday morning. He almost sneered at them. "Another Granite Cliffs murder," he said. "Looks like you two are going backward. I'm sure you've checked Morrissey's whereabouts and are going to assure me he's in the clear" – they both nodded – "so let me ask you this, Harwood. How does this fit with your crackpot Charles Bronson vigilante theory?"

Kate had been practicing looking chagrined in front of her bathroom mirror. "I'll concede the point, Captain. Doesn't fit well at all. The Montgomery murders in Chicago look more and more like a remarkably similar murder a thousand miles away – and that's all."

"We're trying a new tack, Captain," Chapman said. "Spent all day yesterday on it. In addition to searching Thalia Sandberg's history of legal filings and threatened filings for something in common with Bannerman and Kagan, we're looking at social media."

Langdon was instantly alert and interested. "Oh. That's an original thought. High time." *Even his compliments are backhanded,* Kate thought. *Jerk.*

"Sir, I know social media can be a cesspool, but it might be useful here," Kate said. "We're looking at the Facebook and Instagram accounts of Bannerman, Kagan, and Sandberg to see if anyone's been trolling them, attacking them, demeaning them, that sort of thing. Plenty of people have had some negative things to say about their shenanigans, but we're looking for connections in any really vicious stuff."

"That could be promising," Langdon said. "I understand our three victims were very high profile and controversial people out on that island. Anyone else in that category? You could be checking their social media to identify any danger signs – if they might be at risk, and from whom."

"I don't know that there are any other people who would draw the lightning quite as much as our three," Chapman said. "Possibly Judge Cooper."

Langdon flinched at the mention of the judge. *Aha,* Kate thought. *Gotcha. Judge Cooper is definitely your mole.*

Chapman continued. "Apparently the judge thinks he should be treated by his neighbors with all the deference that's his due in the courtroom. Doesn't sit too well. But I don't think he stirs passions the way the other three did. Good thought, though, Captain. We'll check the judge's social media accounts, also ask the bailiffs and courthouse staff if he's received any hate mail."

With that the two detectives were dismissed. They went back to lurking on the fringes of their victims' social media accounts, looking for venom. *What a swamp,* Kate thought. *No cop in his right mind should have social media accounts. But I'll bet Langdon loves them – great territory for him to dig up dirt to use against people.*

Early Wednesday morning Kate received another text from Logan Hutchinson. "Off to the beach in a minute. Zoom tonight? I think I might have found something. Text me with a convenient time."

At 7:30 that evening, Logan's face appeared on Harwood's monitor screen, bubbling with excitement. "You look like the cat that ate the canary," Kate said. "What did you find?"

"I think I might have found the first trigger murder," Logan said. "Amarillo, Texas, in December."

Uh-oh, Harwood thought. *Morrissey was in New Mexico in December.* "I know we opened this up to the entire country, but that's a little far afield, isn't it, Logan? What led you there?"

"I expanded – or maybe the better word is 'revised' – our search criteria a bit," Logan said. "We may have trapped ourselves by defining 'unusual means' too literally. We excluded guns because they're not at all unusual in America. But what if a gun was involved in what looked like an accident, but was a situation that could also be judged to fit our definition of 'unusual means?'

"Anyway, I found this case in Amarillo. A man named Loren Holloway was found dead at his cattle ranch on a Friday evening in December by the call girl who was going to be his plaything for the weekend. Shot in the side of the head at point-blank range, powder burns at the entrance wound, with a .38 Police Special revolver in

268

his hand. The girl's first inclination was to think suicide, even though this guy was a spoiled rich kid, super entitled, living the life of Riley, no reason to take his own life.

"The police found five live rounds of ammunition on the ground at his feet, an open box of blank cartridges, and all the cylinder chambers were empty except for one blank cartridge and the casing of one bullet. And Holloway had an opened bottle of Jack Daniels at his side.

"The cops apparently think he was waiting for his honey, drunk, bored, and decided to play Russian Roulette with a blank cartridge in one chamber. Except he was careless and didn't completely empty the gun of live ammunition, because there were only five rounds on the ground in front of him. He mistakenly left one bullet in the gun, put one blank in a chamber, spun the revolver, pulled the trigger – and lost the real game of Russian Roulette he didn't realize he was playing.

"He might have lost anyway, even with the blank cartridge. Years ago a young actor named Jon-Erik Hexum managed to kill himself playing Russian Roulette with blanks. He put the gun to his head, and when the blank fired, the air hammer from the round fractured his skull and sent bone fragments into his brain."

"Whether Russian Roulette with blanks is foolish is neither here nor there, I guess," Kate said. "Lesson number one: guns aren't toys. Have the police concluded this was an accident?"

269

Logan shook her head. "Don't know for sure. It looks like they believe it was an accident, but I didn't find anything definite or final in the news reports I saw. But here's the kicker for us: the guy, Loren Holloway, had a very sordid history. Spoiled rich guy, like I said, sitting on a ton of family oil money, playing at cattle ranching. He was rumored to have date-raped a couple of beautiful Tex-Mex girls in his early 20's, but those cases were hushed up and made to go away with family influence. Since then he's been in league with some of his buddies in Texas banks, overextending and then foreclosing on poor struggling farm families. A predator all the way around."

Just like Bannerman, Kate thought. *Hmm.* "I think I should talk to the sheriff in Amarillo," she said. "Same low-key approach as with Sheriff Blood in West Virginia. Not second-guessing, but I'd like more details and I'd sure like more information on the lives this Holloway guy screwed up. Do you have the sheriff's contact information?"

"Sure do," Logan said, as she clicked her computer's mouse. "Just emailed it to you. Sheriff Erasmus Dodd." She laughed. "Where do these sheriff types get their names, Kate?"

Kate laughed too. "Probably not an accident. I imagine it's part of the image and persona that get them elected." She paused. "Umm ... one last thing. I'm almost afraid to ask. Does the timing line up with John Morrissey's time in New Mexico? And how far is his ski resort from Amarillo?"

Logan sighed. "I knew you'd ask. His stay at Angel Fire was Sunday to Sunday. This happened on Friday afternoon of that week. In that wide open country, it's about a five or six hour drive from Angel Fire to Amarillo. Doable in one day and evening, I guess. Should we check Mr. Morrissey's rental car records to see that he either did or did not put an extra 750 mile round trip on his car?"

"Good idea, Logan. I'll get on that too. I'll let you know what I find out." She paused. Her face was sad, but she said, "Logan ... listen. You're not to feel bad about this. I'm sworn to go wherever the evidence leads me. If it looks like this is going to come together, one way or the other, could you make another trip to Portland this weekend and help me?"

"Of course, Kate. I get my lobster, and hey, maybe this is just coincidence regarding Mr. Morrissey."

"We've been over this, Logan. Detectives don't believe in coincidences. By themselves coincidences don't produce convictions, but they do seem to be piling up here. I don't have a good feeling about this. I'll call you tomorrow night after I talk to Sheriff Dodd, and we can decide about this weekend."

Kate spent the rest of Wednesday evening pondering her coincidences, particularly those involving Morrissey. Ironclad, unassailable alibis that he was elsewhere for each of the Granite Cliffs murders. That was to be expected given her Strangers scenario. But now the coincidence of Amarillo and New Mexico. And

271

he'd been fishing – apparently alone, in upstate New York – at the time of the crossbow death in West Virginia. It was a straight shot down I-81, no toll barriers, no cameras, from Lake Ontario to Lost River. He wouldn't have been gone, and probably not missed, if he'd quietly taken a day-and-a-half trip.

The one seemingly bulletproof defense Morrissey had was his hotel and skiing footprints at Sunday River the entire week of the Montgomery murders. If those records were unshakable, her Strangers theory – at least involving Morrissey – fell apart. That would be where she set Logan to work this weekend.

Sheriff Erasmus Dodd surprised Kate on Thursday morning. He was soft-spoken and articulate, a far cry from the Texas good ole boy stereotype. He also didn't blockade himself behind intermediaries; he answered his own phone.

"This is Rass Dodd," he said. "How can I help you?"

"Sheriff Dodd, my name is Detective Kate Harwood in the Portland Maine police department. I'm a homicide detective, and I'm looking for some assistance. I'd like to speak with you about your Loren Holloway case. If now isn't a good time, I can call back later when it's more convenient."

A smile came through the phone. "Now's as good a time as any, Kate. What's on your mind?"

Kate, she thought. *Another one on a first name basis right away. These Southern boys ...*

"Sheriff, I'm dealing with ..."

"Call me Rass," Dodd interrupted. "We're colleagues, Kate."

"Fine, Rass. I'm dealing with three sequential homicides here on a small resort island off the coast of Portland. Separated by 2-1/2 or 3 months each time. You'd think a serial killer or someone bent on revenge, but here's the thing – each murder was carefully staged, set up to look like an accident or suicide, but clear pretty quickly that it was in fact murder."

"Not following you, Kate. So you have an artistic or exhibitionistic serial killer, but what does that have to do with Loren Holloway in Amarillo, Texas?"

Kate explained her Strangers on a Train theory of reciprocal murders, the one in Chicago she was relatively sure of, the West Virginia death about which she was suspicious, and now this death on a lonely cattle ranch in Amarillo.

"The other thing my murders have in common," Kate said, "is that they were all people who were really loathed by many of their neighbors, and – frankly – deservedly so. From what I've read, Loren Holloway belonged to the same club.

"I'm not second-guessing you, Rass, but is there any chance Holloway could have been a murder carefully staged to look like an accident?"

There was a long pause, then Dodd said, "I admire the work you must have put in to identify all those dots and try to connect them. Really intricate puzzle, a lot of moving parts. But let me ask you something, Kate. Have

273

you ever heard of Occam's Razor? Do they teach that up there in Maine?"

Kate laughed. "Yes, Rass, they do. It says the simplest explanation is very often the right one. You hear hoofbeats in Texas, you think horses, not zebras. Believe me, that's where we started out. It was only when we'd essentially cleared everyone on the island that we started looking at alternative scenarios. As convoluted as this theory might seem, it's the one that's hanging together the best. I know Amarillo is a long way from Maine, but the timing last December is right, and I can put one of our Maine persons of interests within a few hours drive of Amarillo that day. That's why I'm asking."

Dodd breathed a long sigh. "I wish I could help you, Kate, but this one strikes us as a classic case of 'you can't fix stupid.' Loren Holloway was a complete wastrel who wriggled out of trouble with his family's money and influence and dabbled in cattle ranching for something to do. Hurt a lot of people with some banking buddies of his, too – feeding on mortgages in distress and foreclosures. Nobody's really sorry he's gone. He's the type of guy who perpetuates a bad Texas stereotype. Anyway – drunk, bored, and horny is a dangerous combination, and it killed him."

"Rass, can you bear with me for just a couple more minutes – you said he hurt a lot of people financially, and my researcher said the material she read indicated there might have been a couple of rapes that were hushed up. Did you look at any of those people, or determine their whereabouts at the time Holloway died?"

"Yes, we did. Given the scene, we didn't have much reason to suspect murder, but we checked anyway. The two rapes almost certainly happened, and some of the families who were thrown off their land and impoverished – well, I suspect there were some very bitter people in both groups. So we did try to check, particularly the two alleged rapes and the women in the families who were dispossessed.

"But no one was seen at Holloway's ranch – all his workers were gone once the cattle were sold. And besides, even if someone had been seen – well, this is going to sound awful, but all the women in those families look like sisters. They all work in the hospitality industry – restaurants, bars and lounges, clubs. Very attractive, now in their mid-thirties, I think. God help me, Kate, I'm not racist, but they do all look very similar. No one could pick any of them out of a lineup here with any certainty, and I'm sure they couldn't up there in Maine either – even if your theory proved to be right."

Bingo, Kate thought. *Attractive Latina woman, mid-thirties, at ease in a bar and lounge setting. Mystery woman number one, for Russ Bannerman.* But Sheriff Dodd was comfortable with closing the file on Loren Holloway as a careless fool who ended up dead, and from what he said, a positive identification of her mystery woman wouldn't come out of Dodd's pool of lookalikes.

There was no point in continuing the conversation. She wasn't going to change Dodd's mind in one phone call. But he wasn't the one who needed to be convinced; she was. And now she was sure this piece fit the puzzle.

275

"Rass, thank you so much for your time. You've filled in a lot of blanks for me, and I can rest easier. Please stop by and see us at PPD if you ever get hungry for lobster."

"I'll do that. I'm sure it's better than crawfish, Texas pride be damned. So long, Kate. Good talking to you."

Kate hung up the phone and considered her situation. Neither Sheriff Blood nor Sheriff Dodd were inclined to think their local deaths were homicides, but they didn't determine the actual facts, only the official versions of them. She needed Logan Hutchinson to help her find the truth. She texted the girl and said, "I need you here this weekend. Can you come?"

Chapter 33

Logan arrived on Friday afternoon on the same 4:50 flight she had taken three weeks before. This time Kate Harwood was waiting for her. "What, no handsome hunky guy to pick me up?" Logan asked. "Good thing you're going to feed me lobster, Kate!"

Harwood laughed. "No handsome chauffeur this time, Logan. But we're going to have a home-cooked meal – your lobster – at Dave's condo. He's a Maine boy through and through, and really knows how to prepare it." She looked at Logan. "Strictly social this evening. No business. But I'll tell you this now so you can be thinking about it for tomorrow.

"I checked rental car records – credit cards and cash transactions – for last December for John Morrissey. There aren't any, not in New Mexico or in Texas or Colorado either. He didn't rent a car. What does that tell you?"

"That he drove all the way from Maine to New Mexico in his own car. Long drive, but he had the time. You could say he did it to see the country – or you could think he might have been trying to avoid any discovery of his trip." She paused and thought a minute. "But that doesn't make any sense, Kate. The record of his vacation exchange was right there in plain sight – didn't take much to find it. I don't get it, except it might be a pretty good argument that his ski trip was completely innocent."

Kate nodded. "We're on the same page, Logan. First you think – whoa, no rental car? No way of telling if he made a long side trip? That's suspicious. But maybe not – maybe just a man taking his time to see the country in his own car."

She looked at Logan. "All of which means looking at the record of his presence at Sunday River the week of the Montgomery murders becomes even more important."

Kate waited for Logan as the girl checked into her Portland Regency suite. Then they drove over to Dave MacKenzie's condo and Kate parked in the building's garage. The elevator lifted them to the 17th floor of the high rise overlooking Casco Bay. "Wow!" Logan said. "What a view! Big Sur in California is spectacular, but these islands … really beautiful."

"The ocean floor is beautiful too, in its own way," Dave said. "The bottom of Casco Bay is crawling with lobsters. When you order lobster in a good restaurant, and they say it's Maine lobster … if they're telling the truth, chances are it came from right out there. Not as fresh out of the water as the one you're going to have, though."

"Prepare to be educated, Logan," Kate said. "There's more to eating a lobster than the claws and the tail. You'll be able to go back home and amaze your friends."

278

"I'm for that," Logan laughed. "Amazing your friends is half the fun in life."

Logan already had her computer running when Kate arrived at her suite at 8:00 a.m. Saturday. "Please don't take this the wrong way," Logan said, "but I've been thinking about how to test Mr. Morrissey's presence at Sunday River that week we're looking at. I'm trying to think of a way you could create a false trail or footprint in the system so it would record your presence when you weren't really there. If it looks like it can't be done, end of story. Mr. Morrissey can't be a suspect.

"But it there's a way to pull it off, we have to keep checking to see if he actually did it that way, and created the time for himself to go to Chicago."

Logan had a doubtful, apprehensive look on her face Kate had never seen before. "Kate, I know it looks like I'm assuming he's guilty, and trying to prove it, but it's the best way I can think of to unravel the puzzle. Are you okay with this?"

Kate reached over and touched the girl's arm. "Yes. Yes, I'm okay with it, Logan. This is what we do. No one else is as talented as you at this, so I'm comfortable you'll come up with the right answer, whatever the answer is. Keep going."

An hour later, Logan reacted to something on her computer screen. "Huh. This doesn't prove or disprove anything, Kate, but the ski area has a real estate website, and the condo hotel material on it mentions a mid-week clean for quarter-share owners in residence for their

279

week. Hotel guests get daily maid service, but quarter-share owners only get a linen change and cleaning on Wednesdays of their week. It's apparently an attempt to hold down their quarterly assessments."

"So," Kate said, "that means that John could have left on Wednesday morning after being in the unit through Tuesday night, and not have been missed the next couple of days. If he returned by Friday night, his bed would have been slept in on Saturday morning when the housekeeping crew showed up again."

"Right," Logan said. "Doesn't mean he went anywhere, he could have been there all along, just allows for the possibility he wasn't and nobody knew it."

"Keep looking," Kate said. "We know he worked in ski school that week. If he worked every day, he's in the clear for the Montgomerys."

Later Saturday afternoon Logan said, "Ahh. Finally."

"What's up?" Kate asked.

"I'm looking at the records for ski school days worked, and comparing them with the computer records for the ski lift turnstiles that scan tickets and record days skied. The lift scanners check off days skied for a weekend ticket or a five-day ticket, that sort of thing. But a season pass registers too. I've just been able to set up a comparison of the two data bases side by side for ski school personnel."

"What did you find?"

"There were four teaching ski pros who recorded multiple days worked that week but didn't pass through a lift turnstile on at least one of those days. They weren't on the hill even though they were working. I suppose that's possible – they could have been a greeter in the learn to ski center, helping people get ready for their first time, or they could have spent the whole day on the bunny hill, which has a magic carpet – glorified conveyor belt – instead of a lift. No lift turnstile there to make a record."

"Okay," Kate said. "If John recorded days worked but wasn't on the hill, that still proves he was there, right?"

"That's true," Logan said, "except he's in the opposite category: he worked the weekend and Monday and Tuesday, but didn't work Wednesday through Friday. The lift records show him on the hill all week, though. That's not suspicious itself – he could have taken some time off from ski school just to ski on his own the last part of the week."

"So – those critical days, Wednesday through Friday, not working but showing up skiing on the hill," Kate said.

"Exactly."

"You're a skier," Kate said. "Would there be any way to arrange that – to be recorded skiing – and not be there?"

"The lift turnstiles electronically scan your pass," Logan said. "You no longer have to clip your ticket to the outside of your jacket. You can put it in your pocket and be sure of not losing it. I'm sure the ski pros put the pass in their jackets and never take it out all season."

"So if someone wore your jacket out there, you'd be recorded as skiing," Kate said. "Right?" Logan nodded. "But I've been skiing up there too," Kate continued. "Doesn't the photo on the pass show on the computer monitor at the turnstile? The lift attendant can compare face and photo to see if someone is cheating."

"Sure," Logan said, "but do you think the lifties would check season pass photos for ski pros? I don't. They all know each other."

"So Morrissey would have to get another pro to carry his pass those days. Which brings in, not necessarily an accomplice, but someone who would remember Morrissey asking this odd favor. Almost as risky as having an accomplice."

"Right," Logan said. "But what if Morrissey switched passes with the pro, *and the guy didn't know it?* He carries Morrissey's pass, Morrissey gets recorded skiing, then when Morrissey returns on Friday afternoon or Friday night, he switches the passes back.

"I know that sounds a little far-fetched, Kate, and maybe that's a good thing, because it's the only way I can see to pull this off."

"We're back to all theory, no proof," Kate said. "Is there any way to tell if that might have happened?"

Logan thought a moment. "We can narrow it down. I'm going to look at the four pros who show up as working but not on the hill. If any one of them is in 'working not skiing' status for all three days, he's a candidate for a switched pass. Doesn't mean it happened, I don't know how Mr. Morrissey would do it, but it would put us in the realm of the possible."

"Take a look," Kate said. "Let's get to the bottom of this."

Ten minutes later, Logan said, "One guy worked all three days and didn't register on the hill. A young ski pro named Will Corrigan. Looks like he teaches young kids most days, gets in a lot of hours. That could put him on the bunny slope, not going through a lift turnstile. I'm going to look at his HR record to get his summer contact information." She gave Kate an evil smile. "Don't ask how I'm going to do it, Kate. Exigencies of the situation and all that!"

Kate heard Logan's voice pitched low in a confidential tone a few minutes later. Her voice rose as she ended the phone call with, "Thanks so much for your time, Mr. Corrigan. I appreciate it."

She turned to Kate looking discouraged. "Nothing completely solid, but awfully suspicious. He says he generally works with young kids on the bunny slope, but on those days he still tries to get some runs in before and after class, or one or two runs during the lunch hour. If he has an all-day class he has lunch with the kids, so he says it's possible he doesn't get on the hill on days like that. He doesn't remember that week specifically, but he doubts he was off the hill for three days running – says he'd remember being very frustrated not being able to get some of his own skiing in. But he can't be sure."

"So nothing definite there, but still not good. Here's some even worse news, Kate. I told him I was doing a computer audit of hours clocked and hours paid – he said he already would have screamed if his didn't check out! – and I said I had another pro with a similar discrepancy. John Morrissey, did he know John? 'Oh yeah, John's a great guy! He works adults but we're good friends. His locker is right next to mine!'"

"Makes it pretty easy to switch passes, Kate. That doesn't look good, does it? It's not definite proof, but it's another thing in a long line of 'it could have happened that way.'"

In her mind, Kate could hear the sound of the last few pieces of a puzzle being arranged, ready to fall into place. "I agree. This looks bad. The last bit of protection John has is our difficulty in getting him to Chicago and back in the time allowed – Wednesday morning till Friday night. He didn't fly, he didn't take the train, he didn't rent a car. If he made it out there and back, how did he do it?"

"He wouldn't have driven his own car, as we think he did to New Mexico," Logan said. "With that trip, if he had a breakdown or accident that created a record of his presence, he had a plausible reason for being where he was – going on a ski trip. He couldn't risk taking his own car to Chicago, even on secondary roads with no photos – if anything happened to make a record of that trip, he'd have no good reason to be where he was. From our standpoint, that record would put him on the way to, or back from, killing the Montgomerys."

"So what would he do?" Kate said. "He can't steal a car, the theft might be reported immediately and the police would be on the lookout. Not worth the risk."

"Maybe borrow a car," Logan said. "Maybe borrow a neighbor's car if the neighbor is spending the winter in Florida or something."

"He lives on an island now," Kate said. "All his neighbor's cars are on the mainland."

Logan's eyes took on the thousand-yard stare her father had mentioned. She thought a moment and said, "He could have borrowed – temporarily stolen – a car from the long-term parking lot of an airport or train station. Wait in the lot till he saw someone pull in with a week's worth of vacation luggage. Like a ski trip. He hot-wires and moves that car, pulls his car into that car's space, then puts the borrowed car back in its original space when he returns. Doesn't need the other guy's parking ticket – he can use his own tickets on both trips into and out of the lot. And he can make good time on superhighways in the borrowed car – doesn't have to worry about photos at toll barriers."

Kate felt her legs start to give way and grabbed the desk to steady herself. All the pieces were in place. John Morrissey was guilty. She knew it. He was the puppet master. He'd committed all the away murders, and he'd orchestrated the ones on Granite Cliffs. Yes, a person could conceive of explanations for each step in the sequence, but those would be too convenient to be credible. There were too many red flags. To have all the

285

coincidences be innocent would be like flipping twenty 'heads' in a row.

She started to cry, no sounds, no sobs, only tears running down her face.

Logan saw her dismay, and was close to tears herself. "Kate, I'm so sorry. I got so wrapped up in solving the puzzle I didn't think of what the solution would do to you. I'm just now realizing what he means to you.

"I've probably lost you as a friend. You won't want to have anything to do with me."

The tough cop inside Kate made her presence known. She put her hands on Logan's shoulders, looked her in the eye. "You listen to me. You're one of the most special people on the planet. I'm lucky even to know you, let alone be your friend and have a chance to work with you. Don't ever doubt my friendship."

Kate looked away for a moment, then turned back to the girl. "The toughest times let you know who your real friends are. What will get me through this is my confidence in you – that I know you're right."

Her eyes searched Logan's. "So – we okay?"

Logan nodded, looked at her watch. "I should get ready to go. I'll pack and grab a taxi to the airport."

"Okay. I have things to do. Lot of thinking ahead of me today. Thanks for everything, Logan. You're amazing, I'll be in touch."

Chapter 34

Kate didn't stay as rock-solid as she'd been in saying goodbye to Logan. She was unsteady as she walked the three blocks from the spot where she parked her car to Dave MacKenzie's condo. She felt like she'd been kicked in the stomach. The man she idolized was a murderer.

Inside the condo, she collapsed into an easy chair by the picture window. The idea of making herself at home, thinking of the place as her own, was still new. She and Dave had started living together only last month, at Dave's because it was larger and had by far the better location. Dave was renting with an option to buy – his pay as a fire captain was far north of Kate's as a detective – but with both salaries, they'd started talking about exercising the purchase option.

The move wasn't without complications, because she and Dave wanted to stay a secret to the police and fire departments. Kate maintained her old apartment's street address for department records, but changed her mailing address to a post office box in the downtown station. "Don't want the bad guys looking up where I live," she'd explained to Sally Rinaldo. She'd also dropped her telephone landline at the apartment and continued parking her car on the street, just as she always had.

Their deceit was ironic, she thought, since she'd just uncovered so much of it on Granite Cliffs Island. *How had Morrissey done it? How had he found his recruits? Oh, of course. The same way she and Logan had.* Logan had said it. "You can research anything on the internet."

Morrissey was a brilliant, focused, persistent detective. He could uncover anything if he set his mind to it. He'd simply modernized his methods this time.

Dave knew something was seriously awry as soon as he walked in the door. "Hi honey" wasn't even out of his mouth before it was followed by, "What's wrong?"

Kate cast her eyes down, waved her hand, then looked out the picture window to sea. "Kate," Dave said. "Really, what's wrong? You look like you've lost your best friend."

She turned to him, fighting tears. "It's worse than that. I've lost a hero."

MacKenzie walked over to her chair, lowered himself to one knee in front of her, took her hands, searched her face. "What do you mean? You look shattered, honey. What could be so wrong?"

"I've figured out – well, not just me, Logan Hutchinson and I – have figured out the Granite Cliffs murders."

He gave her a huge smile. "Then that's cause for celebration. That's terrific, Kate. I know you can't talk about the details of an active investigation, but … when are you going to make an arrest?"

"I'm not. I don't have enough proof – any proof, really. Only a lot of pieces of a puzzle that fit together really well."

"Then gather more evidence, Kate. Come on, you're the most dogged, persistent investigator I've ever seen or heard of – except maybe for your pal John Morrissey."

She lost the battle with the tears. "That's just it. It's John Morrissey. He's not the actual killer in all of these murders, but he's the mastermind behind them. I'm convinced of it."

MacKenzie dropped her hands and cradled her face. He lowered his voice to what he hoped was a soothing murmur. "Kate. Listen to yourself. That can't be true. John Morrissey is the straightest shooter and the most honest guy in the history of the Portland Police Department. He couldn't be behind this."

She sighed. "I don't want it to be true, Dave, God knows I don't want it to be true. But it is."

"I know you can't talk about an open case, but …"

"Yes, I can, Dave. I need to. I can't talk to Sam Chapman about it, it would destroy him. I certainly can't talk to Robert Langdon. So it has to be you. I'm breaking the rules – I've been breaking them all along involving Logan in this – but this is even more serious." She took a deep breath. "I have to trust someone, and you're it."

There was desperation in her look. "You have to promise you'll never breathe a word of this, Dave."

MacKenzie took her hands again, pulled her to her feet, and hugged her for a long moment. "I promise. And

… if you say it's John Morrissey – I'm stunned, but I believe you. Hard to believe you, but I do. I know you have your reasons. Come over here and tell me."

He led her to the couch along the living room wall, sat beside her, put his arm around her shoulder and pulled her close. "Talk," he said.

She told him the Strangers on a Train scenario, how she and Logan figured Morrissey had set the dominos in motion, how he'd likely used the internet and social media to choose his 'away' victims, how he'd probably led his 'recruits' through their killings. "It all fits," she said. "Logan gamed out a bunch of other scenarios – like maybe the 'away' murders are totally unconnected and the Granite Cliffs murders were paid hits funded by islanders who hated those horrible people. But that doesn't work – none of those alternatives works."

"Why not? Lots of times the simplest answer is the right one. In this case, you want something done, you hire someone skilled to do it."

Kate shook her head. "Occam's Razor. I had a lesson in that from the sheriff in Amarillo, Texas. He was so pleased with himself that he brought up that idea to a northeast liberal college girl."

She continued. "I'm sure you could easily find some unsavory people on the Portland waterfront who'd hit someone for a few thousand dollars. But you'd be betting your liberty and everything you had that they'd keep their mouths shut and not flip on you the first time they got in serious trouble for something else. Anyone out on the island serious enough to consider hiring out the killing of those people would also be smart enough to know that. Didn't happen that way."

"Okay, Kate, I guess I can accept that. But if your theory is right, there has to be some evidence somewhere. If Morrissey committed the away murders, or at least the first one of them, he had to leave some tracks. And his recruits, coming here to commit the Granite Cliffs murders, surely had to leave some trace of where they'd come from, how they'd got here – "

Kate interrupted him. "Look, we've focused on the away murders because they're so similar to those on Granite Cliffs – some really awful people, lots of enemies and people who hated them, killed in unusual and theatrical ways. But that doesn't prove that they're the connection, or that any connection exists at all. We just think they fit the puzzle – and we have no solid proof that John was present at them. It's only circumstantial."

Kate looked at MacKenzie and, for the first time in their conversation, smiled. "Which is not at all surprising. John Morrissey uncovered peoples' tracks for thirty-five years, no matter how good people thought they were at hiding them. You think he doesn't know how to leave no tracks at all? You think he doesn't know how to manufacture an ironclad alibi – for himself and for others?"

MacKenzie was backpedaling. "Okay, maybe for himself. But his recruits weren't that good. They'd leave tracks."

"Not if he coached them through the whole process, step by step. Which we're sure he did."

"How? He couldn't risk being seen with them, even on their home turf, certainly not on Granite Cliffs. And he probably wouldn't want any of them to see him in person anyway."

Kate smiled again. "Very good, Dave. You're thinking like a detective. You're asking how? The internet. Encrypted emails. Self-destructing evidence. Guides on how to travel, avoid any record or detection, establish alibis, become invisible even in the daytime. What little eyewitness information we have from the island suggests a mystery woman no one ever saw before for the Bannerman murder, and maybe a midday jogger – also who no one knew – for the Kagan killing. And no one saw or remembers anything or anyone in connection with the Sandberg murder. They're all gone, totally in the wind."

"Does Morrissey know that much about the dark side of the internet? That's a young person's game, isn't it?"

"Do you think John Morrissey is smart?" Kate asked. "I sure as hell do. All alone out there in that great big guardhouse, nobody to interrupt him – you think he couldn't become an internet master inside of a few months? He could learn how sophisticated users cover their tracks about where they've been, what they've looked at, even the people they've exchanged emails with. It's way more than deleting emails and saying 'No' to cookies, Dave."

"Okay," Dave said, "he could probably learn enough about navigating the internet – find any information he wanted, do it undetected, without leaving tracks. But what could make him abandon his whole life's commitment to the law and embrace murder as a solution to problems?"

"Think about him out there," Kate said. "Alone with his thoughts, heartbroken at what he sees on that island he and Dottie dreamed about. Maybe it's my detective's cynical view of the world, but I think anyone can become capable of murder if they're pushed hard enough, given the right reason.

"He's a brilliant detective, Dave, but he isn't that complicated a guy. He sees things as right and wrong – maybe he just wanted to put things right, as he sees the right."

MacKenzie was subdued. No wonder Kate was upset. She certainly hadn't talked herself into believing Morrissey was the mastermind because she wanted him to be. The opposite was true. And he was sure that she and Logan had looked at even more alternative scenarios, trying to will them to be more credible. All to no avail. Kate was where she was in her thinking, and she was devastated.

He pulled her close again, then said softly, "What are you going to do, Kate?"

"I can't bring him in as a suspect with the evidence I have. That would be a catastrophe – an accusation or questioning without concrete support would destroy his reputation along with the department's. Sam Chapman would be so torn up he'd probably eat his gun.

"The worst part of it is Langdon has been pushing the idea of John as a suspect, not because of any evidence, only because he hates John and wants to destroy him. Even questioning John informally would give Langdon credibility – in the long run, one of the worst things that could happen to PPD.

"And I certainly can't arrest him. If I did, John would retain Dan Hilliard, and Hilliard would have a field day. All we have is weak circumstantial evidence – 'It could have happened that way.' Hilliard would rip Langdon and the whole department to shreds. He's almost itching to do that anyway. The public would lose all confidence in us, my credibility would be zero – I'd have no career path anywhere. All for the sake of three slimeballs here, and some others elsewhere. The trouble is, even slimeballs count."

She sighed. "I have to go out there, alone – without Sam – and confront him, Dave. If I can't do anything else, I at least have to get him to stop – persuade him that I know enough that we'll be able to nail him if he keeps going."

Her brittle defenses broke again. She leaned forward, cradled her face in her hands, and sobbed. "I shouldn't cry. I'm a homicide detective, for Chrissake. I have to keep it together. Somebody has to make sure there's justice for the dead."

"Kate, the victims on Granite Cliffs were cruel, vicious people. Maybe they've already had their justice delivered to them, courtesy of John Morrissey."

She shook her head. "Sorry, Dave, that won't wash. Logan told me a while ago about a fictional detective who thought of himself as 'God's surrogate on earth.' No such thing. Above my pay grade. Above John Morrissey's too."

She straightened up, squared her shoulders. The tears were gone. "I have to call John tomorrow and go talk to him."

Chapter 35

Kate walked into RHD at 7:30 a.m. on Monday and went straight to Chapman. "Sam, Langdon is still worked up about Morrissey for the Sandberg murder, wants to know if he could have sneaked away from Sebago Lake to do it. Of course not, he was with his friend Rollie all week, but I have to go through the motions of treating John as a person of interest to keep Langdon happy.

"I think it might be uncomfortable for all of us if you were there, as his former partner and all. Do you have a problem if I go talk to him alone?"

"Hell no," Chapman said. "Langdon really makes this job distasteful sometimes. I owe you for taking one for the team."

She called Morrissey and asked if she could talk to him about the Sandberg murder. "I'm getting some pressure from Langdon, John, and I have to put it to bed. Do you mind?"

"Nah, come on out on the noon boat," Morrissey said. "I'll meet you at the pier."

They settled again at the table on Morrissey's back deck overlooking the ocean. "This is a hard conversation to have," Kate said. "Captain Langdon has ordered me to consider you as a person of interest in the Sandberg murder as well as the first two. Really shabby motivation on his part."

Morrissey laughed. "Once a fool, always a fool."

Kate swallowed hard, willed her hands to be steady. "The awful thing is, John, I have the terrible feeling that Langdon might be on to something, for all the wrong reasons. He's driven by his animosity for you, but I've actually wondered if it's possible that you could be playing a role in all this."

She explained the Strangers and reciprocal killing scenarios that she had developed. Morrissey's ironclad alibis for all three Granite Cliffs murders, to be expected. The key proximity in time and space of his New Mexico vacation exchange and the Amarillo Russian Roulette scene. His convenient off-island status at the time of the Chicago and Lost River murders.

"You could – I emphasize *could* – have done this, John. It's logistically possible. And you certainly have the expertise to stage a murder and coach someone through a similar exercise.

"I'm like any homicide detective. I don't believe in coincidences. I have a pretty strong suspicion; it's more than a hunch. I can't prove it, but I had to come out here and talk to you.

"If you're behind this, John, it has to stop. I can't fathom why you'd be doing it, but it has to stop."

He looked at her for a long moment. "Wow. That's a lot to take in on a beautiful summer afternoon, Kate. But … I'm not offended. I'm not angry. You're just doing your job, and you have to consider all the possibilities, even if they might seem far-fetched."

"Thank you for understanding. I want to be wrong, but I have to cover all the bases."

"Yeah. As I said, I'm not offended, but I am disappointed." He looked away, then back at Harwood. "Let me tell you a story about a guy named Richard Feynman. Ever heard of him?" Harwood shook her head.

"No? Well, Feynman was a Nobel laureate, and probably the greatest teacher of physics the world has ever known. He said this about theories – word for word, I've always remembered it. 'First, you guess. I'm serious, you guess. Then you see if your observations conform to your guess – your theory. Then you conduct experiments to create more observations, and see if they conform. Then you try to use your theory to make predictions, and see if your predictions are borne out.

'If at any point your observations diverge from your theory, or your predictions don't come true, your theory is no good. It doesn't matter how beautiful it is, it doesn't matter how much you love it. It's flawed, and you have to discard it.'

"You take my point, Kate? Seems to me you're trying to find some facts to fit your theory instead of using independent observations to confirm it. I have alibis for all the Granite Cliffs murders – I was away for each one, in fact I was probably the last to learn about each one when I returned. As for the other murders farther afield, you seem focused on my ski trip to New Mexico in December and some murder in Texas.

298

"But I've had vacation exchanges for December ski trips to Steamboat and Breckenridge and Aspen too. I'm sure there were other murders in the Rockies at the same time, but that doesn't mean I committed them. And there are so many murders in this country that it would be easy to find a lot of similar homicides where the timing *wouldn't* correspond – they happened while I was here.

"You're trying to cherry-pick facts to fit your theory instead of seeing if all the facts conform to it. You're sliding into confirmation bias, Kate. You know what that is, right?"

Kate nodded. "Langdon has a bad case of it with respect to you. Seems to want to know your movements 24/7."

"Well, look at your supposed trigger for the Sandberg murder. It conveniently came up on your radar screen after the fact. You were looking for murders at the time I was away fishing in New York. That's confirmation bias looking for a place to land, Kate. And you haven't even started to use your theory to make predictions you can check against it."

Kate protested. "My bias – certainly my emotions – are the other way, John. I don't want it to be true."

"Not quite, Kate. You want me not to be guilty, but a part of you wants that bright shining theory of yours to be right. You're back to classic Feynman. You think your theory is beautiful, and you love it.

"I think you've got a good start in spite of yourself. The Strangers on a Train thing is a theory. But those murders on Granite Cliffs actually happened. See if you can check whereabouts of more Granite Cliffs or other Portland people at the time of these murders. That's an awful lot of leads to run down, but something may fall out. And whether it does or not, here's my own prediction: the word will get out that you're checking whereabouts, and the murders will stop."

Kate was not intimidated. She realized she was engaged in a battle of wits with a master interviewer and interrogator. She was verbally jousting with one of the most incisive detective minds in the world. It required all her concentration to keep up with him, but she was determined to do it. Not least because she knew she was right.

She had anticipated Morrissey's argument, and was concerned only with tying his presence to one murder – in Amarillo, the previous December. Then the other pieces of her theory – provable or not – would fall into place.

"John, saying the murders will stop is an easy prediction to make if you've been the one orchestrating them. You simply don't orchestrate any more. Look, if you're doing this, you've been very good at it, and no one will ever be able to prove it. But I'll say it again, John: if you are behind this, it has to stop."

Morrissey looked at her with the saddest eyes she'd ever seen. "I'm sorry you feel that way. It bothers me that you might believe that of me."

"John, I understand these were horrible people. If you've had nothing to do with this, a little tarnish on my hero worship would be a small price to pay knowing that they're removed from the earth. But if there's some 'God's surrogate on Earth' stuff going on with you here, it can't go on."

She reached over and squeezed his arm. "I've said my piece. Take care of yourself. You look even skinnier than the last time I saw you."

He watched her trudge down the long set of stone steps from his guardhouse to the pier, where one of the city fireboats awaited her. He thought about Kate's critical connection, New Mexico and Texas. Goddamn it. Before putting this in motion in December, he'd spent several months the previous summer and fall, mentally choreographing the whole sequence of events – his "objects of justice" both home and away, and the plans for instructions to his recruits. He'd thought he'd been perfect.

He'd been so careful, thought he'd met every contingency. Even getting tetrodotoxin hadn't been a problem – in Boston, from a Japanese restaurant owner with connections to a seedy pawnshop owner, where he'd bought the crossbow and arrows as well.

He was annoyed at his one tiny flaw. He hadn't been as careful as he could have been. Yes, he'd used the 12-day period in December when he'd supposedly been at Sunday River to drive to New Mexico and avoid creating any records of air or railroad transportation. He'd instructed his recruits to do the same, using secondary roads or toll-free highways, staying at cash-only motels, keeping away from security cameras, buying meals at fast food drive-thru's.

But he'd been lazy about New Mexico. He'd used his vacation exchange because it was already there. He could have paid for his lodging as a walk-in early in the ski season, no record of a reservation, cash transaction, illegible name scrawled on the motel register. And he'd have a lodging receipt and a lift ticket in his pocket if he ever needed to prove he was in New Mexico rather than Texas. Not that anyone would ever have traced him there.

But he'd left a trail of his vacation exchange, open to research and to dogged police procedure. Damn it. Thank God he'd been able to undermine her argument about an early season ski trip with his December ski weeks in previous years. But still, not good for him. Not good enough for her to arrest, much less for anyone to indict and convict. Nonetheless, not good.

Still, he smiled as he recalled his own delivery of justice. Maybe the Russian Roulette scene he'd set up for Loren Holloway had been over the top – a little too dramatic when you considered it after the fact – but he liked the memory of the sniveling coward weeping and pleading. He'd deserved his fate. And after all, he'd given the guy some hope, misplaced as it was. "I'm only going to make you pull the trigger once," he'd said. "Let God decide." That was just before he put the gun to the right side of Holloway's head and pulled the trigger himself.

It had been an easy matter to remove the spent bullet's cartridge, place another bullet in the same chamber, put the gun in Holloway's dead hand, Holloway's finger on the trigger, and fire a second round into the sand. Recover that bullet, leave the empty cartridge in the gun, one chamber off dead center, and place a blank cartridge in an empty chamber. Five live rounds on the ground by the body, an open box of blank cartridges, and a half empty bottle of Jack Daniels.

The Amarillo police had concluded what he'd thought they'd conclude. A bored Texas good ole boy, drunk on Mr. Jack, playing Russian Roulette with a blank round. Except he'd been careless and missed a round when he unloaded the gun, and it had killed him.

But Kate – or someone – had the imagination to conceive of what had actually happened. They couldn't prove it, and the Amarillo police apparently didn't buy it, but it had started Kate down the right path. Now she had him under close scrutiny, so the killings would stop. Had to stop. And of course her scrutiny wasn't the only reason.

Chapter 36

Kate spent the evening following her conversation with Morrissey considering her next steps. Despite his facile arguments and gentle support of Kate's efforts, she knew he was guilty. But her decision about what action to take could wait temporarily. Her immediate issue was Robert Langdon.

He'd want to see her first thing in the morning for a report on her session with Morrissey. It would be easy enough to clear John for the Sandberg murder. He had been with his friend Rollie Merron at Rollie's shoreside restaurant on Sebago Lake. Even Langdon wouldn't be able to embrace the notion of a dining room full of people conspiring to provide Morrissey with an alibi.

Kate was sure Langdon would make some snide remark about how fruitless her Charles Bronson vigilante scenario was turning out. That was okay; she and everyone else in RHD were used to Langdon's condescension. But he wasn't as smart as he thought he was, and he was easily placated.

She would swallow her pride and take her lumps, she decided, even though she'd been right with the Strangers idea. She would emphasize to Langdon their continuing efforts in mining social media and researching old legal cases, and tell him they were listening to their informants for any rumblings about anyone boasting about the killings. Once Langdon was persuaded that she and Sam were doing something new – plumbing informants – he'd leave them alone so she could think about what to do about Morrissey.

Her meeting with Langdon went as she'd planned. Langdon had to accept Morrissey's innocence in the Sandberg murder; he sneered at her about the roaming vigilante scenario; and he approved of her ideas for followup work, particularly with informants.

"Captain, if this doesn't involve a revenge motive, and God knows we've looked for that, we think we're dealing with a person who gets his jollies killing well-known local people with bad reputations. Not a vigilante bent on revenge, not a paid assassin, just an exhibitionist. A man – or a woman, if the mystery woman angle is right – who wants his or her art work to be noticed. I ran this past a friend who's an FBI profiler …" – she noticed Langdon start to get steamed, and quickly added – "… not asking the FBI to come in here like a bull in a china shop and upset our case, just a favor from a fellow criminal justice major in college. He says the staging – the meticulous nature of these murders – indicates a highly organized mind. Hallmark of a serial killer.

"But people with highly organized minds tend to be impressed with themselves. We're betting this person, unless he or she is a complete loner, won't be able to keep his mouth shut around his friends or acquaintances or even lovers. We think that will eventually filter through our street contacts."

Langdon nodded. "Well, I'm glad you're off that cockamamie Charles Bronson idea. Cost the department your air fare to Chicago, but I suppose every cloud has a silver lining. If some smartass reporter asks if we've ever considered that, we can truthfully say 'yes.'"

"Yes sir. I should get back to contacting our informants with Chapman."

"Do so. Dismissed."

Nice to know my idea was acceptable to you because it covers your ass, Harwood thought. *What a surprise.*

Kate returned to her desk to consider her options regarding Morrissey. She realized that, in terms of immediate action, she didn't have any.

She couldn't arrest Morrissey for any of the Granite Cliffs murders. He had unshakable alibis that he was elsewhere for each one. Besides, there was the inconvenient fact that he hadn't committed them.

She couldn't arrest Morrissey for any of the 'away' murders either, because she didn't have jurisdiction in those states. And the sheriffs in two of those jurisdictions believed their deaths were accidents, not murders. Even in the Chicago case, all she had to put Morrissey in place was a tenuous 'it could have happened this way' scenario. She was persuaded, but she doubted a Chicago grand jury would be, even if she and Joe Plesnar could get that far.

And finally, she couldn't charge Morrissey with conspiracy to commit murder. Sheriffs Blood and Dodd thought their cases were accidents, so how could a conspiracy for reciprocal killings arise? Even if she could change their minds, she had co-conspirator identification problems. According to Sheriff Dodd, the Tex-Mex women were interchangeable in looks, and that sisterhood would probably cover for one another with alibis anyway. She had nothing for the Sandberg murder; no one saw or remembered anyone or anything out of the ordinary, and she was sure Morrissey's coaching had made sure no travel tracks were left behind. As for Kagan, she and Lt. Plesnar both thought Pat Dufresne was a possibility, but that mystery woman was tan and blonde, and Dufresne in her photographs was a pale redhead. No one had gotten a really good look at their mystery woman, and besides, they had no evidence that Dufresne had traveled to Portland either.

She seemed reduced to letting this go, to doing nothing. The only solace she had came from Richard Feynman. Her theory predicted the killings would stop now that Morrissey knew she was on to him. And that was acceptable to her. In time, PPD would come up with a host of plausible reasons why a serial killer stopped – dead, arrested or imprisoned on another charge, moved away, pulled in his or her horns because of a sense the police were getting too close.

But she was still bothered – why would Morrissey do this, turn his back on a lifetime of upholding the law? Yes, she did believe most anyone could be pushed to

307

murder, but John Morrissey? Yes, the three people on the island were reprehensible, and so were the three away killings, but John had pursued and brought to justice people who were far worse, people who were amoral, violent, murderous. What could have pushed him to do this?

She knew the question would always bother her, but in the end she decided to let it go. No good would come from formally questioning John or arresting him. No good would come from an indictment on the remote chance she could get the DA to pursue and obtain one. And a trial, if it ever happened, would be a circus, destroying lives and careers and reputations.

Maybe what she had said to Dave was right. John was an uncomplicated guy, a straight-arrow in his sense of right and wrong, and he had tried to set things right as he saw it. Maybe losing Dottie had made him a little bit crazy, and his perception of 'right' had slipped just enough.

I'll let it go, she repeated to herself. I'll follow the gospel according to John Morrissey – make it look like you're doing something even when you're not. The killings would stop. And they'd all move on.

Chapter 37

Harwood walked into the RHD bullpen on a Tuesday morning in late August to find Chapman looking shattered. His body was motionless, his face blank, his hands fluttering, shaking, above his desk top.

"Sam, what's wrong? You look like you've been hit by a truck."

"John Morrissey is dead," he told her.

"What? How?"

"Pancreatic cancer. He was diagnosed eighteen months ago, which I guess is what made him pull the plug on the job. I think he probably wanted a little time for his bucket list items.

"I didn't know he was sick until four days ago. He called me out to the island and I found him arguing with his doctor about going to hospice care. Not the first argument they'd had – the first was when he was diagnosed; he said no to an operation, he wasn't going to have his insides scooped out and live out his days as a semi-invalid. Same with hospice care. Said he wanted to die at home, and he didn't want anyone to know till he was gone. Last thing he needed was a stream of visitors saying maudlin goodbyes, he said.

"Needless to say, he won the argument. You know John." A faint smile from Chapman, remembering.

An hour later Harwood got a call from Dave MacKenzie. "You may know this already, honey, but John Morrissey died early this morning. We got called out on the rescue boat to take him back to town where the funeral director is waiting."

"Thanks, Dave. Yes, I do know, just found out. Pancreatic cancer."

"Yeah. His lawyer was waiting for us at the guardhouse. The nurse had instructions to call him immediately. The lawyer would like to see you and Sam Chapman after John's funeral. He's planning to call you this afternoon to confirm. He has letters for both of you, not to be opened till after the committal service."

In any city, the parade is enormous when a police officer dies in the line of duty – the whole department turns out, along with representatives from statewide and regional departments. John Morrissey's parade three days after his death, even as a retired officer, dwarfed them all. It was the largest in Portland's history. Police, firefighters, city workers, politicos, fishermen, lobstermen, all the other denizens of the Portland waterfront, and ordinary citizens. All walked past the throngs of people lining the streets of Munjoy Hill, the Irish neighborhood where John had been raised. They all knew they weren't just burying a cop; they were sending a legend to Valhalla.

Morrissey had left instructions that no politicians, no police chiefs, no police captains be permitted to speak at the funeral service. Instead, Sam Chapman gave the eulogy. He'd worked on his remarks for endless hours in the past week, ever since his visit to the island, when John asked him to speak.

"I've told you this before, for my retirement party," John had said. "Be brief, for Chrissake. The Gettysburg Address is only three minutes long, and unless you're planning to be better than that, don't go any longer."

Sam's speech wasn't Gettysburg, but it was in the neighborhood. The eloquence he'd worked so hard to create, the emotions of this stoic hard-bitten police detective, his eyes glistening – had moved everyone in the Cathedral of the Immaculate Conception to tears.

The distance from the cathedral to Eastern Cemetery is normally only a short walk. But Morrissey's parade took the long route: all the way out Congress Street to the Eastern Promenade overlooking Casco Bay and its islands, past Fort Allen Park, up Munjoy Street and John's childhood home, then back to Congress and the historic cemetery established in 1668.

No one had been buried in Eastern Cemetery in decades; it was ostensibly full, more than 4000 graves in just over six acres.   But the City of Portland had manufactured a burial site for Munjoy Hill's favorite son near members of his family who'd been interred more than a century before. The crowd filled all the open space, cleaned up in the previous three days from debris and the remnants of vandalism. Morrissey's last act of civic improvement.

After the committal service at the gravesite, a chosen invitation list repaired to the Full Clip for an old-fashioned Irish wake. Mick Garnish opened the bar and closed the register: "I've made enough off you clowns that I can offer this gift to John," he said, and the drinks flowed as freely as the stories.

Harwood looked around the bar, recalling the 900 people at the cathedral, the huge parade, this wake that rivaled any in Boston.

"I don't know that John would have been comfortable with such a fuss," she said to Chapman.

"Not of his own volition," Chapman replied. "But he would have laughed at how it's getting under the skin of people like Chief Anthony and Captain Langdon and the Mayor."

As the wake wore down, Morrissey's lawyer found Harwood and Chapman, and handed an envelope to each. "As we discussed. After the funeral. I have no idea what's in these – he didn't share them with me – but he did ask for complete confidentiality.

"I'm sorry about your loss, Detectives. If ever anyone was going to live on in collective memory, it's John. Be well."

Harwood had one more drink with Chapman, then went home. She poured herself a Jameson's in honor of John and settled in her favorite living room chair. Opened his envelope and started to read.

Dear Kate:

Now you know why I was getting so skinny. You're an observant detective. No one else noticed or said anything. I'm proud of you.

On to more important matters. I have no family, and Dottie's gone, so I was going to leave everything to Sam, for his kids' education and to encourage him to get his ass out of there. At least once he has his twenty years in, eighteen months from now. But I'm leaving him just the liquid assets – all the investments that Dottie and I were going to use as our mad money for our bucket lists. A bachelor piles up a lot of money over his working years when he has nothing to spend it on. Sam will have plenty.

I've decided to leave you my house on the island, fully paid for and finally finished. Why, when we've known each other only a relatively short time? Call it returning a favor, to someone I admire and respect. You know I'm not going to write anything that could be seen as an acknowledgement of what I may have done to leave Granite Cliffs a better place. But … you knew. I'm astonished that anyone was able to figure it out. You are an incredibly talented, intuitively brilliant detective, and you've been kind enough to leave my reputation intact, at least in my lifetime. So – consider your favor returned. Thank you. The house is yours.

What should you do with it? I say sell the damn thing. You may love the feel of Granite Cliffs, but you can't commute to police work from there, and the neighborhood is changing – too many insufferable people from away. But … people from away have money, and properties like the guardhouse are few and far between. Very desirable to such people – you'll sell it quickly, I'm sure for a good price.

As for your career, I think you should consider leaving the force. You're wasting your time there as a reluctant pioneer in the gender wars when you're so gifted as a detective. Another city isn't the answer for you either. I think you might very well burn yourself out with the political infighting that's found in most any large department.

Think of the guardhouse money as the venture capital for your own investigative consulting firm. Not a run of the mill private dick chasing cheating spouses, but a consultant helping on intractable cases. Families who feel shortchanged on justice in cold cases, police who have hit a brick wall on their current investigations. In the latter cases – maybe only a few of them until your reputation is built – the PD's won't try to bar the door to you; they'll want you involved and helping them. You'll become very busy, I know you will.

You have a great career in front of you, Kate. Go for it. Who knows, maybe you'll be in position to take on a partner in eighteen months if Chapman retires!

 Keep fighting, kid –
 John

  Kate put the letter down. She hadn't known what to expect from John, certainly not this veiled acknowledgement of what he'd done. Now, having read his letter, she put aside what she'd said to Dave MacKenzie about heartbreak driving Morrissey to the brink of obsession and then to orchestrating the murders. It wasn't heartbreak, it was something else. She replayed

314

the words she'd just read from John about departmental politics and gender wars, and the answer came to her.

This was about bullies. John hated bullies, he'd said so often enough. She should have seen it earlier – she hated bullies too. Now Morrissey's motivations were clear. The away murders all involved bullies: Holloway was a sexual predator and financial vulture; Darlan beat and emotionally abused his wife; the Montgomerys used their authority to bully and steal from their partners.

But the away murders were only a means to an end. The real targets had been on Granite Cliffs. Bannerman was a financial bully, dispossessing and impoverishing struggling families. Kagan was a chiseler of his contractors who abused the legal process against his neighbors. Sandberg sued, threatened suits, and agitated with governmental bureaucrats to subdue anyone who displeased her. The theatrical nature of all the murders was a message: "What goes around comes around. This is what happens to people like this."

I knew he'd done this, Kate reflected, *but I thought it was out of anger. It wasn't. He was keeping a promise.* Morrissey had told Kate about his pledge to Dottie to finish her house. It was more than that, though. He'd not only finished her *house*, he'd protected her *home*. He'd made sure the place she'd loved, the placed she so looked forward to, wasn't destroyed by a few toxic people. One last promise kept, one more mile traveled, and then he'd been free to sleep.

I was right to let it go, she reflected. He was a hero, an icon. No sense destroying his legend just for the ego trip of closing some island murder cases when she knew the murders had stopped.

Morrissey's career counseling, though, was a total surprise. That needed thinking about. But the more she slept on it, and the more waking hours she spent being badgered by Robert Langdon about determining past whereabouts of virtually all Granite Cliffs full-time and seasonal residents – a fool's errand now that she knew the answer – the more sense John Morrissey's arguments made.

And there was another reason for her to leave, something she wouldn't share even with Dave MacKenzie. She had deliberately concealed relevant information about Morrissey – how the puzzle pieces fit together – that she and Logan had developed. It was one thing not to arrest Morrissey because compelling proof was lacking, quite another to leave the information permanently out of the investigative record in the murder book.

That was a career-ender if it ever got out. Maybe even an obstruction of justice charge, even years later. Better to leave the force and not become a high-profile detective with that possibility, however remote, hanging over her head. This had to remain her secret – alone.

She broached the subject of leaving with Dave that evening, and he was actually relieved. He'd started to worry about their parallel career paths in the police and fire departments. "Even if – maybe especially if – we both stayed fast-track," he said, "we'd inevitably become the 'royal couple' of the firefighting and police forces.

And everyone resents the hell out of royal couples. No question you'll be successful on your own, and that makes the most sense because … " – he laughed – "it's very difficult to start a consulting firefighting firm."

He chuckled to himself. "Besides," he said, "your starting your own firm will allow me to do what a lot of people would like to do but never get the chance. Screw a consultant instead of the other way around."

Her tension dissolved, and she laughed. "You're impossible. Lucky for you you're so good in bed."

"Lucky for *you*, my sweet. I think you're just using me for sex."

She walked over to him, locked eyes, and started unbuttoning his shirt. "And enjoying the hell out of it, too. Just one of the things I love about you." She reached down, unbuttoned his trousers, and unzipped him. "And … ooh … here's another."

Afterward, both of them spent, she said, "I don't know how I ever would have come through all this without you, Dave. 'Thank you' will never be enough."

He traced his fingers down her back. "Just …" – his eyes grew soft – "please tell me your firm's headquarters will be in Portland. I'm kind of attached to you, you know. I love you."

"I love you too. You know that, or at least you should. I want us to be like Hank and Arianna Reynolds – together, in love, and succeeding. In fact, maybe Hank can help with that – he might have a few pointers for me about starting a successful consulting firm."

Chapter 38

The following Friday, having checked on space to lease in a month's time, Harwood knocked on the door to Robert Langdon's office. "Captain, do you have a moment? It's a personal matter."

"It would be better if you made an appointment for a personal matter, Detective, but come in." His usual pompous tone, doubtless copied from Chief Armand Anthony.

Harwood settled in the uncomfortable chair across the desk from Langdon. "Captain, I've decided to leave the department and go out on my own. I wanted to check with you as to the protocols of resigning, adequate notice, transition of active cases, things like that."

The last thing Langdon needed was to lose one of his most talented detectives. But he didn't say that, or even "I don't want to lose you" or "What can I do to change your mind?"

Instead he said, "You don't want to do that, Harwood."

"Captain, there's something you should know about me. I do not react well to people telling me what I do or do not want. I find it belittling and demeaning. It's bullying, it's arrogant, it's condescending, and I won't tolerate it. Not from anyone, including a superior."

Langdon looked like he'd been struck. "You want to watch your tone, Detective. People might start thinking of you as a bitch." Then, just in time, his reptilian brain remembered the need for political correctness. "No offense."

"There you go again, telling me what I want. Look, I'm a female detective, Captain. Some people will always think of me as a bitch. I'm not worried. I'll be fine. The cream always rises to the top."

"Keep exhibiting that kind of arrogance, Detective, and you won't need to give notice. You'll be out of here on your ass, with a negative reference clipped to you and your high opinion of yourself."

Harwood smiled at him. The gloves were off. No quarter asked, none given. "Oh, I'm sure people will consider the source, sir. You're the most incompetent police captain in creation, and everyone knows it. 'No offense.'

"You've just blown up any possibility of doing this in a polite manner, Captain. I'm out of here for today. I'll have my union rep handle the details of making it formal." She rose and walked out of his office and back to her desk in the bullpen.

Sam Chapman was looking at Langdon's office window, his mouth half agape. "Christ, Kate, he looks like he's about to have a heart attack. What the hell did you say to him?"

"Wait a decent interval, Sam, and then meet me at the Full Clip for lunch. We have things to discuss."

Chapman walked into the Full Clip at 12:10 and found Harwood at the corner table. "What did you say to him? Sally Rinaldo has it all over the squad that you told him to go fuck himself."

She cocked her head to the side and smiled. "Sam. I'm a woman of good breeding. I would never say something like that to a superior. I would, however, be quite willing to stick a hot poker up his ass. What a complete shithead.

"I tendered my resignation, and he made it easy. Validated the decision. No second thoughts or regrets at all."

"Jesus, Kate, what are you going to do?"

"That's what I want to talk to you about. John said he was leaving you all his liquid assets, all the mad money he and Dottie had accumulated. I don't know if he told you, but he's leaving me the guardhouse. Encouraging me to sell it and use the proceeds as the venture capital for an investigative consulting firm. He thinks I'd be good at it.

"He thinks you'd be good at it too. And I think he was great at career advice. He said I should start the firm now, wait eighteen months for you to complete your twenty years, then take you on as a partner.

"I think it's a great idea, Sam. I'm excited. What do you think?"

"Wow. That's a lot to digest, Kate. I want to go home and think about it, talk it over with Mary Sue, sleep on it. But I'm inclined to think it's a pretty good plan …

hard part will be lasting another eighteen months without you."

Kate smiled at him. "Morrissey told me over a year ago, when Langdon stuck us with his old cases, that a good detective can make it look like he's doing a lot when he's actually just going through the motions. You'll be fine, Sam. And we'll probably be seeing more and more of each other as D-Day approaches."

"Okay. Let me go back and piss away the afternoon and then go home and talk with Mary Sue. Will you be in the office Monday?"

"I don't know. My next appointment here in my temporary office is with Larry Griffin, our union rep. I've filled him in on my communication with Langdon; he'd like to arrange a few days of transition where I come in for two or three hours each day while Langdon makes himself scarce. Keep at least a semblance of professionalism and make sure we have an adequate transition of cases."

"If you come in and he's not there, cheers are going to go up, Kate. You have no idea how much Sally's rumor has improved morale!"

She laughed. "That's great. My grandfather used to tell me, 'If they don't tell stories about you, kid, you're not worth a shit!'

"I'll see you Monday, Sam, one way or the other."

Chapman stood and looked at her, a sly smile on his face. "You sure you didn't tell him to go fuck himself?" She laughed and waved him out of the bar.

Larry Griffin was a former detective lieutenant in Vice, now president of the police union in Portland. He entered Armand Anthony's office at the appointed time, carrying a small tape recorder under his arm.

"What's that machinery you have there?" Anthony asked. "And what does it have to do with Detective Harwood's departure?"

"It's a recording of a recent subject interview conducted here at PPD, Chief," Griffin answered. "But before I play it for you, I'd like to make a suggestion about Detective Harwood's transition out of the department. She's willing to come in for a few hours a day for five days, ten days, however long it takes, to transfer her active cases and informants to other officers – as long as Captain Langdon isn't in the vicinity while she's here in department spaces."

"That's highly irregular," Anthony harrumphed.

"Yes, sir, it is, but warranted, I think. Aside from the fact that Detective Harwood has lost all respect for Captain Langdon, she – and I – are concerned that he would disrupt the transition process in the work she'll be handing over." He paused. "Let me play this tape now, if you're agreeable."

Griffin played the tape of Dan Hilliard's incendiary interview with Harwood and Chapman about Ron Roberts' whereabouts at the time of the Bannerman murder. He concluded with, "It appears that Detective Harwood is not the only person who has Captain Langdon's number, sir."

Anthony was incensed. "How did you obtain that tape? All interview tapes are catalogued, archived, and guarded. Whoever took it from archives has committed a crime: obstruction of justice by stealing evidence and corrupting the chain of custody."

Griffin sighed. The chief was a pompous ass with bureaucratic blinders on. "Not the response I was hoping for, Chief. As it happens, this tape did not come from the evidence room archives. If you check, you will find no record of any tape at all. Captain Langdon ordered the tape destroyed immediately after the interview. I think you should be more concerned with his behavior.

"Fortunately, professionalism and integrity prevailed within the ranks of the police department, and a copy was made before the original was tossed. I need hardly tell you that this is not the only copy. And I'm sure you can foresee the repercussions if this tape were to become public – which it may if any aspersions about Detective Harwood follow her out the door."

Anthony's voice was ice. "Be very careful, lieutenant. Don't threaten me."

"Farthest thing from my mind, Chief," Griffin smiled. Threatening the fat bastard was exactly what he was doing, and he was enjoying it. "I'm sure we'll have a smooth and professional transition in the manner I've suggested, with Detective Harwood's exemplary reputation untarnished. This tape and its copies will then be destroyed." He paused and smiled. "Unless, of course, you'd like to have it to support any action you may wish to take concerning Captain Langdon."

With that the meeting was essentially over. Griffin left Anthony's office, stowed the tape in the police union's safe deposit box at TD Banknorth, and went to meet Harwood at the Full Clip.

Their conversation lasted five minutes. Chief Anthony had agreed to their proposal, Griffin told her – five days of transition in which Harwood would be in the office for 2-1/2 hours each day while Langdon absented himself. "The Hilliard tape was an eye-opener for him," Griffin said, "even though he played it pretty close to the vest. He didn't say so outright, but I think the Chief now realizes what a zero he has in Langdon. I don't know how low the number is, but I have a feeling the captain's days are numbered.

"In any case, he accepted our suggestion and you can do your transfers without that jerk on the premises."

Chapter 39

Kate spent the next week occupied with her transition work, handing off cases and informants. One set of cases, of course, was the Granite Cliffs murders, now solely on Chapman's desk.

Sam didn't know about Kate's second weekend with Logan, nor was he aware of the actual subject of her last conversation with Morrissey. Not telling her partner the whole truth was a horrible betrayal, of course, the moral equivalent of leaving information out of the murder book. She could justify it to herself only because she knew the truth would destroy Sam.

She told him she could conceive of a series of events that would support her Strangers scenario, but stitching them together was a long shot. "John and I agreed there's a reason Occam's Razor has stood the test of time," she said. "Simplest explanation is generally the right one. Either a long-ago revenge motive we haven't uncovered, or a serial killer getting his rocks off killing high profile slimeballs in artistic and creative ways. Either way, chances are pretty good someone will talk sometime. Be ready when they do."

Once her transition activities were completed a week later, Kate thought about her consulting firm's start-up activities. Maybe Morrissey's open cases were a possibility – this time from another direction. She was sure the families and loved ones of the victims in those cases had looked into the background of the people they suspected were their guilty parties. Maybe Kate could identify some disgruntled inner circle people – there were always disgruntled inner circle people – to flip, change sides, provide more evidence to get the DA's office off the dime. It was worth thinking about, and maybe the thinking required a fresh look.

There was also the unsolved disappearance of the Atlantic Estates dockmaster three years ago. With an unmanned boat found floating at dawn, and no body ever recovered, the tentative conclusion had been an accidental fall overboard and subsequent drowning. But the dockmaster's friends were convinced it was murder, and they believed the murderer was a husband retaliating against his wife's lover. *That's a long shot,* Kate thought, *but maybe worth looking into. A big splash if I can solve it.*

Aside from a big splash, she considered what else could get her firm moving. She doubted she could do all the work alone. She'd be spread too thin chasing down leads to do much research. *My first inspired move,* she thought. *Put Logan Hutchinson on retainer.* The true "intuitive genius" Morrissey had written about was Logan, and the Zoom arrangement and hotel weekends she and the girl had shared had worked well.

We could do a lot even at a distance with Zoom, she thought. Exchanging files would be easy. Wouldn't matter that there was a continent between them. I'm going to call her tomorrow. I'm sure she'll be busy with her senior year courses and her honors thesis, but it's worth a shot. Kate's father had often reminded her, "If you really want something done, ask a busy man." "*Woman,* Dad," she now thought. "Ask a busy *woman*!"

That same afternoon Logan Hutchinson sat atop her lifeguard tower on a Georgian Bay beach. Today was September 15, the last day of manned lifeguard stations. It was two minutes till 5:00, then the summer's work was done. An eventful summer, much more than simple lifeguard duty. Good thing too; life might have become boring if not for the challenge of Kate Harwood's puzzle.

She sensed a presence approaching the side of her tower and heard a male voice say, "It *is* you. Wow."

She turned and recognized her visitor, gave him a brilliant smile. "Well, hey there. Long time."

"I guess it is," the man said. He looked down at the ground. A little shy. She thought he might actually scuff his foot in the sand, like the proverbial barefoot boy. "They told me at the lifeguard station I'd find you here. You're … ummm … sort of beyond anything I imagined," he said.

Logan laughed. "Oh, I grow up nice? You really are a silver-tongued devil, Billy. Hang on a second, I'm off duty right …" – she glanced at her watch – "… now." She donned an Oxford cloth shirt as a cover-up and hopped down from her tower and stood in front of him. She faced him, took both his hands in hers, and said, "Let's have a look at you. See what ten years have done." Her eyes swept him from head to toe and back again. Six-three,

185 pounds, a hardbody, a younger and blonder version of her movie-star handsome father.

He's become a man, she thought. *All man. Holy shit. Try not to stare, Logan.*

She smiled at him. "Wow yourself. Come with me, I have to sign out and drop my equipment at the lifeguard shack. Won't be a minute, then we can walk along the beach and catch up."

Signed out, equipment stowed, she walked down the beach to the water's edge and turned to face the sun, now low in the western sky.

"Hey," the man said. "Your house is the other direction."

"Yes, I know, I don't get lost on the beach any more. You've heard that story, right? About the way my parents met, courtesy of a lost little girl?" She smiled. "Anyway, I thought we could go this way for a bit, give us more time to catch up."

"Oh ... okay." He couldn't believe his luck. More time with her than he'd hoped for.

They walked and talked, she about what she was doing, he about what he was doing, she about what she hoped to do, he about what he hoped to do. "Big dreams," she said. She cast a sly smile at him. "Have you been dreaming about me, Billy?"

He burst out laughing. He'd been trying his damnedest to muster all the aplomb he could, walking beside this spectacularly beautiful woman clad only in a bikini and a half-buttoned shirt, trying not to stare at her.

But she was as funny and sassy as he remembered her, and it settled him a little.

"Well, you have crossed my mind a few times. Just wondering what you might have become."

He's as sweet as ever, she thought. *And a whole lot more, methinks.*

They turned around, walked back toward her house, talked some more, both of them losing the battle not to stare. As they reached her parents' beachfront home, she rose on tiptoe and brushed a chaste kiss across his cheek. She squeezed his arm once, smiled, and walked up the lawn to the ground-level deck of the house.

Her father sat in a large white Adirondack chair, beer in hand. "That guy looks familiar," he said.

Unbuttoning her shirt, his daughter glanced up at him. "He should," she said. "That's Billy Donovan."

"And I know that name too. Just can't place it."

"He was the DJ I helped at Dr. Valentine's party the night you and Mom finally figured out you were in love." Her eyes danced at the memory. "God, I'd thought 'never' ... also the night Gramma met Harry and Harry held his 29 hand in cribbage. Pretty good night all around."

Hank Reynolds laughed. "Now I remember. You dumped me for a newer model — a good-looking blond lifeguard. He was the lifeguard."

"I didn't dump you, Dad. I loved you then just as much as I do now. It was just ... Billy was so easy to look at that night."

329

Reynolds considered her carefully. "Still is, apparently."

Logan appeared to be studying the buttons on her shirt, but her eyes were distant. A breathy exhale. "Yup."

Her mother had just walked on to the deck from the walkout basement and caught the end of the exchange. "Who's easy to look at?"

"Billy Donovan," father and daughter said together.

"Oh, yes," Arianna Reynolds said. "I remember that party."

"Me too," her husband said. "Especially after." He pulled his wife down across his lap, her legs dangling over the arm of the chair, she bursting into laughter. He kissed her. Thoroughly. Arianna Reynolds then stood and gazed into her husband's eyes for a long moment.

"Geez, guys," Logan said. "Get a room, will you? It's a little unnerving for me to see old people that much in love."

"Well, I think someone else may be halfway there already," her father said. "I saw the way he looked at you as you walked up here."

"Oh, come on," Logan said. "We ran into each other on the beach this afternoon, and spent a half hour walking and talking after I got off duty. Not much duty anyway, this time of year. Anyway, it wasn't romance, it was just old DJ's reconnecting."

"I remember ten years ago you thought he was really gorgeous and very sweet," her mother said.

The girl looked at her mother and laughed. "Well, even then, Mom, I was a good judge of man flesh." She turned to her father. "Maybe even a little quicker on the uptake than you were with Dad. Remember, I was the one who said Dad was a hunk."

She fell to her knees in mock supplication. "Please don't start kissing again ..."

Her mother smiled. "But I also remember that, even at age ten – he was seventeen, wasn't he? – you thought he might not be smart enough for you."

Logan stood and looked off into the distance. "And I was wrong. He's now a captain in the Canadian Air Force, a fighter pilot and squadron leader, just seconded to test pilot school at Edwards Air Force Base in California. He's on the candidate list for astronaut selection in two years – International Space Force pilot for translunar missions from the space station to the moon colony."

"Wow," her father said. "That's a lot of resume to cram into a half hour."

Big smile from Logan. "I'm a good listener, Dad. Runs in the family. Got it from Gramma."

"How were you so wrong about him ten years ago?"

The girl studied the decking in front of her. "I think that ... underneath those recruiting poster looks and that fighter pilot image ... there's a quiet guy who's among the best in the world at what he does. How else does a young captain get on the short list for piloting missions to the moon?

"He told me he has to work at meeting new people and being at ease with them. I think when he was younger that came across as a little goofy. Probably why I underestimated him. Now his quiet comes across as intense" – she smiled – "but maybe he's still a little shy."

I know a guy like that, Arianna Reynolds thought. *Intense as hell but still a little shy. It's irresistible. I should know.*

"You going to see him again?" she asked.

"He's home on leave for a few more days, then he's off to Edwards. Maybe I'll be able to see him when I get back to Cal Tech; Edwards isn't that far from Pasadena. But this week there's one last retrospective at the movie theater, so we're going to see 'Gone with the Wind' tomorrow night."

Ohmygoodness, her mother thought. "You know, 'Gone with the Wind' was the first real date for me and your dad ..."

"Yes," the girl said, a faint smile crossing her face. Her eyes took on a faraway dreamy look. "Yes, I know."

She excused herself to take a shower. Her mother looked at Reynolds. "Yikes. The cute boys haven't been smart enough. The smart boys haven't been attractive enough. The few who've been both haven't lit up her world enough. But that boy ..."

Reynolds laughed. "That boy is in a lot of trouble, Rini."

"You think so? Did you see the look on her face when she was talking about him? She may be the one in

332

trouble, Hank. She was protesting a little too much about 'just reconnecting.'" She paused. "What should we do?"

Reynolds laughed again.   "Leave them alone, honey. We know Logan's going to change the world. Maybe the two of them will change it together. Let's just keep cool and enjoy the show."

Epilogue
The Next Day

As his family sat down to a late Saturday morning breakfast, Hank Reynolds said to his daughter, "So – big date tonight, huh?"

Logan shrugged. "Not that big a deal, Dad. Just an early dinner, then the movie."

"Where are you going to dinner?" her mother asked.

"Billy said he was going to make reservations at Enrico's."

The girl glanced up to catch the look that flashed between her parents. She stared at both, back and forth. "What?"

Arianna Reynolds smiled. "Enrico's is where your dad and I had dinner on our first date, before we saw 'Gone with the Wind.'"

"Huh. Whaddaya know ..."

Her father gave her a knowing smile. "They'll seat you and Billy in the middle of the room, in front of the bay window. Let all the people, inside and outside, know that Enrico's is where the beautiful people dine."

Logan looked quizzical. "How do you know they'll do ... Oh."

Her father laughed. "Rumor Central will have a field day with that. Billy Donovan and Logan Hutchinson.

Your ears – both of you – will be burning all the way in California."

The girl gazed into the middle distance, thinking. "Well … what the hell. Let 'em talk."

The kitchen phone rang and Arianna Reynolds answered it. "Dr. Reynolds," a familiar female voice said. A quiet chuckle. "Arianna. You asked me to call you 'Arianna.' It's Kate Harwood. How are you?"

"Fine, Kate. What can chez Reynolds do for you this morning?"

"I was hoping to catch Logan before she left for Cal Tech. Is she still around? Does she have a few minutes?"

"She's here, and I'm sure she has time for you, Kate." Mother handed the phone to daughter. "Kate Harwood."

Logan took the phone and walked to the end of the kitchen, looking out at Georgian Bay. "Hi, Cuz!"

"Hi, Logan. Ummm … I know you're about to become really busy, but … I have some news, and I have a proposition for you."

Logan pitched her voice lower to keep her parents from overhearing. "Okay. You first, Kate. But I …" – a trace of a smile – "I have some news too."

About the Author:

Adah Armstrong lives on a hillside in Vermont with a dog named Abby and two felines named Barncat and Spike. Her house is close to the woods where Robert Frost stopped on that snowy evening, and very near the road he didn't take. She is a former management consultant, an amateur astronomer, and an insatiable fan of puzzles and detective stories. "Return the Favor" is her second novel. She is currently at work on a third.

337

Made in the USA
Middletown, DE
16 July 2022

68962078R00189